Sugar Baby

Sugar Baby

A True Love Story

Ryan Lee

Papillon Publishers

Copyright © 2014 by Papillon Publishers

All rights reserved. This book or any portion thereof may not be reproduced or used in any manner whatsoever without the express written permission of the publisher except for the use of brief quotations in a book review.

Printed in the United States of America

First Printing, 2014

ISBN: 978-0-9916161-3-8

www.PapillonPublishers.com

"When love is not madness it is not love."

— Pedro Calderón de la Barca

Contents

Prologue _____ vii

Date 1: October 24 _____ 1

Date 2: November 3 _____ 17

Date 3: November 17 _____ 29

Date 4: December 1 _____ 39

Date 5: December 14 _____ 53

Date 6: December 22 _____ 65

Date 7: January 12 _____ 77

Date 8: January 24 _____ 83

Date 9: January 31 _____ 101

Date 10: February 7 _____ 113

Date 11: March 14 _____ 125

Date 12: May 2 _____ 141

Date 13: May 28 _____ 157

Date 14: June 12 – 13 _____ 181

Epilogue _____ 205

Prologue

I never quite fit in. Not that I was unpopular growing up. By all appearances, it was quite the opposite. Class president, homecoming king, valedictorian, captain of the varsity baseball team – from a titular perspective, I could have been the popular boy from a John Hughes movie. But while I had all the trappings of social success in high school, I was completely missing it in one crucial respect: I could not get laid for the life of me.

I mean, forget laid. I couldn't get a date. I remember clearly the painful experience of asking a girl to the prom in my junior year of high school. The dismissal bell rang, and students ran to their lockers to put books away and get ready for the bus ride home or after-school activities. With sweaty palms, I fumbled to open my combination lock while watching this girl out of the corner of my eye. This poor girl, whose only crime was being in the wrong place at the wrong time. And by "wrong place" I mean being assigned the locker next to mine. And by "wrong time" I mean deciding to come to school that day. My nervousness rose as I waited for the right moment, but I waited too long. She closed her locker, and I knew she would be gone in an instant. So I turned in desperation and blurted, "Vanessa, would you go to the prom with me?"

Silence. The universe stopped in that moment – but not in the way you fantasize about. Rather, in that moment of raw emotion, nervousness and surprise, we let our guards down completely and peered into each other's souls. And what I saw there, I'll never forget: pity. "Okay," she whispered in a stunned voice, too nice to say no.

So that was it. My lone date in high school – a pity date. We had a fine time at the prom, but that's not really the point. It's like my high school life was this strange dichotomy, where on the one hand I was popular, personable and successful athletically and academically, but on the other hand, I couldn't get any of that to translate into success with girls. None, zero, zippo.

College was better. By then, the braces had come off. I got rid of my high school bowl haircut, and I replaced my coke-bottle glasses with contacts. For the first time, girls were genuinely interested in me physically. Honestly, it was a strange feeling. It took me awhile to even know how to react to this sort of new attention. But I eventually figured it out. I dated one really nice girl for four years during and after college. I broke up with her in my mid-twenties when I realized that I couldn't possibly get married after having had only one real relationship in my life. So I messed around a bit after that.

Eventually, I met another really nice and beautiful girl in my early thirties. Fell in love, got married, and had a few kids. I had run the gauntlet of growing up and had come out the other end successfully. I had a picture-perfect family, a high-paying job, and lots of friends. By all appearances, I had it all. But just like in high school, appearances could be deceiving – which is why, after six years of marriage, at the age of 38, I started to cheat on my wife.

Date 1: October 24

I hurried into the Italian restaurant – late, late, late. As I walked in, I surveyed the tables, looking for her. Kristina. A nineteen-year-old girl whom I had never met before. A girl with whom I had only exchanged a few pictures and brief messages over the Internet. We had met on one of those "sugar baby" websites. You may have heard of these Internet "dating" sites – where rich, older men go to meet beautiful, financially challenged girls. Basically it's a business model based on the principle that at a primordial level, 1) men want beautiful women, and 2) women want men with resources. There are plenty of supportive analogies in the animal kingdom, and also plenty of counter-arguments that humanity has evolved beyond these sorts of basic instincts. But regardless of your moral or religious compunctions, there does seem to be a robust market for this service. There are dozens of these "sugar baby" sites on the Internet, some of which have memberships that run into the hundreds of thousands or even millions.

As with any Internet community, the sugar baby subculture has its own vocabulary. A typical sugar baby profile might read: "Hot young college student, seeking financial support for school and shopping. Loves traveling and fine dining. NSA (no strings attached), mutually beneficial relationship. Discretion required. Low drama. You have your life, and I have mine."

Of course, a "typical" sugar baby profile is really a misnomer, since there is a wide spectrum of girls on these sites who are seeking very different things. On one end of the spectrum, there are girls who are really just escorts seeking purely transactional relationships. You pay me $Y, and I'll do X (or XXX, as is more often the case). To be honest, these escorts who are fishing on a sugar baby site are probably on the wrong site. There are escort sites that service those sorts of purely transactional relationships much more efficiently (believe me, I know). On the other end of the spectrum are girls who have watched *Pretty Woman* too many times and are seeking their "soul mate" (who, by the way, happens to be rich, tall and incredibly handsome). I almost feel sorry for these girls. I mean, escorts are *probably* on the wrong site, but these girls are *definitely* on the wrong site.

The appropriate sugar baby / sugar daddy relationship is really about having an arrangement that emotionally sits somewhere between visiting an escort and having a real, committed relationship. But it's a tricky act to stay emotionally balanced between these two extremes, which I would find out firsthand.

I had messaged Kristina (a.k.a. "Isabelle" in her profile) a week ago after reading her profile and, of course, viewing her stunning personal pictures. Her profile read:

Username: Isabelle
City / State: Los Angeles, California
Age: 19 years old
Height: 1.6 meters (5' 3")
Body Type: Slim
Eye Color: Green
Hair Color: Light Brown

Hi, my name is Isabelle and I just moved to the Los Angeles area. California is actually the 12th state I've lived in. I guess you can say we're just a bunch of gypsies!

I am a full-time student and I aspire to be a geriatric psychiatrist. I love the outdoors and traveling, although I don't get to do so often. I love being spoiled – what woman doesn't?! However, I am much more attracted to intellectual stimulation than money. The added security a sugar daddy brings is just a bonus.

That being said, any "allowance" you feel compelled to share with me after we've established a relationship will be greatly appreciated. Unlike many girls on this site, I won't spend your hard-earned money on crazy shopping sprees or drugs/alcohol. I live a modest life and am independent enough to pay my own bills, but I simply can't afford to put myself through college – let alone medical school.

I consider myself down-to-earth and fairly low-maintenance. I love to laugh and experience new things. I don't drink alcohol but have no problem if you do, as long as you're not pushy or obnoxious when you drink. I am 420 friendly and got my medical card after having back surgery last year, but I don't sit around all day and get stoned. Basically, don't judge me and I won't judge you!

Please do NOT contact me if:

- You are going to tell me what a shame it is that I have a (cigarette) smoking habit. I understand it's not healthy, and I legitimately am trying to quit. If you want to meet up with me but don't want me smoking in your presence, I respect that 100%.

- You expect to sleep with me on our first encounter. I am not a hooker, I am a lady. However, I do know how to have fun once I am comfortable with someone.

- You either don't have pictures on your profile or are not willing to send pictures before we meet up.

- You are a mass murderer who plans on chopping me up in little pieces.

Feel free to start a conversation if it seems like we're looking for similar things. I promise I'm not as uptight as I sound! :)

Beautiful pictures. Elfish nose and smile. Something about her profile hooked me, so I messaged her.

Hi Isabelle,

First off, I loved the honesty and humor in your profile. To introduce myself, I'm a businessman in my mid-thirties who is kind, funny and good-looking . . . at least I think so (granted, I am very biased). Asian-American, I was born in Pennsylvania, but I moved out to the Bay Area about fifteen years ago.

I believe it's best to be honest and upfront about what we're each seeking, so in that spirit:

- I am seeking someone fun and smart to meet a couple times a month. On our dates, we could have dinner for a few hours and talk about our dreams, fears and passions. We could hopefully learn from each other and maybe even help each other see the world a little differently. To be straightforward, I am seeking a relationship where there is physical intimacy, but only when the relationship has progressed to a point where it feels natural to both of us.

- Also, I said I'd be honest, so I should let you know upfront that I'm married. I guess that is sort of an oxymoron since I'm being honest about being, y'know, dishonest. But regardless, it's the truth. So I am seeking something with low drama.

- I'd be happy to provide an allowance of $2,000 per month for these two dates a month. As we get to know each other, if we want to increase or decrease the number of dates a month, I'd be open to that also.

Well, that's about as honest as I can be. If the above doesn't interest you, I totally understand. But if you are interested, it'd be great to get to know you better!

Best wishes,

Chris

"Chris" wasn't my real name, of course. But given some of the crazies on these sugar baby sites, I was cautious with revealing my true identity until I got to know the girls.

Isabelle messaged back and told me that her real name was "Kristina," so I told her my real name was "Ryan." We exchanged a few pictures, and we seemed to have a nice rapport over email. We set up an initial date for the following week. The plan was that I would fly her up from Los Angeles to San Francisco. We would get to know each other over dinner, and then she would go home that same night. I offered $300 for this initial "meet and greet" date and, to put her mind at ease, I made it clear that I did not expect (nor really want) anything physical on this first date. If we got along, we could transition to the "arrangement" with a full allowance.

So that is how I ended up at this random Italian restaurant on this particular day. Nervous. Excited. Late – yikes. I had made reservations for 6 P.M., but was running twenty minutes late. I texted her during my drive in order to update her on my ETA. As I got close, she texted me back.

Text from Kristina (10/24):
Got way too excited to get out of the cab and forgot my jacket. LOL. Just my luck! I hope you don't mind, I got us a booth in the back and sat down already. I realized I've been too nervous to eat all day so I'm munching on some bread before you get here.

As I hurried into the restaurant, I scanned the booths looking for a girl who hopefully matched the photos. Then I saw her. She hopped up from the horseshoe-shaped dining booth and walked over toward me with a big smile. We gave each other a quick hug.

"Thanks for making the trip up," I said. "And I'm sorry that you lost your jacket in the cab. I can't guarantee that I will be worth it."

"No worries," she smiled. She paused a moment and then added, "I have a feeling we're going to be seeing a lot of each other."

I mulled over this slight odd statement as we walked to the table. We slid into the booth, she from one side of the horseshoe and me from the other, until we were close enough to almost touch. Kristina was so pretty in a completely natural way. In her pictures, she had been blonde, but she now wore light brown hair with gentle waves that fell just below her shoulders. Large green eyes, button nose, and an easy smile that revealed one dimple in her right cheek. She was the epitome of the "It" girl in high school, the one whom all the adolescent boys pined over.

"So your profile says you lived in twelve states. How does that happen? Military family? Criminals on the run?" I asked.

"Criminals on the run. I'm actually trying to figure out where to hide your body after I take all your money tonight," she laughed easily. "Actually, we just moved around a lot. I was born in Pittsburgh. But my dad left us when I was four. So my mom raised me all over the place, wherever she could find work. I spent a lot of my childhood in Henderson, Nevada. Then, in my teen years, when my mom and I were fighting all the time, I reconnected with my dad. So I went to go live with him in Lubbock, Texas for a while. That was tough because he already had a new family by then, and they weren't exactly happy to have me intrude on that. So after I couldn't take that anymore, I went to Florida to live with my grandma for a while. Then I moved to Calabasas, California to live with my dad again. Then back to Florida for a couple years, and then a few weeks ago, I just moved to the Los Angeles area to live with my grandparents."

"Wow. That's a lot of living in nineteen years. Can I ask, why did your parents separate?"

"My mom found out that my dad was cheating on her, and she kicked him out."

I paused for a moment in order to reflect on the irony of that statement and then laughed, "That's just horrible."

"I know, right?"

"Well, embrace the horror of who we actually are, I always say. Look, to be crystal clear, what your dad did to your mom was wrong, and by extension, me being here with you is also morally wrong. I acknowledge that."

"Then why are you here?"

"I suppose, if I were to psychoanalyze myself, it has something to do with the fact that I always grew up the perfect kid. Class president, captain of the varsity baseball team, homecoming king, valedictorian . . . but for all that, I could not get laid in high school for the life of me. I was pretty ugly, to be frank. I grew up this little Asian kid in the countryside of Pennsylvania, where the only things around were farms. And my high school was homogeneously Caucasian. Literally, I was the only Asian in my entire high school class. I had this awful bowl haircut. On top of that, I had the coke-bottle glasses and the steel wire braces. Yes, it all looked as bad as it sounds. Worse actually. So I was popular in one respect, but not in the most important respect as a teenage boy. Not in the romantic sense.

"I eventually outgrew that in college. I got contact lenses, got a new haircut, had my braces taken off, and much to my surprise, for the first time, girls were legitimately attracted to me. I also started dating Asian girls, and life was much better. But I think some of those scars remained from high school . . . and some of those fantasies," I said and then paused for a few moments before continuing.

"The other aspect of all 'this,' I guess, is that I support my family really well. I've studied hard and worked hard my entire life. I'm proud that I can support my parents, help my sister who doesn't exactly have a financially rewarding career, and provide a life for my wife and kids where they don't have to worry about anything ever. I know the stereotype of a guy having an affair is someone with a really unhappy marriage and family life, but that's actually not the case with me. I love my wife. We still enjoy being together, and we have a decent sex life for having been married six years. And my kids are my world. I just decided that in this one little piece of my life, I'm going to be a selfish. Since I'm not very religious, for me, life is really just a collection of all of my experiences, and I want to maximize those experiences."

Kristina looked at me with eyes that did not judge. "I guess I feel a little bit the same from my side. Not the part about growing up ugly. But the part about as long as this is separate from our real lives, it is what it is. And I don't want to inflate your ego, but you look better than your pictures, by the way."

"Thanks. You're blind, but thank you."

We reviewed the menu. We both ordered minestrone soup to start. She ordered penne pasta with tomato sauce. Not a big meat eater, and definitely no meat on the bone, she informed me. She hadn't had beef in over seven years. When she ordered, she said the word "penne" like "puh-NAY." I don't know why I remember that, but it made me wonder for a second if I had been mispronouncing it my entire life.

"So why this most recent move from Florida back to California?" I asked.

"My boyfriend in Florida went a little crazy. Smashed up my car and broke the windows into my apartment, and I just had to get out of there. Plus I help take care of my grandparents here in California now. I cook for them, drive them around. In the spring, I'm going to attend community college, and then hopefully transfer to a university."

"Boyfriend troubles?" I asked. "I can totally imagine boys going crazy over you. What type of guys do you typically go for?"

"For me, it's all about the personality and emotional connection."

"Sure, sure – pretty girls always say that, but then they all somehow end up dating the high school quarterback."

"No, really. See, in tenth grade, I was dating the most popular, best looking guy in high school. The one who all the girls wanted to date. Everyone thought that we were the perfect couple. But then I fell in love with my neighbor, who was in eighth grade. So I dumped the popular kid to date this younger boy. And can I tell you, people were really pissed at me. People were mad that I would somehow dump this beautiful class stud for this kid who was three years younger."

"Probably because you invalidated or threatened their own perspectives on the world. All of these other girls wanted to date your boyfriend. Then you dumped him, so they had to believe that something was innately wrong with you. Otherwise, they would have had to acknowledge that something might be wrong with them. Cognitive dissonance and all, you know."

"I know. This popular kid, Derek, was really hot and was really nice, but he would just say the stupidest things. Taylor, the eighth grader who I fell in love with, would hide in my closet when Derek came over, and we'd laugh afterwards about all the silly things he would say to me."

"Derek must have taken it pretty hard when you dumped him for Taylor. I'm sure that made no sense in his view of the world."

"You have no idea. After I broke up with him, he showed up at my house in a suit, with flowers, trying to get back together."

"Wow. Did he also stand outside your house holding a big boom box over his head?"

Kristina laughed.

"Do you know what movie I'm talking about? I forget the name of the movie."

"Yes, I know what you are talking about," she laughed again. "And no, he didn't."

"So did you get back together with Derek after he showed up at your house in a suit?"

"No. I started dating Taylor. And we've been on-again-off-again for years. Right now, we're off again. Taylor was the boyfriend who went a little crazy in Florida, and so I had to leave."

"So you're nineteen and Taylor is now sixteen? At least he's older now, but I guess you'll always have that three-year age difference."

"I know," she said with a slight whine. "And I think girls mature faster than boys, so right now, it feels like an even bigger gap. I think that we both need this space to be apart and grow on our own, but we'll be together in the end, I know."

We finished our minestrone. The waiter brought out our pasta dishes, her puh-NAY, and my sausage rigatoni. I ordered a glass of Cabernet.

"Would you like a glass of wine also?" I asked.

"No thank you. Only nineteen, remember?"

"Oh right. Man, I feel like a dirty old man," I laughed wryly. She laughed warmly with me.

"So your dad," I started again. "He left when you were young, but you reconnected with him in your teenage years. How is your relationship now?"

"Okay, I guess. He lives in Southern California with his eighth wife, only about an hour away from my grandparents. So I see him most weekends. Our relationship is relatively good compared to a few years ago when I lived with him in Calabasas."

"What happened in Calabasas?"

"It was just a tough time. I was really lonely having left all my friends in Florida. And I just started doing a lot of drugs."

"What types?"

"Cocaine mostly. I was doing meth for a while too."

"You smoked meth?"

"No, because I care about how my teeth look. One day, my roommate had meth lying on the table, and I asked if I could snort it, and she said sure. It hurt so bad. But like I said, I was pretty lonely and it helped. Then two weeks later, I tried to commit suicide."

"Jesus. How? Was it like some big emotional breakdown, and you just wanted to end it?"

"No, I was pretty calm actually. One day, I just decided 'no more,' and I started taking sleeping pills, one after another. I took twenty in a row, and then just lay down to let them take effect."

"Then what happened?"

"Then I started freaking out, and I woke up my dad and told him he needed to take me to the hospital. He didn't understand, and I said, 'No, like right now!' So he's driving me to the hospital, and I start throwing up in the car. And all that I can think about is how horrified I am that I'm throwing up in my dad's company Mercedes. He worked at a Mercedes dealership as a salesman. After that, they say my heart actually stopped in the hospital, and they had to shock me back to life with those paddles."

"Jesus, then what?"

"Well, they made me go to a mental institution for a couple of months for therapy. It was horrible. There were all these really crazy people who were scary to be around. My dad would come to visit weekly, and after three weeks, I was supposed to be released, but my doctor and my dad decided that I wasn't ready to leave yet. And I just remember holding onto my dad's leg crying, 'Dad, please don't go. Take me with you. Please don't go.' The nurses had to wrestle me free from my dad and sedate me."

I sat silent for a few seconds. I contemplated if I should go any further. I contemplated if I even wanted to go any further. Hard core drugs? Suicide? Mental institution? Just by sitting with her and talking to her, I was risking everything – my family, my job, everything I had worked so hard for. Was this girl even mentally stable now?

But then I looked into her eyes. I know it sounds stupid, but in that moment, I felt her soul and it gripped me. Completely. So down the rabbit hole I went.

"So what happened after you got out of the mental institution?"

"Well, my first day of high school back, I could feel everyone staring at me and whispering. One classmate, who was a drug dealer and had been trying to hook up with me for a long time, came up to me and said, 'Look, if you are trying to stay clean, I totally respect that, but if you want to meet up after school and do some coke – we can do that too.' I was like, 'Yes, please. Let's do that.' So we did. Then I decided that I couldn't take all those stares at high school anymore, so I transferred to this program that was more of an independent study, and I got my high school diploma through that."

"So you graduated from high school in Calabasas, where you were living with your dad. Then what drove the decision to move back to Florida?"

"Well, as I mentioned, my dad has been married a lot. But he was single at the time, and he just met this woman who he started to date. Actually, he was dating two women at the same time. One woman, Sharon, was nice and totally age-appropriate. And then one night, he brings home a different other woman, Mary, who's much younger. I just got pissed and started to scream at her, 'I don't know who the fuck you are, but you're just some skank who my dad is going to end up screwing over again.' And I started yelling at my dad about Sharon right in front of this new girl, Mary. My dad got really pissed, so I left the house. I went to Barnes and Noble and was just hanging out there when a guy, Kaden, approached me, and we started talking. He asked if I wanted to go see a movie and I was like, 'I don't even know you. You could be some crazy murderer.' But something about him seemed safe, so we ended up going. Then midway through the movie, I got a text from my dad that said, 'You need to grab all your stuff and go.'"

"What do you mean? How did your dad even know you were in the movie theater with a stranger?"

"Huh? Oh no, he meant that I needed to pack up all my stuff in his house and get out. Not that I needed to grab as much popcorn as I could and run," she laughed. "So I just started crying in the theater, and Kaden asked what was wrong. So I showed him the text, and he said, 'Okay, let's go get your stuff.' So we went to my dad's house and packed up my stuff. I didn't have much, and I went to stay with Kaden. It was kinda crazy because Kaden himself lived in this small room he rented from another family, so we were cramped in there for a few weeks. I would spend all day . . . literally all day, on the phone talking with Taylor. Since my dad kicked me out, I made plans to go back to Florida to be with Taylor and my grandma, who I love, love, love. My grandma is the best. I mean, it's not like she's super successful or anything. She basically lives on Social Security now, but she's got a huge heart. If I end up with half the heart of my grandma, I'll be really happy with my life."

"So did you and Kaden hook up while you were staying with him?"

"No. Right as I was leaving to go back to Florida, Kaden told me that he was in love with me. But nothing ever happened."

"Would you have hooked up with him if he tried something?"

She paused to consider the question. "I think I probably would have just because I felt like I owed him a lot. Which is a terrible reason to hook up, so I'm glad he never tried anything."

We were just picking at our pasta at that point, so the waiter came by for the plates.

"Would you like dessert?" I asked.

"Maybe. Would you?"

"Sure, let's split something," I said. I ordered a tiramisu and two spoons.

"Know what I like to do?" she asked.

"Break guys' hearts, I suppose."

"No," she giggled. "When I was in Calabasas, I used to like making friends with the homeless people on the beach. And I would try to give them a little money or food. Which is funny because growing up, we were always poor. So it wasn't like I had any extra."

The tiramisu came a few minutes later. We dug in. She seemed to get more of a thrill from the dessert than from her pasta.

"So, question," I said. "Have you ever dated an Asian guy?"

"Yes."

Somewhat surprised, I smiled. "Was he the valedictorian?"

"No, he was a drug dealer," she snorted. "Breaking the mold!"

I burst out laughing. Trouble. At that moment, I knew this relationship was going to be more than I had planned for and maybe more than I even wanted.

"So tell me a little more about your perspectives on this sort of arrangement," she asked. "Have you had one before?"

"Well, I've already told you a bit about my perspective on this. I only have one friend, Andrew, whom I tell everything to. Anyway, he's been having some marital problems, and he has a girlfriend who lives in Korea whom he sees every couple of months when he travels. We were having dinner a couple months ago, and he was describing the thrilling emotions that a new love brings. 'But,' he said, 'that passion always fades after a while. Six months. A year. It always fades. So why can't we live the rest of our lives just repeating that passionate, fun period over and over again with new, different people? I mean, if this is all there is to life, why not?'" I made a motion with my hand of one wave cresting into another wave, into another wave, and into a final wave.

I continued, "I'm not sure that I totally subscribe to that, but in my own amoral world where this arrangement is totally separate and not impacting anyone in my real world – I guess I'm looking for that in-between."

"In between what?"

"Well, on one end of the spectrum, having sex with an escort, which is purely transactional. And on the other end of the spectrum, finding the person you end up falling in love with and marrying. In-between."

Kristina was quiet for a few moments. I guess she was trying to figure out what "in-between" would actually look like. Truth is, I wasn't even sure myself.

"Well, I better get you to the airport to catch your flight back to LA," I said as I stood up. "Here, take my jacket for the flight back since you lost yours. By the way, the envelope with tonight's allowance is in the pocket." I wrapped my navy-blue Gap jacket around her delicate shoulders.

We walked outside together. The valet pulled up my car, and I started driving her to the airport only a few miles away.

"You can tell I don't really care about spending my money on cars," I said, pointing to the dashboard of my aging Honda. "Never been that important to me."

"What do you like to spend your money on?"

"Oh, I dunno. Other, less moral things, apparently," I said, and we both laughed.

"By the way, how is this going to work?" she asked.

"I guess, if you're still interested, I could fly you up next week. I want you to always feel comfortable, so the physical aspect of this arrangement can come when it feels natural to both of us."

"I actually meant, like how is this going to actually work – like where? I mean, would we just do it in the restaurant on the table?" she laughed.

"Oh. Well, ideally, for our next date, we could have dinner in a hotel room. It will be more comfortable to talk that way also, since we had so much trouble finding things to talk about this time," I said wryly.

"Okay, that sounds fine," she said calmly. "Next week should be fine also. I'm interviewing with Urban Outfitters tomorrow, but I don't know if I'll get the job or what my schedule will be if I do."

At the airport, I pulled up to the curbside for Southwest departures. I turned toward Kristina, and we both leaned in simultaneously. We kissed. Exciting, new, passionate. I felt the heat of Kristina's closeness as we probed gently with our tongues. It couldn't have lasted more than twenty seconds, and then we separated, just barely. I gave Kristina a little rub on her nose with mine. She laughed lightly, reached over, and gave me a bear hug.

"Oh no, why are you hugging me like a Teddy bear?"

"Because you're cute," she said, slightly embarrassed. I hopped out of the car and popped open the trunk. I pulled out a small Tiffany's bag and said, "Just a small gift to thank you for coming up. Text me when you get home so that I know you arrived home safely, please. And good luck on the Urban Outfitters interview. But I hope that the new job won't get in the way of you coming back up to visit."

She smiled and said, "It's okay. I'll find a way to come up. You pay better anyway."

We hugged once more, and she walked into the airport. I got back into my car and started to drive home. Home. To my wife and kids, and my real life. But I was already anticipating the next date with Kristina. I could still hear her easy laugh. I could still smell her perfume. Mostly, though, I could still sense the kindness of her heart. To have had such a tough childhood and to still be so at ease with the world . . . I was enthralled.

I arrived home. Kissed my wife. Told her briefly about my business dinner, and then went into the bathroom to take a shower and get ready for bed. As I sat on the toilet, I checked my text messages. I felt a little spark of excitement when I saw a message from Kristina.

Text from Kristina (10/24):
Tonight was great. Thank you so much for everything. Can't wait to see you next! :)

I texted back.

Text to Kristina (10/24):
Y'know – what makes life great are those rare moments that sparkle, that break apart the sometimes ordinary everyday. Thank you for making tonight one of those moments for me. If anything, ironically, the only risk I see is not the lack of a connection, but rather some level of unexpected (perhaps unhealthy) emotional bond. But I will do my best to remain emotionally unassailable in that respect. And as far as I can tell, the only way you'll REALLY fall for me is if I become, y'know, a drug dealer. (not currently in my plans).

Text from Kristina (10/24):
I just got your "verbose" text and I agree completely. :) Was it next Thursday you wanted me to check on?

Text to Kristina (10/24):
Yes, what I like to call "verbose" others sometimes call "verbal diarrhea." Oh well. Yup, next Thurs. Off to bed!

Text from Kristina (10/24):
Sleep tight!

I didn't sleep very well that night. Not at all.

Date 2: November 3

In retrospect, I know what this relationship with Kris would look like to an outside observer: some combination of infatuation mixed with an early midlife crisis. A pathetic thirty-eight-year-old man trying to relive his youth just one more time and right the wrongs from his awkward teenage years by finally getting the "It" girl from high school, even if he had to pay massive sums of money to do it. Truth is, I don't know if this relationship, as it eventually developed, was infatuation or love, and I stopped caring about the difference a long time ago.

After our first date, we emailed back and forth practically daily. I spent my formative teenage years in the '80s when there was no Facebook, no Twitter, and no Instagram. So I would write lengthy letters to girls whom I liked. On actual paper. Given my significant disadvantage in the looks department during high school, I worked hard at making writing a competitive advantage. It didn't help all that much, but regardless, writing notes was a skill that I practiced out of necessity:

Email to Kristina (10/25):
So to continue my text – I would love to see how deep this rabbit hole goes. If you're game, keep next Thursday open. I'll look into flights tomorrow. Generally though, it would be great to fly you up in the afternoon, meet for an early dinner in a suite, and order room service. We can watch a movie, listen to music, and just see how it goes. I'll need to leave around 9:30, so I can book you on a late flight back (around 10:30 or 11 P.M.). I will assume that we'll start the full arrangement gift next time. But I also want you to know, as I said, the physical connection (hopefully we have one) – I want that to come when it feels natural for both of us. I'm not stressed about it. Good luck with the Urban Outfitters interview tomorrow. I am also already looking forward to seeing you again.

Email from Kristina (10/25):

Hey you. I'm definitely game for next week! Of course, my interview got rescheduled to this Thursday so no good news to share yet. How is your day going so far? P.S. I probably would have died last night without your jacket on the way home.

Email to Kristina (10/26):

Know it's a bit sophomoric, but it makes me happy to think of you wearing my jacket for some reason. I'm glad it kept you warm.

Long day of driving today. Took the kids up to Tahoe for a few days to learn to ski. They're pretty excited. Then Monday, I'm off to your old hometown (or at least one of them, if I remember correctly) Las Vegas for a couple days for work.

Sorry your interview got postponed. How was your day otherwise? Full of inquiries from freaky sugar daddies that make me look good by comparison, I hope. Not ashamed to admit that I thought of you more often than was probably appropriate. Guys are so predictable in that way. You, on the other hand, most likely woke up this morning and said, "Hmmm . . . whose jacket is that?" C'est la vie.

Hopefully see you next Thursday? In the meantime, I wish you sweet dreams that are filled with short, cute Asian guys . . . well just one . . . no, not your ex-boyfriend...

Email from Kristina (10/26):

I've only lived in Henderson! -5 points for Ryan. ;) My day was actually pretty boring, hopefully today will be better. Right now the puppy and the kitten are cuddled up together in my lap as I fill my head with paternity test results on Jerry Springer. I have a feeling this is as exciting as my day is going to get. Hope you're having a wonderful time with the kids, and yes, I've been thinking about you a lot as well. :)

Email to Kristina (10/27):

Totally not fair. We covered so much ground over dinner, how could one simple man possibly remember all of it? Plus I was in the geographic vicinity, so I should at least get partial credit.

Also, I believe it was Freud who said that most of our dreams are based on events or ideas from the day prior (called it "day residue"). So anyway, last night, I had a nightmare I was on Springer, you were sitting there, and he was yelling at me "You are NOT the father!" Egads – thanks for that horrifying vision also.

Fine, fine. Kristina 1. Ryan 0. (or -5 if you must)

Email from Kristina (10/28):
At least he didn't say, "you ARE the father"!

We made plans for the following Thursday. I reserved a suite at a hotel near the airport, and I asked Kris to take the hotel shuttle from the airport. I arrived early that day, checked into the room, went to pick up sushi per her request, and then waited in the room. She texted that she had landed and was on the hotel shuttle. But the rush hour traffic on the highway was bad, so the driver was taking a convoluted route on back roads instead. Shit.

I brushed my teeth, set out the food, and opened a bottle of wine. Finally, there was a knock on the door.

"Hi," I said as she walked into the room. I leaned in to give her a hug and kiss. She dodged the kiss and gave me a hug back. A little bit of an awkward start given how we ended things last time.

She took off her jacket. I noticed she was wearing the Tiffany's teardrop pendant that I had given her last time.

"Glass of wine?"

"No, thanks. I don't really drink much. I don't like the taste of it. The only alcoholic beverage that I will drink is Smirnoff Ice. I know, very girly."

"I'll remember that for next time. First off, here is your gift for this visit. I really meant what I said about you always being comfortable. So I wanted to give this to you up front. You can literally leave now anytime you want," I said as I slipped the envelope with $1,000 in hundred dollar bills into her handbag.

"Great, I'll be seeing you later then," she laughed.

"Oh no! At least stay for dinner," I smiled. "Shall we eat?"

We sat down on cushions around the coffee table and dug into the edamame and sushi. She needed a fork, so I ordered one from room service. We caught up on our respective weeks generally. She had gone to Texas with her dad to watch Game Three of the World Series. Turns out her dad worked as a sales rep at a Mercedes dealership in Long Beach, and he had won the trip for being one of the top sales reps that month.

"So how was the game?" I asked.

"Okay, but San Francisco lost. We had this sort of funny moment on the trip, though. When we checked into the hotel, they asked for a credit card. I guess the hotel needed to charge four hundred dollars for the room. My dad didn't know he was expected to pay up front and get reimbursed afterwards. So we were kind of stuck because he didn't have four hundred dollars, and he doesn't have a credit card because his credit sucks. I actually had enough in my account because of the money you gave me last time. So I said, 'Dad, you can use my debit card.' And he just looked at me, kind of embarrassed and kind of like, 'How the heck do you have four hundred dollars?'" she laughed.

"That's funny. So did you get good bonding time with your dad on the trip?"

"Sort of. I mean, it was nice spending time together, but I kept waiting for us to have a serious talk about our relationship. But it never happened."

"What did you want to have a serious talk about?"

"I don't know. There are just a lot of unaddressed things from the past."

"Like when he left your mom and you when you were four?"

"Yeah, but not just that. Like when he kicked me out of his house in Calabasas, which I told you about last time. It felt like he was kicking me out because of his new girlfriend, Mary. It hurt a lot for my dad to kick me out of his house for someone else."

"And Mary eventually became his eighth wife, you said? Jesus. How old is your dad?"

"He's sixty-one, so pretty old. He was forty-two when he had me, and he was fifteen years older than my mom when they got married. She was wife number four, I think . . . though she didn't know it at the time."

"Did he have any other kids with his other seven wives?"

"Not that we know about. But my mom and I always joke with each other that we're going to hire a private detective to see what else he's hiding."

"Wow, eight wives. Your dad is a stud. I hope I'm still going like that when I'm sixty-one," I joked. "I know you've had your ups and downs with your dad, but there's got to be something charming about him that he could actually convince eight women to marry him."

"My dad has a big personality and just gets along with people. Most people, I guess," Kris said quietly. Then her thoughts seemed to drift. I sensed that it would be best to shift the conversation away from daddy issues – paternal daddy issues, at least.

"So I was wondering, have you ever had a sugar daddy before?" I asked.

"Sort of. When I was eighteen, I was working for this guy in Florida, Bill. He was probably in his fifties. I swear his business must have been a front for something else, because me and this other girl would just sit in the office all day and literally do nothing except surf the web and check Facebook. Nobody ever called or came into the office. He did something to do with diamonds, I think. Anyway, after a few weeks, he started to jokingly ask the other girl, 'Susan, when are you going to set me up with some of your hot young friends?' And Susan, who's kind of heavyset, would point to me and say, 'Well, I've got one right here.' This went on for a while, and he eventually started asking me directly if I would be open to him paying me for that sort of arrangement. At first, I said no. But my roommate Katy and I were behind on rent. So Bill started working on Katy to convince me to do it. Finally, one day, I just did it."

"How was it? Was he good-looking? By the way, I'm not judging, obviously," I said as I pointed around the room at our surroundings. "As far as I'm concerned, two consenting adults should be free to decide what they want to do."

"Well, I was barely an adult. And no, it wasn't good – not at all. I don't remember much, honestly. I just remember going on his boat and walking into the bedroom. And then afterwards, I remember breaking down and crying. I was dating Taylor at the time. I didn't tell Taylor everything, but he kind of knew. So that's when we started selling weed to try to make some extra money, and eventually I broke things off with Bill. I couldn't deal with having a sugar daddy who was so close and lived in the same town. Then I discovered the sugar baby website.

Through that, I met a guy named Max in Las Vegas. He seemed pretty good-looking from his pictures. Katy and I needed to make rent again, and she kept telling me, 'C'mon, Kris, take one for the team,'" Kris said with a snort. "Max would fly me out, and I'd spend the weekend with him in Vegas. He was a total douche and ended up being a lot older than his pictures implied. But at least he had good drugs that we'd do together. Again, we needed to make rent, so I did it until I couldn't take it anymore. I only saw Max two or three times."

I thought for a minute. Two prior sugar daddies, and she obviously held both in great disdain. Was I kidding myself that I had felt something genuine from Kris on our initial date?

"And this? Us, I mean. How do you feel about this?"

"I feel really good about this. You don't understand. Most guys on the site are creepy, a lot older, and look nothing like their pictures. I actually told Katy about you after our last date. I told her that you're really good-looking, funny and rich. And she asked me, 'Then why is he doing this?' She's right, you know. I mean, you could get girls on your own without paying them."

"That's nice of you. Whether true or not, the fact is it would be really hard to form a new relationship with a girl since I'm married. For example, even if you do genuinely like me, it's not like you would be here if there wasn't this common understanding of what this is and what we're both seeking."

Kris was quiet for a bit.

"What about you?" she asked. "Have you had other sugar babies?"

"No. I've really only been looking for a few months. It's funny. The way that I found out about the site was from a friend who emailed a group of us an article written about the founder of this sugar baby website and how he built this empire based on connecting rich men with beautiful girls. All my friends were emailing back and forth, joking about the site. You know, stuff like, 'That guy's my hero!' Anyway, I joked along with them, but in the back of my mind, I was like, 'Hmm . . . very interesting.' So then I subscribed to the site and started looking. Before you, I met with two other girls. I made plans to meet with four, but two of them were no-shows. Literally, I bought them plane tickets, and they just didn't show up. Impending reality has a way of crystallizing things, I think. Of the two that I did meet, they were nice and attractive, but we just didn't click. So we didn't go any further than the initial date."

"Did you have sex with them?"

"No. One of them was pretty aggressive, actually. She thought that I expected sex, and I basically had to push her off of me on the first date. You see, if you have money, it's easy to find sex. And I don't mean sex with some scary streetwalker. I mean if you have the money, there are escort services that can set you up with legitimate college girls and models. But I wasn't looking for sex on these previous dates. I could get that if I wanted. I was looking for that in-between."

"I remember," she said thoughtfully.

"So you mentioned that over the last few years, you've been on-again-off-again with this younger guy, Taylor."

"Yup. We're actually on-again now."

"Got it. Hmm . . . does he know about this whole thing?"

"Well, he knows about the site, and he knows that I met you. I told him a little bit about our first date, but I basically said that you were an old Chinese guy just looking for someone to talk to and that you didn't want anything physical. I said that you broke down crying after telling me about your life," she laughed.

"Wonderful, Kris. Sounds like you made me out to be an emotional wreck," I chuckled. "Well, whatever you need to tell him is fine. I can hardly call the kettle black. One question that I had from our last date was that you told me that Taylor busted up your car and broke a window in your apartment. What were you guys arguing about?"

"Long story. One thing I didn't tell you is that I'm attracted to both boys and girls. And there was this girl, Heather, from my high school who is really cute. Anyway, we kind of hated each other during high school, but after high school, we became friends. I had a party at my house one night, and Heather and her new boyfriend, Evan, and me and Taylor went into my bedroom to smoke weed. Then Heather started making out with Evan, and Taylor and I started making out. And then we all started hooking up. But Taylor got overwhelmed and couldn't really, you know, keep it up. So he got really upset and ran out. I ran after him, but he drove off. Anyway, after he left, I was still high, and I went back to my bedroom and ending up hooking up with both Heather and Evan."

"Nice. Ménage à trois. Evan must have been psyched. It went from a foursome to a threesome with just him and two beautiful girls."

"Yeah, he was pretty happy. But then he started paying more attention to me and ignoring Heather. And then he started to have sex with me, and Heather got upset and ran out of the room. So I ran out after her."

"Poor Evan. Went from two beautiful girls to none," I laughed.

"Yeah, and he didn't even get to finish. I basically kicked him out of the room when Heather left and, then I found her on the porch and tried to make up."

"So Taylor found out and basically got pissed."

"Basically."

"And then he went psycho. Do you think he was more mad that you cheated on him, or more embarrassed that he had to run away because he couldn't keep it up beforehand?"

"That's a good question – I'm not sure. Probably a bit of both."

"And what was harder for him – you cheating with Heather or with Evan?"

"Both, actually. He was really pissed at me having sex with both Heather and Evan."

"That's interesting. Most guys have fantasized about lesbians at some point. For me, I would have just been pissed that you had sex with Evan. So Taylor went psycho, busted up your car, and then he broke into your house through the window. What did you do when that happened?"

"Well, I was just watching TV with Katy, and when I heard the window break, I just ran."

"Were you afraid he was going to hurt you? I mean, has he hit you before?"

Her eyes left me for a moment. "No," she said quietly. "He hasn't hit me before, but still, I just ran. He's a smart kid. Gets straight As. He wants to go to Berkeley to become a doctor when he graduates. But he just has no common sense."

"So you left Florida again recently to live with your grandparents in California because of that?"

"That was a big reason. Also, I had no money and nowhere to live in Florida, and my grandparents were able to take me in. I help them around the house in return. But the truth is that if Taylor and

I hadn't gotten into that big argument, I would have found a way to stay in Florida with him."

"But now you're back together doing the long distance thing?"

"Yup. Like I said, I always just assumed we'd end up together. We met when we were just kids, and we basically grew up together. So no one knows me like he does."

"But he doesn't know everything about you."

"What do you mean?"

"Well, this. Us. He doesn't know everything. Kris, my view is that we all have to wear different masks in different parts of our lives in the real world. Even with those people whom we love dearly. So for example, I wear one mask when I talk with my parents. A different mask when I talk with my sister. Another mask with my wife – I mean obviously, she doesn't know that I'm here. A different mask with my friends, colleagues, and so on. We're constantly adjusting and gauging how much information to share. The one nice thing about our arrangement is that we can decide to wear no masks. We can be completely ourselves because it doesn't matter. I'd like to try to do that. No masks at all. Just completely who we are . . . like we are when we're alone in our most vulnerable moments."

Kris nodded and smiled thoughtfully. By now we had worked through about a third of the massive amount of sushi that I had ordered, and we were both stuffed. I reached over for my iPad and started to play some soft music.

"Oh, congrats on getting the Urban Outfitters job. How was the interview?"

"It was fine. I wore the Tiffany's necklace that you gave me to the interview. So, I guess it brought me luck. I've never really had anything nice like this before, by the way. Certainly nothing from Tiffany's. I was so excited that I took a picture when I got home and posted it on my Instagram. The only funny thing from the interview was they asked me what I didn't like about my previous job, and I almost responded 'My boss sexually molested me.'"

"What did actually you say?"

"No opportunity for career advancement."

We laughed freely together.

"So I have a random question that I like to ask people," I said. "If you had 100 points to allocate across three characteristics for your future spouse, and those characteristics were looks, personality and intelligence, how would you allocate those points? For context, 33 points is average. So if you said, 33 looks, 33 personality, and 33 intelligence, you basically would be marrying Mr. Average. Also, of course, some people actually are better than average across all three characteristics, but the question is more about your relative prioritization if you only had 100 points to allocate for your spouse."

"Hmm . . . I'd go 40 looks, 30 personality, and 30 intelligence. Looks are pretty important to me."

"Really? But on our last date, you said that you date guys based on personality. That's why you supposedly dumped Mr. Wonderful in high school to date Taylor, who is three years younger. Is Taylor really good-looking too?"

"No, he's not. I mean, he's not bad-looking, but I think that he gets insecure about it sometimes. Like one time went to McDonald's. While he was standing in line, some other guy approached me and was like, 'Hey beautiful, come hang out with us.' When I pointed out that I was with Taylor, he was like, 'Him – really? You're way too hot for him. I'm a Hollister model, you should be with me.' I basically told him to fuck off, but it really bugged Taylor. I tend to look for average to above-average guys who I really connect with. So maybe my overweighting of looks only applies for this sort of relationship," she giggled.

"Well, if you're focused on looks, I'm sorry to disappoint."

"Hush. I already told you I thought you were handsome. What about you? How would you allocate 100 points for your spouse?"

"I'd go 80 looks, 10 personality and 10 intelligence."

"So your wife is basically a supermodel, but she's dull and dumb as a rock."

"Well, I figure you might as well have a superhot wife because it's socially acceptable to go outside your marriage to get intellectual and social gratification, but not acceptable to go outside your marriage to get sexual satisfaction. Our situation, of course, notwithstanding," I smiled.

"Of course," she said thoughtfully. "But you don't really mean that, do you? About your allocation, I mean?"

"No, I don't really mean it. Course, like everyone else, what I really want is someone who is 100 on all three characteristics."

I glanced at my Blackberry. I groaned silently – it was already 9:10 P.M. I'd need to drive her back to the airport in twenty minutes, and we hadn't even kissed yet. On the one hand, it was wonderful that we could get lost in our conversation for hours. On the other hand, this was a sugar baby arrangement and the physical aspect was part of the understanding. I didn't want to be shy about that, either.

I took her hand and stood her up. I drew Kris close with one arm around her waist and one hand gently placed under the back of her delicate jaw. I kissed her deeply. I felt a slight pause and then submission as she kissed me back. I recalled her slight hesitation when she had first walked into the hotel room. I suddenly realized that while I had built up in my mind the romanticism around our second date in the privacy of an elegant hotel suite, from Kris's point of view, she was walking alone into a random hotel room hundreds of miles from home to meet with some guy she barely knew. I drew apart for a moment.

"So, Kris, I have one request."

"What?"

"Let's not have sex tonight, okay? I've got to drive you to the airport in about fifteen minutes, and I don't want to rush this. Think you can handle that?"

"I think so. I'll try to control myself," she smiled.

I took her hand and led her to the bedroom. We kissed again deeply, and then I slowly pulled her blouse over her head. As I reached around her back and unclasped her tan bra, she said, "One thing I forgot to mention."

"What?" I asked breathlessly. I could already feel my cock throbbing inside my jeans.

Kris let her bra fall away as she reached up with her fingers to gently fondle two small gold hoop rings in each of her nipples.

"Very nice," I said. My god, Kris's breasts were perfect. Size-wise, they were solid C-cups. They were perfectly proportioned for her slim frame, and they rested firmly and naturally on her chest.

I laid Kris on the bed and put my mouth onto her small pink nipples. I used my tongue to gently play with her nipple rings. Kris slowly unbuttoned my oxford shirt. She paused when she got to the last button.

"What?" I said.

"Geez, you have a six-pack. Didn't expect that," she said teasingly. "You say you are thirty-eight, but have the body of a twenty-year-old."

"It's an Asian thing," I smiled as I kissed her harder this time. I unbuttoned her blue jeans and then tugged them slowly down. She wore pink lace panties, and I slowly pulled those off also. As she lay on the bed on her back staring up at me, I was almost paralyzed by her beauty.

I crawled down and put my tongue against her left ankle. I slowly drew my tongue up her leg, pressed harder with my tongue as I licked the inside of her thigh, and then hovered my head between her legs to let her feel my hot breath on her pussy. After a few long seconds, I pressed my wet tongue against her clit. She moaned.

Salty, sweet, and musky. More musky than I had expected and more than I usually like. But with Kris it didn't matter – I wanted her. I licked her gently and could feel her grind against me for a few seconds before she pushed my head away gently.

"No, please," she gasped. "If you keep doing that, I'm going to want to have sex tonight, and we need to get to the airport."

"Sure, something to look forward to next time."

We got dressed. Both unsatisfied. Both longing. I left a ten-dollar tip for the maid on the coffee table since we had made a mess with all the sushi boxes. As I drove Kris to the airport, I took a wrong turn and we ended up on a back road that ran parallel to a bog.

"Where are you taking me?" she laughed lightly. "Smells awful."

"That smell is from the outside, by the way. That's not me. I didn't fart."

"Uh huh, sure."

I turned the car around, got back on the highway and found my way to the airport.

I gave Kris a hug in the car. She hopped out and was gone.

Date 3: November 17

Anyone who is considering becoming a sugar daddy needs to be very mindful of developing a "hero" complex. It's quite an emotional high to be suddenly adored (or at least, appear to be adored) by a beautiful young girl whom you shower with money and gifts the likes of which she has never experienced before. But that emotional high can get addicting in an unhealthy way. Before Kris, I had met with a couple other potential sugar babies, and they both had stories of sugar daddies who had become too dependent and obsessed, to the point where they had tried to control the "real life" of these girls outside of their arrangements. These sugar daddies would get jealous over new boyfriends and constantly ask where they were and why they weren't immediately responding to messages.

I was determined not to let that emotional boundary be crossed – in either direction, frankly. I could already sense the emotional bonds forming between Kris and me on our dates and in our emails. So I had to remind myself that I was paying her a lot of money to hang out with me, and I would constantly tell Kris that she should remember that I'm the type of guy who cheats on his wife. I felt like as long as we remembered those two facts, we'd be able to maintain a certain level of disdain for each other that would act as an emotional shield from our becoming too close. From our becoming emotionally unbalanced.

But, as Woody Allen said, in reference to his own optically inappropriate relationship with his stepdaughter, "The heart wants what the heart wants." Kris began to fill my waking thoughts. I would wait anxiously for her reply emails, and I would fantasize about our next date. I remember late one night, as I tossed in bed, I mentally slapped myself. "You are paying her to hang out with you. Don't forget that! Don't lose that disdain for her, or for yourself," I thought. But then another thought popped into my head. "If there ever comes a day where I have a date with Kris and she tells me not to pay her, then I'll know I have crossed some important emotional line. Some emotional barrier will have broken down, and I will be in real trouble."

Kris and I set our next date for a couple weeks away. That was the original pacing we had discussed, and it felt like the right cadence in order to avoid our arrangement feeling like too much a part of our real lives. But we messaged often in between.

Text from Kris (11/11):
Is it weird to say I miss you?

Text to Kris (11/11):
Only if I replied back with something awkward, like "thank you." I miss you also. There – all good.

Solution is one of two options. A) come visit or B) grab the next Asian guy you see as a reasonable replacement (trust me, he'll be happy).

Email from Kris (11/14):
When I go into work tomorrow, I will see what my schedule is like and let you know about visiting. I'd like to come visit!

My weekend was expensive lol. Christmas shopping. Of course. I gave in halfway through and ended up buying myself a jacket to ease the tension of trying to figure out what to get for grandparents and parents who claim to want nothing at all.

Why do all of you elderly people do that?! ;)

Email to Kris (11/14):
My dear – the reason I say "nothing" when asked what I want for Christmas is because what I want, you can't buy in a store (though, as it turns out, I may have found it on a less than reputable website . . . I guess we'll both see). Hopefully the reason your grandpa says "nothing" is different than mine – because otherwise that would be really weird.

We set our date for Thursday. Same plan. Kris would fly up, take a shuttle from the airport to the hotel, and meet me in the hotel suite.

This time, she would arrive before me, so I put her name on the hotel reservation so that she could check in when she arrived.

When I got to the hotel, Kris texted me the room number, and I went directly to the room.

"Hi!" she said brightly as she opened the door. I grabbed her waist and pulled her close for a deep kiss. We smiled at each other for a few seconds, and then she said, "Let's order room service. I'm starving!"

We ordered a pizza and salad from room service, and I put her envelope for this date into her handbag. I then took a quick shower while we waited for the food to arrive.

"So how was your day?" I asked as I finished toweling off and pulled my jeans back on.

"Mmm . . . okay. I had a physical checkup today. It sucked. I haven't had health insurance for a while. But my dad is working now, so I have coverage through him. I figured I should take advantage of it while I can, so I went in for a physical exam, which I haven't done in years. I also need to go in for a dental checkup, which I haven't been able to do in years either."

"What sucked about the physical exam? Just typical poking and prodding?"

"No. He asked me if I was sexually active. When I said 'yes,' and told him that I'd never been tested for STDs, he had me do a battery of tests, including a blood test and a Pap smear. The Pap smear really hurt, so I'm kind of sore down there, by the way."

I reflected on the implications of that for a few seconds.

"How long did you not have health insurance before your dad got this job?"

"Oh, I can't even remember. Years."

"So what do you do when you get sick?"

"I try not to get sick. Here, let me show you something." Kris stood up in front of me and straightened both of her arms out in front of her with her wrists pointed up. I saw a distinctive bend at the elbow of her right arm. Instead of the elbow pointing straight down, it kicked to the inside.

"What happened?" I asked as I helped myself to a slice of pizza.

"When I was thirteen, I went to a birthday party for my friend, Dylan, at his parents' country club. Dylan was driving me around the golf course in one of those souped-up golf carts that don't have a speed limiter, and he started going really fast over hills and making sharp turns. He was showing off, I guess. I started freaking out, and I was screaming for him to slow down. But he kept driving like a crazy man. So I jumped."

"Jumped?"

"Jumped out of the cart. Landed on my arm and broke it. Dylan felt so bad, he carried me all the way back to the clubhouse. Which is silly, because it's not like my leg was broken, and we had a golf cart right there," she said, laughing. "Anyway, I got home, and my mom was really pissed. We didn't have health insurance, so they just wrapped my arm tight in a towel and let it heal on its own."

"Jesus, you never saw a doctor?"

"We couldn't afford it. God, it hurt like hell. Eventually it healed, but my arm's crooked now, and it limits my range of motion. I had to give up a bunch of things that I used to do, like ballet and tennis."

"That's horrible, Kris," I said sadly. "Ballet? You were a dancer?"

"Yes, ever since I was four. I used to think that I would pursue it as a career. But after the accident, I gave that up. I've had to give up a lot of dreams because we were poor," she said, her eyes distant. "You know what really pisses me off? Kids who have parents willing to pay for their college, but who don't go. They don't know how lucky they are. And to just waste it . . ." she said as her eyes squinted in frustration.

"I'm sorry, Kris. That's really sad."

"Could have been worse," she said as she shook herself back into the moment.

"Yeah, I guess you could have been unattractive along with being poor. It just seems so unfair. Honestly, it makes me mad, and I'm not sure at whom. Just mad at the world, I guess. For me, it was different. My parents were typical immigrants who worked hard to give their kids all the opportunities they didn't have. So we were middle class growing up, but we were always very frugal. My parents saved every penny in order to send my sister and me to college and not burden any of us with student loans. So I was able to graduate from Princeton with no debt. That was a huge gift for which I can never repay my parents. And in exchange, my only job was to study. That was my only responsibility

– get perfect grades. And since, as I already told you, I couldn't get a date in high school, I had plenty of time to study . . . and read a lot of fantasy and science fiction books also, of course," I laughed.

"I wish I could have had your high school experience."

"What do you mean? I told you, my high school life sucked."

"I know, but if you hadn't gone through that and instead were out partying . . . maybe you wouldn't have studied so hard, gone to the best school, and eventually made a great career and perfect family. It's like all that was the sacrifice to get you to where you are today. And I'm the prize," she said with a laugh.

"Well then, it was all worth it," I laughed with her. "I've done okay, I guess. I've sort of always felt this filial piety, where I need to do well in order to honor and take care of my parents, which I'm really proud that I can do now. But I don't know if I'll ever have the same drive my parents have. Particularly my dad – he grew up poor in Shanghai during the war. He knew poverty at an entirely different level, where he was literally starving and going to bed hungry every night. I think that creates a drive that is pretty hard for me to ever replicate. He came to the U.S. with nothing, and sent his two kids through Ivy League colleges with no debt."

I paused for a moment. "Have you ever known that type of poverty? I know you were poor, but was there a time when you were ever physically hungry?"

"There was a period in elementary school in Nevada when my mom lost her job. We had to sleep in her car for a few months. We really couldn't afford food, so I remember going to elementary school with nothing for lunch. Or sometimes, I might have a pack of those orange peanut butter crackers. My friend, Jennifer, would sometimes share her lunch with me. She had just moved to Henderson and didn't know anyone, and I was hungry, so it worked our perfectly," Kris said with a light laugh.

I was stunned. Kris. This beautiful nineteen-year-old girl, who had been through so much pain in her young life, was sitting here calmly talking about living in a car and going to sleep hungry without an ounce of self-pity.

I suddenly felt an urge to help her . . . to protect her. I could feel the hero complex start to erupt in my heart. Careful, careful, careful.

33

"That's heartbreaking, Kris. No kid should be hungry like that."

"Happens all the time."

"One out of six kids is the statistic in the United States, I believe. And did the other kids in school ever make fun of you? For being poor? I know how mean little kids can be."

"No. No one really knew, and I tried hard to stay clean. After a while, my mom finally found a job. We moved in with a close friend of hers for a bit, and then we finally moved into our own house."

"That must have been exciting, to have your own place. Your own room."

"It was," she smiled. "It had a real yard and everything. Jennifer and I are still friends, actually. One time, in elementary school, I gave her this sticker to thank her, and she still has that sticker today."

We had finished eating, so she suggested we go into the bedroom and watch TV while we talked. There was some teen comedy on about a girl who agrees to pretend that she had sex with the class nerd in order to elevate his social standing. The irony there wasn't worth dwelling on. We lounged next to each other on the bed with our backs against the headboard, holding hands.

"So what about now, Kris? You've had to give up some dreams because you were poor, but what are your dreams now? You're only nineteen, after all."

"Well, I told you I moved back to Florida after my dad kicked me out of his house in California. And I mainly moved back to be with Taylor, but he was and still is in high school. So last year, I attended community college in Naples. I finished the first year. Then all that shit with Taylor happened, and I moved back to California to live with my grandparents. Right now, I'm planning to finish my second year of community college in California and then hopefully transfer to a university. My dad has a pretty decent job now, so hopefully he can help with tuition. But we'll see. He's always been unreliable in that respect. Taylor wants to go to Berkeley, so if I don't get into Berkeley with him, I'll just attend some other college in the area."

"And if I remember your profile correctly, you wanted to be a doctor of some kind?""

"Close. I originally thought I'd be an elementary school teacher, but now I'd like to be a geriatric psychologist."

"That's pretty specific. How did you decide on that?"

"My grandma in Florida practically raised me when my mom left for a number of years. And I was also super close with my great-grandmother, my Nanna. She passed away last year, but they were both my best friends. So I just really feel comfortable around older people. In a lot of ways, when people get older, they kind of become little kids again. Anyway, I like being with and helping older people."

"Great," I said, raising one eyebrow. We both burst out laughing. "At least, when I'm a senior citizen, you can be my psychologist."

"What about you?" she asked. "Did you always know you wanted to . . . what do you do again?"

"I work at a hedge fund. It's fine, and I'm decent at it. But I never expected to have a job where I woke up every day and couldn't wait to get to work. I guess that I never had that expectation of loving my job. They call it 'work' for a reason, right? I mainly chose this job because I can make a lot of money in a short period of time and create the financial independence to then go do something I'd really like to do."

"And what would that be?"

"I'm not sure yet specifically, but I want to build something myself. You know, start a business. And I don't have to build a hugely successful multi-billion dollar company. Honestly, I think I'd be happy if I just built a successful restaurant or some other small business. Just knowing that I created something that wasn't there before – that's what I'd like to do."

I glanced at the bedside clock. "Jesus, it's already 8:45. I need to drive you to the airport in forty-five minutes. I don't know how this keeps happening. Talk, talk, talk, talk, talk, talk, talk, and next thing you know, we're out of time. Just like last time. Well, I'm not making that mistake again," I said with a smile.

I leaned over and let my lips brush against hers. Then I pressed my lips harder against hers and explored her inviting mouth. Our tongues danced around each other and our breath grew heavier. I lightly probed her ear with my tongue, and she moaned in return. I gripped her breasts through her flower blouse and then pulled it over her head. She had on a turquoise bra speckled with small sparkles. I unclasped it and just stared at her perfection.

Kris sat up, unbuckled my belt and tugged off my jeans and boxers. She pushed me back onto the bed and bit my nipples gently. I could feel my cock press against her stomach. She moved downwards, and I felt a rush as she wrapped her moist mouth around my cock. She alternated between bobbing up and down my cock with her mouth and stroking my cock with her hand.

I could barely control myself. I reached down and pulled her up towards me so I could feel her mouth against mine again. Then I gently turned her onto her back and worked her jeans and panties off. I kissed her ears, then her neck, running my tongue from her chin down to the valley between her breasts. I licked my index and middle finger and caressed her left nipple as I sucked on her right nipple. I moved slowly down her perfect body, explored her belly button with my tongue, and then ran my tongue down her left thigh. I heard her moan as I licked the inside of her thigh, and she moaned louder as I lifted her left leg from the bed and began to suck on her toes . . . one by one.

I moved back up her leg slowly and then pressed my tongue onto her swollen pussy. She gasped. I found her clit and lightly worked my tongue in circles. Then I sucked on my middle finger before slowly pushing it inside her pussy. I felt her wince.

"Pap smear?" I asked.

"Yes, it hurts a little from that."

"So no sex?"

"I'm sorry," she said with an apologetic frown.

"That's okay, we'll have fun in other ways," I smiled as I reached over the edge of the bed for my duffel bag. I pulled out a bottle of Astroglide lube that I had brought. I poured a quarter-sized amount onto my index and middle fingers. Then as I kissed Kris tenderly, I slowly and rhythmically rubbed her clit. Up and down, just a fraction of an inch in a small oval pattern. I could feel Kris's breath accelerate. As I felt her body tense beneath me, I rubbed her clit more vigorously and sucked on her nipple as she moaned loudly. She suddenly let out a loud gasp and grabbed my hand, which was massaging her clit, with both of her hands. She shook uncontrollably as she came hard on my fingers.

After about twenty seconds, she regained control and then pushed me onto my back on the bed. I arched my back in ecstasy as her mouth enveloped my cock again. She took my shaft all the way down, and I could feel my cock hit the back of her throat. "Let me see your beautiful eyes," I groaned, raising my head to look at her as I simultaneously grabbed her hair into a ponytail behind her head. She looked up at me with her luminous green eyes, and I came hard into her mouth. As she felt me cum, she sucked harder and faster until I was completely spent. She swallowed . . . all of it. She looked up at me and smiled.

I pulled her upwards, and she laid her head onto my chest as we both breathed each other in deeply.

"That was amazing," I said.

"You felt amazing also. I've never had someone use lube on me before. I thought lube was just for old women, but it was really fun," she smiled. "I was wondering what you brought in that black duffel bag."

"Right," I laughed. "The whole bag is just full of lube." She laughed with me.

"So let's see each other again soon, please," she said sweetly. "I'm nervous about the next couple of weeks because my mom is coming from Nevada to visit for Thanksgiving. When we were younger, we would fight all the time, but it's better now. Still, spending that much time with my mom makes me nervous. And then my dad and his wife are going to be around also, so that could make things awkward because my mom still has a lot of anger towards him."

"Yikes. Okay, we'll plan our next date soon. And good luck with your mom's visit."

I hopped in the shower to quickly rinse off as she got dressed. I gave her a deep kiss before we left the hotel suite, since I knew it would be risky to kiss her at the airport. I drove Kris to the airport and she hopped out of my car. As I watched her walk through the automatic sliding doors of the terminal, I was already planning our next date.

Date 4: December 1

Kris had consumed an ever-increasing portion of my waking thoughts since our first date, but after our last date, she started to infiltrate my nocturnal dreams. Sometimes they would be sexual in nature, which is quite predictable. Most times, though, we would just be hanging out doing normal stuff. Watching a movie together, going to the supermarket, cooking dinner.

The rational barriers that I erected to keep this relationship separate from my real world were breaking down quickly. In a way, my obsession with Kris started to become my real world, and my work and family life started to become just the stuff in between. I intuitively knew how dangerous this was becoming, but I was like a boat with no oars in the middle of a storm. Kris's storm. I'd email or text her constantly. At work. On the toilet. At my kid's birthday party.

I wanted to turn it off – at least rationally I wanted to turn it off. But I couldn't, and I knew it. All I could hope for was to ride out this storm until we reached calmer waters, and pray that my boat wasn't smashed against the rocks before then.

Email to Kris (11/18):
So I woke up this morning and had a question pop in my head. If you rarely eat hamburgers, what do you order at McDonald's (which you've mentioned before)? I was like, "man – if she didn't tell the truth about not eating hamburgers, maybe that calls into question everything she's told me." Maybe she's not really 19. Maybe she's actually old . . . like 20. Chicken nuggets – but I never really considered that a full meal? Could she possibly just order fries without getting a hamburger – but fries are just an appetizer?? Filet-O-Fish – I thought only Asians ordered that??? Egads.

Glad you got home safely. Did you tell Taylor I was even MORE of an emotional wreck this time? Perhaps, I just asked you to hold me as I sobbed uncontrollably on your shoulder for several hours. :)

Hope you have a wonderful time with your mom next week. Do something fun with her like go to Disney or indoor ice-skating or Universal or something. Really, plan something your mom will remember from the trip.

Maybe we can plan our next date the week after Thanksgiving, if you're free? My work / travel schedule is moving around a bit, but I'll let you know once I figure that out and hopefully we can coordinate. Our next date, btw, is watching a movie and eating McDonald's (so I can see what you REALLY eat, hmmm?).

Email from Kris (11/18):
I really do just get a large order of fries every time I go, with ranch and ketchup, of course. Sometimes when I'm feeling adventurous I'll order a fruit and yogurt parfait. Promise I haven't had a hamburger in 10 years!

Indoor ice-skating is a wonderful idea.

Email to Kris (11/24):
Good luck with the parents today – hopefully it all goes smoothly. As I was preparing / molesting this poor raw turkey today – I thought to myself, so does Kris not eat turkey on Thanksgiving (it being on the bone and all)? We'll have so much ground to cover next Thursday.

BTW – this year, I'm thankful for you . . . well, just being you.

Email from Kris (11/24):
My stepmom and I gave my mom a makeover today and . . . well . . . she now has red hair. I had lots of mashed potatoes and green beans and rolls and a ridiculous amount of pie, but no turkey.

By the way, I'm trying to stifle a grin sitting over here in the corner imagining you molesting a bird. It's actually making me feel a little dirty.

Wish me luck tonight, I'm going into work at 2am for Black Friday. Hopefully I don't get trampled by coupon-clipping soccer moms Christmas shopping for their overly hip daughters. Fingers crossed.

Email to Kris (11/24):
2AM. Ouch – brutal. Who can possibly need Urban Outfitters clothes so badly at that hour? Just insane. Gotta be crazed moms, as you said – so your womanly charms will be useless tonight. (so now you'll know how normal people feel every day)

I picked up Smirnoff Ice and sushi on the way to the hotel. Kris had arrived early and checked in first again. The plan was that she would stay overnight in the hotel and fly back the next morning, though I didn't plan on staying overnight with her.

"They didn't have any forks," I said apologetically as I put the take-out bag onto the dining table. "Just chopsticks and plastic spoons. I can call down for a fork for you, though."

"That's okay," she smiled. "I'll make do with the spoon."

"Also, your envelope," I said as I put her allowance into her handbag. "So tell me about Thanksgiving. How were the family dynamics? Any drama between your mom and your stepmom?"

"Actually, I was really nervous about it, but they got along pretty well. By the end, my dad's wife, Mary, and my mom were making fun of my dad together. It was nice that my mom and I got to spend quality time together also. I took my mom ice-skating. Thanks for that suggestion. It was really fun. At first we had to use those walkers on the ice to stand up, but we got the hang of it by the end," she laughed. "Still, I could tell my mom was sad at times. She would see my dad and Mary happy together, driving around in their Mercedes. She won't admit it, but I know she was thinking that was supposed to be her life. She really thought she and my dad were going to be together forever."

"I imagine that has to be hard on her. She never remarried?"

"No. She would sometimes bring home these guys from the bar, but they were all bad guys," she said, and her eyes darkened from the memories. There was something deeper there, but I had other things I wanted to discuss today.

"And how are you feeling about this whole thing? Us, I mean – this relationship."

"I feel really good about us. If anything, it's a little confusing. I've been having dreams about you. In one dream, I came up from L.A. and visited you. You were at some party in a ballroom with your wife, and I dreamed I was just hiding in the crowd. I just wanted to see you. But then I was discovered somehow and all hell broke loose," she smiled. "In another dream, I was dancing with you. I was in a wedding dress and I was crying."

"Was I the groom?" I asked in mock horror with my eyes wide.

"No, I don't think so," she said thoughtfully. "After those dreams, I actually wanted to see if my dad's insurance covered psychotherapy, because I felt like I needed to talk to someone. On the one hand, I have my boyfriend, Taylor, but then on the other hand, I have all these feelings for a married man. But then I decided against going to a therapist, because I felt like their advice would be biased depending on if they were a man or a woman."

"How do you mean?"

"Well, if the therapist was a woman, she'd probably be really prejudiced against a man cheating on his wife. A male therapist might have a different view. And I just felt like their advice shouldn't be based on that. Anyway, I've been thinking about you a lot. Too much."

"Me too," I admitted with a wry smile. Too much, indeed. "So I'm glad you feel good about us. I do also. But I was thinking that if we're going to pursue this, we should probably do the responsible thing and talk about, y'know, our sexual history. As I said from the beginning, we should be maskless with each other. So I am going to tell you everything. Some of it may be pretty shocking or despicable, but it will be the truth. I'd ask you to do the same."

"Yes, let's do that."

"Okay, I'm happy to go first," I said as I took a deep breath. "Where to begin? Well, I told you that I couldn't get a date in high school because I was ugly."

"I would have dated you."

"Sure, Kris. That's easy to say now, but you didn't see me back then. Trust me, you wouldn't have dated me. So my first real girlfriend was in college after I started to . . . hmm . . . blossom, I guess is the best word. We ended up dating for four years, from junior year of college through after graduation. Believe it or not, we actually didn't have sex until the very end of our relationship. Because I had very few romantic experiences growing up, I read all these fantasy books and developed a completely storybook concept of love. In other words, I sort of sanctified sex as this holy thing, and I just felt like we should wait. That was a mistake in retrospect. We satisfied each other sexually in other ways, but we never actually had intercourse until the very end. And by then, it was actually kind of sad. At the end, when we both could feel our relationship dying, we had sex almost out of desperation as a last-ditch effort to save it. We had sex a few times, but emotionally, it just felt really sad. So I guess I didn't lose my virginity until I was twenty-four or twenty-five."

"Wow," she said non-judgmentally.

"I know, right? After we broke up, I kinda went a little crazy. I had decided to switch careers, so I quit my old job and took the summer off to just play before seeking a new job. So I went to Asia to hang out with some friends. Have you ever been to Asia?"

"No."

"Well, the guys would love you over there. Especially in Japan. Japanese guys are so dirty, and you would be able to fulfill their particular fetish for screwing the prototypical American prom queen," I said with a laugh. "If I were to psychoanalyze myself, maybe I'm trying to do the same thing. Y'know, maybe I'm trying to make up for being ostracized in high school by now dating the Caucasian American prom queen."

"I've thought about that," she smiled.

"Anyway, I spent that summer between jobs partying it up in Asia. That's the first time that I really did drugs. Ecstasy, weed, mushrooms. We would do drugs and then go to these rave parties. It was a pretty crazy summer. In terms of sex, if you're a successful businessman in Asia, it's really part of the culture to meet professional girls. You have business meetings during the day, and then you go to these places called 'room salons' at night where girls drink and sing karaoke with you. And depending on the place, they may sleep with you also. So I had sex with one of those girls while I was in Asia. When I got back to the States, I found a job at a hedge fund. I met my wife in the same company, and we were sexually active right from the beginning. So really, my wife was only the third girl that I ever had sex with."

"That's not many."

"No, not many at all. But that's probably part of the problem. It gets worse. So after a few years of marriage, I started to think that it was unfair that all my friends in Asia were having sex with different girls every week as part of the culture over there, regardless of whether they were married. And here I was, destined to die having only slept with a grand total of three girls in my life. I think I was faithful to my wife for five years of marriage, and then one night when I was traveling, I called an escort and the dam kind of broke."

"Escort? What's that like? I mean, how is that different from this?"

"Oh, it's night and day different. Escorts are basically prostitutes. But not nasty streetwalkers, like you see in movies. If you have money, there are services that will hook you up with beautiful, legitimate women. College students, models, actresses. But it's still purely transactional. They show up, and you pay them for an hour or two. You have sex. They leave, you go to sleep."

"Wow," Kris smiled with her eyes wide. "By the hour? How much does that cost?"

"Well, you can pay pretty much whatever you want. Since I had the money, I'd always pay for top quality, which could be up to a thousand dollars per hour. So I went through this escort phase of my life, where every time I would travel, I would use one of these high-end services to deliver an escort to my hotel room."

"How many?"

"Honestly, I lost track of the exact number, but probably somewhere between fifteen and twenty."

"In my mind, that sounds like a lot."

"It does to me also. But when I compare myself to my close friends in Asia, it's nothing. They have slept with literally hundreds of women. The more important point, though, is that the actual experience with escorts was never as good as the anticipation. Right after I would cum, I would think, 'Shit, that wasn't worth it.' To be clear, I wouldn't be wracked with guilt. I would just feel like I should have saved the money and avoided the hassle by masturbating. Faster, easier and cheaper. Not only that, but I was always afraid of catching an STD, so I was very careful about using a condom every time. Even then, after each experience with an escort, I would wait a couple of weeks and then get a full

STD blood test. To a certain degree, I can deal in my own screwed-up moral view of the world with cheating on my wife as long as it doesn't affect her. But if I ever gave her a STD, I would never forgive myself. So after each experience with an escort, I would avoid having sex with my wife for a couple weeks, and then get a blood test to make sure that I hadn't caught anything. And, of course, I didn't actually want to use my work insurance for all these STD tests."

"Because it would go on your medical record, and you didn't want to explain why you were getting STD tests every month?" Kris grinned.

"Damn it, I sat on another dirty toilet seat!" I said sarcastically.

Kris burst out laughing. I laughed along with her, a little surprised that she didn't appear disgusted with my sexual history.

"So I had to go to private clinics in order to get these blood tests done, and they would cost hundreds of dollars each time. And they would stick me with a needle to draw blood each time. I mean, it's not too painful, but it's still uncomfortable, like a bee sting. And the entire time, I would be thinking, 'This is your punishment for being so morally weak.' Last year, I finally told myself, 'Ryan, just stop this. It is so not worth it.' So, I stopped seeing escorts. However, when I thought back about which experiences with escorts were actually enjoyable, the only ones that came to mind were the experiences where we talked almost the entire allotted time before we had sex. So when my friend forwarded that article a few months ago about the sugar baby site, I thought, 'Well, this could be perfect.' I was curious to try it.

"Well, that's it. My sexual history in all its naked glory and ugliness," I said as I exhaled deeply. "Now what about you?"

Kris thought for a second, and then stood up. "I'm going to go have a quick smoke outside, and then I'll be happy to answer all your questions about my sexual past."

"Sure. Make sure to take a card key," I said.

The suite door shut behind her.

Shit, I thought to myself. I hope she comes back.

Ten minutes later, I heard the click of the card key in the door, and Kris walked back in. She smelled of smoke. Usually I found that a turnoff, but somehow it was alluring on Kris.

"I was afraid that you might not come back," I smiled. "I just told you all of my darkest secrets, and then you literally walked out."

Kris laughed. "Sorry, I didn't mean to scare you. Some young guy approached me as I was smoking outside. We talked a bit. He asked me if I was here alone and if I wanted to hang out. I told him I was staying with someone."

"The guy has good taste."

Kris grinned. "Okay, what would you like to know about my sexual history?"

"Just start from the beginning, I guess. How old, first time, et cetera."

"Well, my first was a boy named Stephen, who I dated when I lived in Lubbock, Texas. He was older. When we first started dating, he was eighteen and I was twelve."

"Jesus, is that even legal? I know this behooves me to say, but I think the maturity gap between an eighteen-year-old and a twelve-year-old is bigger than . . . oh I don't know, the gap between a thirty-eight-year-old and a nineteen-year-old."

"Oh, I totally agree. But we didn't have sex until I was probably fifteen or sixteen."

"What was the first time like?"

"I don't remember much. I remember the walls were yellow," she offered. "He was uncircumcised, which was a little gross, and I didn't really know what to do with it. We only had sex a few times. Pretty bad experience overall."

"Why did you guys break up?"

"Well, I was in Lubbock for a few years, but then I moved back to Florida in tenth grade. After a few months, I begged my aunt to buy me a plane ticket to visit Stephen for the holidays, which she did. It also gave me a chance to visit my dad, who was still in Texas. I didn't know it at the time, but Stephen had gotten into heroin. It was a pretty bad visit. We broke up for good after that."

"What happened?"

"We were driving in Stephen's car, and he started asking me about other boys in Florida. He started to get really mad and called me a 'slut' over and over again. Finally, I warned him, 'If you call me a slut one more time . . .' And of course, he did. I had one of those Big Gulp grape Slurpees, so I just threw it at him, and it exploded all over Stephen and the dashboard. He immediately pulled over and started to punch me. I didn't know it at the time, but he was probably high on heroin, which didn't help. After beating the shit out of me, he threw open my car door, literally kicked me out and drove off. I had taken off my shoes in the car, so I was basically standing by the side of this empty road in Texas, barefoot and bleeding badly down my face. So I just started walking. After a long time, I saw a light in the distance, and I made my way towards it. Luckily, it was the house of a family who let me use their phone to call my dad."

"What did your dad say when he saw you?"

"Nothing. He just kind of stared at me." Kris shrugged. "Anyway, after that, I just wanted to get back to Florida. My relationship with Taylor had started to blossom. We hadn't become romantic yet, but we were talking every day. He used his savings to get me an early ticket home, and he came with my aunt to pick me up from the airport. When we saw each other at the airport, we both just started crying."

"Jesus, Kris, that's horrible."

"Yeah, it kinda sucked."

I paused for a moment to assess if she was emotionally okay to continue. She seemed fine, actually.

"Okay, so after Stephen, who was next?"

"Let's see, after Stephen, I dated Derek in Florida. Remember, the good-looking boy I told you about?"

"Oh right, Mr. 'Say Anything' who went to your house in a suit to try to win you back."

"Right," she giggled. "Anyway, we only dated a couple months, but I took his virginity."

"Wow, no wonder it was so hard on him when you broke up with him."

"Then I moved to Calabasas, California to live with my dad again during my junior year of high school. I was pretty lonely and missing Taylor, and that's when I started getting into cocaine and meth. There was this boy there, Warren, who I had sex with. He was really good-looking and had sex with a lot of girls. We weren't even boyfriend and girlfriend. He would basically come over to my house, and we'd do cocaine and have sex."

"How was that?"

"Well, it wasn't 'not good.' I mean his technique was pretty good," she smiled, giving me a playful thumbs-up. "But I was high each time, and we only did it a few times before I tried to commit suicide."

"Oh."

"So after finishing high school, I told you that I moved back to Florida to be with Taylor and my grandma. Taylor and I had been long-distance dating, but it was really only about a year ago, when I got back to Florida, that we started having sex. I took his virginity also."

"Look at you, deflowering all these guys. So Taylor was the last person you had sex with?"

"No, Taylor and I were always getting into these big fights and were constantly on-again-off-again. And in between, we would date other people to try to hurt each other. Actually, it was mostly me that would date other people. During one of those 'off-again' times, a friend introduced me to Charles."

"Right, the Asian drug-dealer. A.k.a., my Asian nemesis for your affections."

Kris laughed. God, I will never get tired of that smile, I thought.

"So I had sex with Charles when I was dating him. But that only lasted a month, and then I was back together with Taylor."

"Was Charles really upset?"

"No, he said he kind of knew that I'd end up going back to Taylor. Everyone in Naples has seen Taylor and me break up and get back together so many times, it's sort of assumed now. So Taylor and I got back together until I had that threesome with Heather and Evan that I told you about," Kris said and then paused to reflect. "After that, Taylor and I broke up again, and I dated another guy, Linus, for a brief period. He was also a drug dealer, like Charles. We would basically just smoke weed all day. We never had sex. It's funny to mention Linus. I haven't spoken to him in months, but I just got a text from him late last night."

"What did it say?"

"It was a long text saying stuff like how much he missed me and how much he missed holding my small hands in his big hands," she said as she scrolled through her iPhone to locate the message.

"What did you say back?"

"I haven't replied yet. Not sure what I should say. Thank you?"

I laughed. "Thank you is not the response he's hoping for, I'm sure."

She laughed also, and then breathed in deeply. "So that's it. I think that's my complete sexual history."

"No, you're forgetting someone."

"Who?"

"Your former boss, Bill, right? You had sex with him on his boat."

"Oh right. Yeah, I don't really count that in my mind, but yes, you're right. Then there was Max also, the sugar daddy in Vegas. But we just did drugs. We never had sex. We tried one time, but he couldn't perform because of all the drugs."

I did the math in my head. "So seven? Stephen, Derek, Warren, Taylor, Charles, Evan, and Bill."

"Do you count Heather? I've had another threesome with a different girl also."

"Nah. I don't count girls."

"Interesting. Taylor counts girls equally. Yes, seven then."

"Who was the best? I mean in terms of sex?"

"Probably Charles. He was pretty good. Though it's a little hard to compare because when Taylor and I first had sex, he was a virgin. So the first twenty times were pretty bad. But he's gotten better over time."

"Did you ever fake an orgasm with Taylor?"

"I did in the beginning, so he wouldn't feel bad. I don't know. Sometimes he would go down on me for a long time and try really hard, but I just couldn't cum. I would be thinking about bills or rent or other stuff. We've tried some different things recently."

"Like how different? Like *50 Shades of Grey* different? Have you read that book?" I asked.

"Oh my god, yes. I would be reading it in my apartment, and then I'd suddenly tell my roommate Katy, 'I need to go to the bathroom to be by myself,'" she said with a laugh. "Yeah, he's tried spanking me and choking me recently. I like it, but I kind of feel like we shouldn't need that now. Like we should be saving that for later when we need to spice things up."

Choking and spanking. Interesting. "Well, thanks for sharing all that," I said as I cleared the table of take-out boxes. "I'm glad we were able to be totally open with each other."

"Anytime," she said with a small smile.

I took a sip of my Smirnoff Ice. "These are very fruity."

"Yup, that's why I like them. I don't like beer or liquor. What do you typically drink?"

"Not this," I laughed. "I brought a portable DVD player and one of my favorite movies, *The Little Mermaid*. Would you like to watch it?"

"Sure," she said brightly.

I held her thin waist as we walked into the bedroom. I hooked up the DVD player, and we snuggled on the bed. She put her head on my chest as we watched the movie. About twenty minutes in, I noticed her eyelids getting heavy. Time to wake her up.

I cradled her head towards me, and I gave her a deep kiss. I pushed my tongue slowly and deliberately into her mouth, over and over. I could feel her heartbeat accelerate against my chest. I quickly stripped off her clothes and then worked my way down, from her ears, to her nipples, to her belly button, to her inner thighs. Then I licked her slowly up and down her legs until she was moaning and squirming. Finally, I pressed my tongue flat onto her pussy and massaged her clit gently with my tongue.

"Oh my god," she gasped as she covered her open mouth with her hand.

I licked my middle finger, and then slowly pushed it inside her wet pussy. I pressed my finger upwards, and I brushed her special spot from inside as I licked the outside of her clit with my tongue.

"That feels amazing," she moaned.

I increased the rhythm of my finger and my tongue. Within a few minutes, she gasped, "Oh my god!" as she clenched my head against her pussy and came hard on my mouth.

I pulled myself level with her as she regained her breath, and I kissed her deeply again. "We're just getting started," I smiled.

She turned me over on my back and slid down on top of me. She hovered above my erect cock for a second and then engulfed me with her mouth.

"Look at me, baby," I groaned. She stared up at me with those mesmerizing green eyes as she worked my stiff shaft with her mouth and played with my balls in her left hand.

I pulled her up so that I could kiss her, and she ground on top of me with her hips. Then I saw her reach down to grab my cock. Somewhere in the back of my brain, I heard the word "condom," but it was too late. She inserted the tip of my hard cock into her dripping pussy, and slowly impaled herself onto me.

"Oh Ryan," she moaned.

My body spasmed. I've had sex many times before, but it had never felt this intense. It was like she was honoring me completely as she leaned back and slid up and down my cock. Her perfect breasts bounced rhythmically, and I lay flat on my back and just stared up at her perfection. She reached back with one hand and grabbed my balls as she fucked me. My whole body ached as I tried to hold back. I didn't want to cum yet.

I flipped her off of me and positioned Kris on her hands and knees. I thrust my cock back into her pussy from behind. She gasped, "Oh my god," and covered her open mouth with her hand as I slammed her desperately from behind. I felt her cum on my cock again, and seconds later, I came hard inside of her, filling her up with my hot cum. We collapsed onto the bed. I held Kris cradled from the side with her back against my chest. Our bodies were covered in a sheen of sweat that made our skins feel seamless against each other.

"I can't believe I'm getting paid for this," she laughed lightly, as our breath and heartbeats slowed.

"That was unbelievable. I'll be honest. I brought condoms for us. But in the heat of the moment, before I could get a condom, you just slipped me right inside."

"Are you saying that I raped you, Ryan?" Kris smiled.

"Something like that," I laughed. I felt complete as we lay there and I held her in my arms. Or maybe "completed" is more accurate. "Y'know, Kris, it's really hard for a guy to disaggregate his romantic feelings for a girl between his sexual desire and his true emotional connection. Even if a guy believes that a beautiful girl is funny or smart, it's very likely that his sexual desire is coloring that perspective. And so the only time that a guy really has a clear view of his emotions toward a girl is during what I call "the five minutes of clarity." That's basically the five minutes right after orgasm when his brain is briefly clear of that sexual desire."

"So how do you feel?"

"Wonderful, Kris. Just wonderful being here with you," I smiled.

She suddenly sat up. "Hey, my nipple ring came out. Help me look for it, please."

We searched under the blankets and on the floor for a few minutes until we found the ring. "That's never happened before. I can't believe you did that with your tongue."

"Never?"

"Never."

"I guess I'm quite skilled," I laughed. As she stood up naked to go to the bathroom, I noticed a small one-inch scar at the base of her spine. When she returned, she crawled back into my arms so we could snuggle.

"Can I ask you a question, Kris?"

"Sure."

"Where did you get that scar on your back?"

"In high school in Florida, I started having back problems that got increasingly worse. I'm not sure if it was from cross-country running or the golf cart accident or what. But by the time I moved from Florida to California in my junior year, it had gotten so bad that I literally could not walk up a flight of stairs. Luckily, when I moved to Calabasas, my dad had health insurance and so I was able to finally get back surgery to fix it."

"My dad had back surgery before. It didn't turn out so well for him. That must have been scary for you."

"It was a little scary, but mainly I was desperate to get the surgery because I was so tired of the pain. It's a lot better now, but it still hurts some days, especially if I sit down for long periods of time. Weed helps," she smiled. "I hate the scar on my back, though."

"Barely noticeable," I whispered. I kissed her lightly on the lips and stood up. I cleaned up in the bathroom and then walked back into the bedroom to put on my clothes.

"You'll be okay taking the shuttle to the airport tomorrow morning yourself?" I asked.

"No problem," she said. She stood up and wrapped her arms around my neck as I pulled her waist toward me for another deep kiss. We breathed each other in for a few seconds, and then I walked out the door.

Date 5: December 14

Email to Kris (12/2):
You are exquisite. Even in that "5 minutes of clarity," I still thought so (which is kinda rare). And I'm glad we had such an honest discussion yesterday. My only regret is we talked for so many hours (how does that keep happening), I was frankly exhausted by the time of the . . . ummm . . . main event. Sure you were a bit tired also. Next time we save all that silly talking for later. Then we can go like Energizer bunnies. Or at least make it through a movie. :)

I sent you a massage gift card also. Figured you could use a massage after the intense workout last night. What's that you say? No, not much of a workout at all??? Huh. Oh well, anyway, figured you could use it after running or whatnot.

I actually dreamed of you last night. I can tell you about it next time, but it's scary that you're entering my dreams. Ahh Kris, "what am I going to do with you." (using my best Christian Grey voice)

Not good, not good.

Email from Kris (12/2):
You only must have gotten a few hours of sleep, huh?

You should've seen me after you left last night. I'm glad you got your 5 minutes of clarity in when you did because as soon as you shut the door I grabbed the popcorn and another Smirnoff and went to work on shoving my nipple ring back in before it closed up. Not so elegant. Maybe I should've tried using the lube.

Thank you for the massage. I really don't know if I've ever met someone so thoughtful. Lee > Grey in my book, although I'm still holding my breath for that helicopter ride.

I found Kris's Facebook page and obsessively scoured it. Even without actually "Friending" her (which would have been difficult to explain to my wife), I was able to read her historical Timeline which had some posted pictures, notes and comments from friends going back a few years. I read every note and every comment several times. It was fun to triangulate the "in the moment" color commentary on her Facebook Timeline with the oral history that she had shared with me. For example, as it relates to Derek (the beautiful, but dull boyfriend in high school), I could trace the entire arc of their brief relationship through her posted notes from a few years ago.

Falling in love:
"I officially have a date for Friday! Full-fledged date!" (January 12)

"He kissed me!!!" (January 16)

"I am falling HARD!" (January 25)

To struggling with mixed emotions:

"Confused. Sleepy. Sixteen." (March 18)

To looking for an exit out of the relationship:

"I really don't want to hurt anyone, but I'm afraid I'm going to anyway." (March 23)

Facebook stalking. Creepy, I know. But I had already embraced the fact that I was completely obsessed. So Facebook stalking was just another incremental baby step towards insanity.

We continued to message back and forth between dates on practically a daily basis.

Email to Kris (12/5):
Hello my dear,

How does your next Wed look? Could fly you up Wed afternoon and fly back the next morning.

Anything exciting on tap for you this week? I'm off to New Orleans tomorrow for a couple of days. Can't remember – was that one of your prior hometowns? I'll keep an eye out for the telltale signs of broken men by the side of the road waxing poetic about holding Kristina's small hands in their big hands. (I will tell them that Kris says "Thank you")

To be 100% honest, I miss you more than I probably should. But will work my way through it eventually, lest I end up one of those broken men by the side of the road. I mean, I won't even have the luxury to poetically say that I miss holding your small hands in my big hands, because my hands are, y'know, quite modest themselves. So I'd have to say, "I miss holding your SMALL hands in my SMALL hands" – and that doesn't sound romantic. It just sounds kinda creepy. Anyway, when I reach that vegetative state – please don't ask questions, just shoot me.

(honestly, Kris, I have no idea how you put up with my verbal diarrhea at times).

Email from Kris (12/6):
Wednesday sounds great. Will it be our last meeting before Christmas?

The most excitement I've had so far this week was taking the puppy to get his second set of shots. I cried, of course. New Orleans isn't one of my hometowns, but you can tell all the guys I say hello anyway if you'd like. Maybe they've heard of me. ;)

I really do miss you too. AND your not-so-huge hands.

Email from Kris (12/7):
In New Orleans now – I checked with all the guys here. Yes, they've heard of you and are just waiting for you to swing through at some point wreaking devastation in your path ("Hurricane Katrina was nothing," they keep muttering to themselves like some crazed ancient Greek oracle).

Just in my hotel room doing work . . . ahh, Kris, if you were here with me, the things I would do to you. (in my best, raspy "Christian Grey" voice again)

Y'know – like make you watch age-inappropriate animated movies and eat sushi with a spoon. Just kinky, crazy stuff.

Sadly, I think it's reasonably likely next Wednesday is our last date before the New Year (and we each head off to our respective holiday trips). Unless we break our "every two week" pattern, and see each other the week after again (which is possible, but a slippery slope – next thing you know I'll be asking to join you and grandma in Florida over the holidays).

Okay, Kris – counting the days until our 5th date. :)

Email from Kris (12/7):

I always get so excited when I see an email from you. :)

So we'll be going from the 14th of December to at least the 9th of January without seeing each other? I have to admit, that makes me more sad than it probably should. I've been desperately trying to think of a Christmas gift for you but 1. You can afford just about everything you'd ever want from a materialistic standpoint and 2. I can't give you anything personal because you wouldn't be able to explain it to your wife (for example a Christmas ornament made from my panties) so I'm in a bind here.

5th date! Where's the ring? Ahh, I suppose I'll settle for dinner and conversation.

I had my massage this evening and it was wonderful. Thank you again. My masseuse was an Asian woman, go figure.

Hope you're not too lonely there in New Orleans.

Email to Kris (12/8):

Seems like a long break, but I will remind you that you will be in Florida for a lot of the time being constantly circled by three ex-boyfriends (not even including the "Say Anything" dude with the suit and metaphorical boom box over his head). Plus, two of your ex-boyfriends can offer weed, and one of them is Asian even. Not sure how I compete with all that – so I'm confident that I'll just be a distant memory by the time New Years rolls around.

In terms of gift, nothing material please. If my wife found your panties, I'd be forced to claim that they were, in fact, mine – and that would raise all sorts of other uncomfortable questions. But I won't say that I want "nothing" like other old people (I remember you talking about how frustrating that is) – so if I might be so bold as to make a request for a gift – it would be this. See, at some point, our lives will likely diverge again. And I actually worry, believe it or not, that at some point, I won't remember "all the faces" of Kris. So if, instead, you sent me a montage of a few pictures of happy Kris (nothing racy, just ones where I can remember your personality and smile) so that I can always remember back to when I met someone really special in this crazy life (even when I'm an old, wrinkled man) – I would love that.

Email from Kris (12/10):
I can definitely work with that.

Just got back from Urgent Care and I'm basically dying. Either that or I have a sinus infection, one or the other.

Hopefully I'm better by Wednesday so we can have our early Christmas/5th date anniversary two-person party!

  I stood in line impatiently in Papyrus, waiting to get Kris's Christmas gift wrapped. She had already checked into the hotel just a few miles away, and the thought of her so close made me anxious to start our date. After ten long minutes, a sales rep was finally able to help me. As she wrapped the gift, I hurriedly scripted a personalized card, and then I was on my way.
  I opened the door to the hotel suite and entered. Since this was our last date before the holidays, I had booked an extra large suite with a whirlpool to celebrate. Also, this would be the first night that we actually slept overnight together.
  I didn't see her when I entered the living room. I set down the gift bags and my overnight bag.
  "Hello?" I called.
  "Hi," she said groggily as she walked out of the bedroom in jeans and a sweatshirt. She coughed a couple times, looked at me sweetly, and then gave me a big hug.

"How are you feeling?" I asked.

"Okay. The doctor gave me antibiotics, so I feel a little better. I get these sinus infections a couple times a year. I'll live."

"Well, I'll take care of you tonight," I smiled. We ordered pizza and a salad from room service, and I opened a couple of bottles of Smirnoff Ice for us. "So, are you excited to go back to Florida for the holidays? You're going to be there for ten days, right?"

"Yup, ten days. I'm pretty anxious, actually. I'm not sure why. For one reason or another, Taylor and I have never been able to spend Christmas together. We haven't seen each other for so long that I'm nervous about what it will be like now. Also, Taylor really wants me to move back to Florida. He moved out of his parents' home because he was constantly fighting with them, and so he's just been crashing on the floor of various friends' apartments. But it's a little selfish of him to ask me to move back in order to make his life easier. If he really thought about it, being in California is the best thing for me in terms of hopefully going to university someday. So I'm nervous about getting into all that with him also," she said with uncertainty in her eyes.

"I bought a bunch of presents for Taylor that I've already wrapped and packed into my suitcase. One of his presents is this skateboard that he's wanted for a long time. I'm really afraid that airport security is going to unwrap it, so I attached a note explaining what's inside and begging them not to open it. I also got my grandma a Coach gift card. She's wanted a Coach purse her entire life, but she would never spend that kind of money on herself. I even took a picture of the gift card and posted it to my Instagram," she laughed.

I thought a moment about how disorienting it must be to grow up so poor, and then suddenly have thousands of dollars in cash given to you every couple of weeks. I found it sweet that her first instinct was to spend it on the people she loved.

"Speaking of gifts, here's your Christmas gift," I said as I handed her the gift bag with the presents inside. "Your envelope is in there also."

"Thank you," she said sweetly. "Should I open the gift now?"

"No, open it later. I actually prefer not to be present when people open gifts from me because if I'm there and they don't like the gift, then they have to act like they do."

The pizza arrived a few minutes after, and we sat down at the large dining table to eat.

"What about your mom? What did you get her for Christmas?" I asked.

"I got her a massage gift card. I just felt like it was the most thoughtful gift when you gave it to me. She's been having a rough time. She lost her job after she came to visit me for Thanksgiving. It's bullshit because she had gotten approval for the time off, but her boss claims she never asked."

"That's terrible. Well, at least you should have some money now to help her out if necessary."

Kris was silent for a few moments.

"She's looking for another job. Hopefully, she'll find one soon. Y'know, except for the presents that I bought for my family, I put all of your money into a separate bank account for my tuition next semester. Actually, I sent a check to my grandma and she put it into a separate account for me. I feel like I deserve to be a little selfish in this one area."

Interesting notion of being selfish, I thought to myself. Paying for your own college education because your parents either can't or won't. Still, I could tell by the pensive look on her face that she was uncomfortable at the thought.

"First off, Kris, it's your money, not my money. Second, I agree, you deserve to be selfish in this respect. Frankly, I don't consider it selfish at all. Did your grandma ask how you suddenly had thousands of dollars?"

"No," Kris smiled. "My grandma is cool. She knows that she probably doesn't want to know."

"Well, at least your mom got fired for a good reason. I mean visiting you over Thanksgiving must have meant a lot to her."

"It did. Growing up, we fought all the time, and she'd beat the crap out of me. But now that we're older and not living together, we have a better relationship."

"What were your best childhood memories with your mom?"

Kris thought for a few moments.

"I remember camping with my mom and aunt. We used to have this large E.T. doll that we would bring, and we used his finger as a toilet paper holder," she laughed. "I love E.T., by the way."

"That sounds fun. Did you guys go camping a lot or do other trips?"

"Not really. We didn't have any money to take vacations. Though one year, we went to Disney World. My mom had saved all her money for months to buy everyone nice Christmas presents, and then all the presents got stolen out of her car literally a couple days before Christmas. She was so heartbroken and desperate, she basically said, 'Fuck it, let's go to Disney World,' even though we couldn't really afford it. That was pretty fun, though we basically ran around the entire day from ride to ride because she wanted to make the most of it. I just remember being exhausted by the end."

"And what does your mom do now?"

"Drink," Kris said with a sad laugh. "Some kind of accounting, I think."

"Is your mom still drinking a lot?"

"Still? She's never stopped. I mean, I was basically raised in a bar. I would go to the bar and wait for her after school until she was drunk enough or until she met some guy."

"But you said that she never had a serious relationship again, right? None of these guys from the bar worked out?"

"No, they were all . . . not good guys."

Her voice sounded odd when she said that. "No masks, right Kris? And we can ask each other anything?"

"Sure."

"So did any of these 'not good' guys ever abuse you? Physically or sexually, I mean."

Her eyes left me for a few moments.

"No," she said softly. "My mom had this one boyfriend who once snuck up from behind me when I was in the kitchen. He picked me up and was horsing around, and then he dropped me by accident. I got hurt pretty bad. So I have this fear now of being picked up. Like if I'm at a party, and someone picks me up to throw me in the pool, I will literally start screaming and going crazy. Also, I don't like big guys. I feel like they can hurt me."

"Well, I'm glad to help out in that respect . . . you know, with me being small and all," I smiled. Kris's eyes were still distant, but I decided not to press the topic any further. After all, this was supposed to be our holiday celebration.

"Do you like bubble baths?" I asked.

"I love baths," she said as her face brightened. "I probably take a bath once a week to relax. I saw the huge whirlpool in the bathroom."

"Yup, that's why I got this room. Let me go get a bubble bath ready for us, and while I do that, you can open your gift."

I took the bubble bath soap out of my overnight bag, and went to run a bath. The whirlpool was huge and elevated on a black marble platform, so you actually had to walk up a couple of steps to get inside. Just as the whirlpool was about full, I turned around and saw Kris standing behind me. She gave me a huge hug and whispered, "Thank you. I love it."

"I'm glad you do. I figured you'd like an iPad to go along with your iPhone. I'll show you how to use it later. Remember, you still owe me my gift – a collection of pictures of you so I can always remember you."

"I won't forget."

"Let's get in the bath, shall we?"

We both undressed, and I took her hand to help her into the steaming bubble bath. She sat cradled with her back against my chest, and in between passionate kisses, I massaged her shoulders and gently rubbed her breasts with foam.

"What about you?" she asked. "Ready for your family trip to Shanghai? What are you going to do there?"

"Mainly just spend time with my parents. My dad's not in good health, so it's important to take the kids to see him while we still can. But I'm not looking forward to the thirteen-hour flight with three kids."

"So with our holiday schedules, we won't see each other for almost four weeks," she said sadly. "I'm going to miss you."

"Me too," I said thoughtfully. "You know, Kris, this relationship is a lot more emotionally intense than I originally planned. I don't know what to call it. Obsession doesn't seem right, but it's probably close. So maybe this four-week break is good for us. Give us some time to breathe individually again."

Kris just stared straight ahead in the bathtub as I held her in my arms. After a while, she gave me a little nod.

We showered together after the bath, toweled off and then retired to the bed.

We made love again. She straddled me and rode me hard. Then I flipped her on her back and fucked her deeply with her legs propped over my shoulders. Finally, I pushed her legs off my shoulders to one side, cradled her body in mine from the side, and penetrated her from behind. I increased the rhythm of my thrusts to keep pace with her increasing excitement, and then I reached around with my hand to gently rub her clit.

"Oh my god!" she screamed and then clasped her hand over her mouth as she came hard on my cock. I came just a few seconds later deep inside her.

As we lay there holding each other, she started laughing gently.

"What?"

"You told me that you were always really careful and used condoms in the past, but you just plow ahead every time and cum inside of me."

"Well, you started it," I laughed. "You know, the difference in how much better it feels without a condom is not like fifty percent better, it's like ten thousand percent better. I also figured that you just got an STD blood test at the doctor's when you had your Pap smear, and you said it came back clean. And you're still taking your birth control pills, right?"

"Of course, but I think we should still be careful."

"You mean, I should wear a condom?"

"Or just pull out when you cum."

"Okay, I'll try," I smiled, a little doubtfully.

I turned Kris onto her stomach and began to give her a back massage.

"Mmm . . . that feels good," she said with a laugh. "Asian hands are so good at all these things."

"What things?"

"I don't know. Massages, manicures, pedicures . . ."

"Making dumplings," I added with a laugh. "I'm not sure, but I think I should be offended."

I pressed firmly into her lower back and noticed her back scar again. I gave it a gentle kiss.

"By the way, where does your wife think you are tonight?" Kris murmured. "I mean, how are you able to sleep over this time?"

"I told her I had a business trip to Portland. I know, I know – I'm going to hell," I said with a sigh. "What about Taylor? Does he know you're here?"

"He does, but not that I'm spending the night. That reminds me. I should call him to check in. I'll go on the balcony. The street traffic in the background will make it sound like I just got back to the Los Angeles airport."

As Kris went to make her call, I pulled on my clothes and went into the living room to call my wife to say goodnight. We reconvened after about ten minutes in the bed and turned on the television.

"Do you ever feel bad about this?" she asked.

I thought for a few minutes. Did I feel bad? I worked hard. My family had everything they could ever want. I loved my wife and children. And this relationship with Kris only existed in a fantasy world that, in my amoral mind, didn't seem to be hurting anyone.

"I feel bad that I don't feel bad," I said finally with an apologetic shrug. "Does that count?"

"No," she sighed.

"Do you feel bad about lying to Taylor?"

"That's the weird thing. I don't. I'm going to hell also, I guess."

"At least we'll be there together."

We got up to brush our teeth and get ready for sleep.

"One thing you should know," I said. "I'm not a big cuddler when I sleep. I like to have my space."

"Oh no, I love cuddling. We'll have to see about that."

I swallowed an Ambien before lying down next to Kris. I knew that without chemical help, I would just toss and turn all night with this young goddess beside me.

I have vague memories of sleeping next to Kris that night. There are hazy images of partially waking up several times to find Kris's arms wrapped around me, or my arms and legs entangled around her lithe body. Finally, I opened my eyes for good and scanned the bright, sunlit room. Kris lay cradled in my arms with her back towards me.

Gently, I began to kiss her ear. Then her cheek. Then her eyelids. She gave me a smile, still half asleep with her eyes closed, and she pulled my head down to kiss her lips. I worked my way down to her breasts and she moaned. She was fully awake now. She rolled on top of me with a bright smile and said, "Well, good morning, Mr. Lee!"

We made love again. As if nothing existed outside of this bedroom. As if the only reality in the universe was Kris and me together.

I came inside her again.

Date 6: December 22

Text from Kris (12/15):
Return flight got cancelled. :(They moved me to a later flight.

Text to Kris (12/15):
Okay. At least you have your iPad to keep you entertained at the airport. I'm tired – just got back from Portland myself.

Text from Kris (12/15):
Wow I bet you're exhausted!

Text to Kris (12/15):
You have no idea. I actually went to Portland TWICE last night! (believe it or not) Okay, focus, focus – shoot me a quick text when you get home safely. :)

Up until now, we had kept a two-week cadence between our dates. In the beginning, that seemed like a sensible schedule so that our dates would not become a burden to either of our real lives.

By now, however, the two-week cadence seemed like a prison sentence during the time in between. Yet I had remained disciplined. As intoxicating as being with Kris was, I recognized that I had a job, a family and responsibilities. I knew that if I spun out of control into Kris, my real world could come crumbling down quickly.

That's what I told myself logically. But emotionally, I knew I had stepped over some unspoken line in the sand a long time ago. And now I faced the daunting prospect of not seeing Kris for almost four weeks over the holidays. "It will be good for you to take a breather," I told myself. "Regain that sense of balance that you've so clearly lost." But I struggled with the idea of not seeing her for so long. I literally felt a tightness in my chest thinking about it.

I was like a man desperately hanging onto the side of a cliff by his fingernails. Knowing that he's already a goner, but still barely clinging on.

And then I slipped.

Email to Kris (12/20):

Ahh, Kris. Is my obligatory 2-3 day "cooling off" period between emails over? :)

But don't you worry, I've kept myself busy. I dug up all of my old grade school pictures, and I threw together a little pictorial history for you . . . since you make such outrageous claims like "I would have played Truth or Dare with you in middle school" despite never actually knowing what I looked like back then.

No, Kris, I don't think you would have. (please see attached pictures)

The second thing is . . . and I can't believe these words are even coming out of my mouth (or technically my hands as I type . . . y'know, my versatile, skilled Asian hands) . . . are you busy or do you have to work on Thur?

Email from Kris (12/20):

I can't even respond to anything else you've said without finding out why you're asking if I have work on Thursday. Because I don't. And I'm not busy. So explain!

Email to Kris (12/20):

Short explanation is I'd like to see you, of course. If you're not sick of me yet. And if there are still flights available. Course, I'm not sure on either of those points.

Email from Kris (12/20):

Well go see if you can book a flight! Of course I want to see you again. :) By the way, I really liked all of your pictures. You were so adorable in middle school!

Email to Kris (12/21):
What do you think about me coming to visit you this time?

I don't know that many folks in LA (I think), so we could go out on a normal date . . . maybe even go to a club? I could get a room and stay overnight (be great if you'd stay with me, if you'd like), and I'd fly back the next day.

Email from Kris (12/21):
And I could drive you around and everything! Wow. Okay!

Text from Kris (12/21):
What time is your flight home the next day?

Text to Kris (12/21):
Flight home? I thought I'd just move in with you. Go to Florida for the holidays also. Kidding. 12:10PM on Friday.

Text from Kris (12/21):
Oh! Yes, well then I'll have to elaborate on the foreign exchange student story. :) You do realize that's almost 20 hours together? Yet last time we saw each other you insisted on distancing ourselves. I think you might be having a midlife crisis!

Text to Kris (12/21):
No, no . . . you totally misunderstand the "Taoist" inverse philosophy on these matters. In this case, I'm sure the Taoist proverb would go something like "in order to distance two souls, they must first be drawn close together." See . . . perfectly consistent with what I asserted last time. Course, I have no idea what that jibberish means . . . egads . . . yes, definitely midlife crisis. Anyhoo, no cuddling this time – you kind of ambushed me with that last time. The Ryan doesn't do cuddling (at least not again)

Text from Kris (12/21):
THE Ryan? Impressive. Not to rain on your midlife crisis parade but I'm having some cramps so either I went too hard with my Brazilian Buttlift DVD today or my internal clock is off and my time of the month is starting early in preparation for the holidays. Our activities at the

two-person party tomorrow might be limited. That being said, feel free to cancel if you're unwilling to spoon-feed me ice cream in bed. I really wouldn't blame you.

Text to Kris (12/21):
I'll see you tomorrow, Kris. We always seem to do just fine hanging out, no matter the physical limitations. :)

Text from Kris (12/21):
:)

I stared out the window as the plane descended into Los Angeles.

I knew that I should have been wracked by guilt. I knew that the "good" part of me should have been pulling on my conscience with all of its might. The "good" part of me that had always followed the rules and done everything right my entire life should have been scornfully reprimanding my conscious mind. "You are pathetic, immoral, and selfish. You have risked everything that you worked so hard for, and you have betrayed the love and trust of your family," the good part of me should have been saying. But it wasn't. It was silent.

I think some people imagine that a person having an affair is constantly struggling between a devil on one shoulder leading him into temptation and an angel on the other shoulder trying to save his eternal soul.

But I didn't feel any of that struggle. As the plane touched down, I just thought to myself, "Wow, I can't believe that I'm here. Life can be really beautiful, exciting and unpredictable."

I know that old adage that when a spouse has an affair, someone always gets hurt. Even if the spouse doesn't find out, YOU will always know. Maybe I'm just built differently, but I guess I was comfortable that I would always know. If my wife never found out, then ME "knowing" didn't really seem to bother me.

I love my wife. She is my best friend and my loyal partner. We still enjoy living together, raising our kids, having long talks, and making love. But it wasn't enough, clearly. In my non-religious view of the world, my short time on earth was really all that I had to work with. Really, I was just a collection of my experiences, and I selfishly did not want to waste that time struggling over these moral questions.

Take escorts as an example. When I went through my phase of fucking escorts, I wanted to experience meaningless sex with beautiful women in order to see if it was as exciting as I imagined. I was always careful. I got tested after each encounter, and I didn't have sex with my wife again until I was sure that I was clean. I'm not religious, so I didn't necessarily think that I was jeopardizing my afterlife, and I didn't feel like I was hurting my wife as long as she didn't know. Disappointingly, I didn't derive any great joy from fucking escorts, but neither did I feel any great guilt. Like I said, maybe I'm just built differently.

This relationship with Kris was different, of course. I still could not force myself to feel guilt, but I knew it was much more dangerous in terms of where it could lead.

Kris was getting a massage that I had booked for her in the spa of the hotel when I arrived. So I dropped off my bag in the suite, went to pick up some drinks and snacks, and then headed to the hotel gym for a quick workout.

When I walked back into the suite, I heard Kris call from the bathroom, "I'm in here."

I put Kris's envelope into her handbag in the living room and then walked into the bathroom. I took a moment to savor the vision of Kris relaxing in the bubble-filled tub. She was drinking a Smirnoff Ice and eating the bag of cheese popcorn that I had bought.

"Hi gorgeous," I said as I peeled off my gym clothes and slipped into the bath behind her. "You must be totally exhausted after your arduous massage."

"Totally," she laughed.

We were quiet for a few minutes and just enjoyed the feeling of being together in the warm bath. Finally, I said, "Kris, I've been thinking about our prior conversations. One thing that's really hard for me to fathom is how you could have reached the point where you tried to commit suicide in high school. I mean, you are beautiful. You have all these friends. What could have gone so wrong in Calabasas that you felt you had nothing to live for?"

"I don't know. When I moved away from Florida to Calabasas in high school, I just felt really lonely. I mean, I've always been pretty. But sometimes I wonder if people like me just because I'm pretty. So I have a hard time trusting people."

"I know you moved around a lot growing up, but I guess I figured being beautiful would ease your integration into new schools."

"In some ways. But in other ways, it's harder. Not that I'm complaining. But when I moved to a new school and started to get attention from the guys, some of the other girls would usually get upset."

"I could see that. It's like as a new beautiful girl, you are upsetting the established hierarchy or pecking order in high school. It's like everyone thinks they know their place, and then suddenly there's this new attractive, and threatening, variable thrown in."

"Something like that."

"You don't ever have to answer any questions you don't want to. But I was wondering, when you tried to commit suicide and your heart stopped, you said that the doctors had to shock you back to life with a defibrillator. Do you remember what that felt like?"

"It felt like somebody pulling me up from underwater."

"Do you remember who pulled you up?"

"I do. It was Warren's prior girlfriend. Warren was the guy that I was doing cocaine and having sex with at the time. Anyway, his girlfriend had committed suicide a few months before I got to the school, so I never met her or even saw her picture. But somehow, I knew it was her that pulled me back up."

I thought for a few moments about how different Kris's life experiences were from mine, and yet somehow, despite these dramatically different paths, we had connected in such a fundamental way.

"Kris, that's heartbreaking. I hope that if you ever reach that point again where you feel like you have no way out, you reach out to me. No matter where I am . . . or where 'we' are, for that matter."

She turned around in the bath, gave me a light kiss on the lips, and then stood up. We hopped into the shower together, where I alternated rinsing myself off with giving Kris passionate kisses on her lips, her neck, and her breasts.

We toweled off and migrated to the bed. I gently pushed her onto her back so that her butt was lying on the edge of the bed. I stood with my feet on the floor between her legs. I lifted up her right leg to my mouth and began to suck on her toes. She gasped as I worked my tongue between her toes and rubbed my hard cock against the inside of her lifted right thigh. Then I spread her legs and pushed them both back towards her, as my mouth moved slowly from her toes, down her calves, and along the inside of her thighs, and then hovered with my hot breath over her pussy.

"No, Ryan," she moaned as she grasped my hair and tried to pull me up towards her. "My period."

I pushed her hands off my head and thrust my tongue flat against her pussy. I tasted the distinct metallic flavor of blood mixed with her salty sweetness. It was intoxicating. I licked her clit gently as I slowly fucked her with my middle finger, pressing up on her special spot inside her vagina. I could feel her hips grind against me faster and faster, until she screamed, "Oh god!" and clasped her hand over her mouth as she came on my finger and mouth. I stood up and pushed my cock slowly into her wet pussy. She moaned as she wrapped her legs around me and pulled me deep inside her. As I thrust in and out of Kris, she took my hand and placed it around her throat. I pressed down and choked her. She closed her eyes, and when she opened them I saw . . . excitement. I released her throat after a few seconds, and she breathed heavily in ecstasy. Finally, I crawled on to the bed, bent her over on all fours facing the headboard, and began to fuck her from behind. I could see the blood on my cock as I pumped her hard. I was in another world. I saw her clasp one hand over her mouth again as she came on my cock, and then I exploded inside her moments later.

We collapsed onto the bed, facing each other, with our arms and legs intertwined. We didn't say anything for a long while. We just held each other and savored this moment of complete release.

By and by, she said, "I've never done that before. I mean, while I'm having my period."

"Was it okay?"

"Amazing," she said as she leaned forward and gave me a soft kiss. "By the way, I don't want to inflate your ego, but you have a big penis."

I burst out laughing.

"Some of those escorts must have told you that too!" she said.

"They have, but I always figured it's because I'm paying them tons of money. C'mon, Kris, you don't have to lie to make me feel good."

"No, I wouldn't do that. I mean it's really thick. It's not the longest, but it's the thickest I've seen."

"Is that good?"

"Oh yeah. Thick is good. You feel amazing. Too long is not good. Sometimes that can hurt, and it feels like it's hitting the back of my uterus."

"I see. Were any of your past boyfriends too long?"

Kris thought for a moment. "Stephen was too long."

"Plus he was uncircumcised," I added.

"I know. Just . . . yuck."

"I was wondering a little bit how I compared. A guy can't help but wonder sometimes. I remember the first time we had sex, immediately after you put me inside of you, you said, 'Oh Ryan!' I was hoping that was because you were surprised that it felt good."

"I thought it would feel good. I just didn't expect it to feel SO good," she smiled. "And I guess I didn't expect your penis to be large. I mean, Charles, my prior Asian boyfriend – small penis. Fits the stereotype."

"I know, right? The irony is that in high school, my baseball teammates used to call me 'Rice' as sort of a semi-derogatory reference to me being Asian and the assumption that my cock was small. Oh, what I would pay to have you go back in time and spread a rumor around my high school that my cock is actually large," I laughed. "But you also said Charles was probably the best sex of all your boyfriends, so I guess that was despite his small penis?"

"I think a guy that has a small penis tries harder. Really," she said with a light laugh.

We rinsed off quickly and then got dressed for dinner. We typically ordered in when Kris visited me in order to avoid the risk of running into someone I knew. But I hardly knew anyone in Los Angeles, so I thought this date was a low-risk opportunity to take her to a nice restaurant. I had made dinner reservations at Nobu.

The hotel valet pulled up her silver Toyota Camry and we hopped in. To be honest, it was filthy and smelled heavily of cigarettes and weed. There were paper cups of ash in both center cup holders, and the mileage on the car read over 200,000 miles. But I didn't care. Nothing seemed to matter when I was with Kris except being with Kris.

"So I thought we might smoke weed together before dinner," she said with a mischievous light in her eyes as she started to drive.

"I've only smoked weed twice in my life, and that was over ten years ago when I had that crazy summer in Asia," I said. "But sure, let's do it."

"Really?" she smiled. "I thought I'd have to try harder to convince you."

"Nope, I'm all in."

We got lost trying to find our way to Nobu despite turn-by-turn directions from her iPhone. We laughed at our own ineptitude at not just following directions, but trying to communicate with one another.

"Should I turn left here?"

"Right."

"Turn right?"

"No, I meant 'correct' – turn left."

Cue adolescent laughter. Silly, I know, but it was fun to be silly in the moment. Eventually, we found the restaurant, and we parked a few blocks away to smoke weed.

She stuffed a pinch of weed into a small bowl and showed me how to burn the weed with a lighter as I covered the ventilation hole on the side of the bowl for a few seconds before releasing and breathing in the concentrated smoke. I tried a few times as we passed the bowl back and forth.

"That's not bad, but I don't think you're doing it quite right," she said. "It took me a while to get the hang of it."

"Well, this is the third time that I've smoked weed, and I haven't felt anything any of the times. Maybe I am doing it wrong."

We passed the bowl back and forth a few more times, and then walked to the restaurant holding hands.

I ordered several of the signature dishes on the Nobu menu, including the cod with miso and the sashimi with jalapeno, and I made sure to ask the waiter for a fork for Kris also.

I pulled out my Blackberry and stared at it for a few seconds.

"Work?" she asked.

"No," I said with a guilty smile. "I have to admit that I create a running list of questions that pop into my head in between our dates. We have such limited time together that I want to make sure I don't miss anything. Otherwise, I'll have to wait another two weeks to ask you."

Kris smiled, tapped her iPhone and held it towards me to see the screen – her running list of discussion topics, apparently. We both laughed.

"We're fucked up, you know," I said.

"I know."

"So here's one of the questions that I had on my list. I was trying to trace your moves all around the country growing up. I think you moved from Florida to Lubbock, Texas to live with your dad, and then back to Florida and then Calabasas, California to live with your dad again, then back to Florida and then back to California to live with your grandparents. Did I get all that right?"

"Right."

"Well, what I couldn't figure out is why did you move to Lubbock, Texas the first time to live with your dad and then move back to Florida? I'm not sure I ever got that story."

"Well, I moved from Florida the first time because my mom and I couldn't live together anymore. She was drunk all the time, and so we would just fight constantly. Physically and verbally. So I went to live with my dad in Lubbock when my mom decided to move back to Nevada. But I hated it in Lubbock. As I mentioned, my dad had remarried and had a new family there. They didn't really want me there."

"So they were mean to you. Your dad also?"

"Yeah. Sort of," Kris said softly. Then I saw tears suddenly well up in her eyes. Kris had shared with me a lot of the difficult situations that she had faced growing up, from an untreated broken arm, to her alcoholic mom, to her abusive, heroin-addicted boyfriend. But I had never seen her cry before.

"Oh Kris," I said, my heart breaking. "I'm sorry."

"I just want my dad to say he's proud of me. Just once. I told you that I want to become a psychologist, but I haven't shared that with my dad because he would never believe that I could do it."

"Well, you'll do it, Kris," I said as I reached across the table to put my hand over hers.

Kris gave me a weak smile, and then pulled her hand away and wiped her tears. She took a deep breath.

"I was going to write you a letter for Christmas," she said. "I wanted to explain how much this friendship means to me. How much you mean to me. But then I realized you couldn't keep the card, and you'd probably have to throw it away."

I nodded.

She sat silent for a while, and then added, "And actually, I didn't write the letter because I didn't know if it was appropriate."

"What do you mean?"

"I'm worried with how deep we're getting into this relationship, so sometimes I force myself to try to keep a little emotional distance. So I might not respond to an email right away, or my response might be a little cold on purpose. Plus, I would never want to be an emotional wedge between your wife and you. I know you still love her, and you have kids. I would feel terrible if somehow our relationship screwed that up."

"I understand, Kris," I said with a sad smile.

We had talked about going dancing after dinner, but we were too exhausted. So we made our way back to the hotel.

When we entered the room, we immediately began to kiss passionately. Then I pulled away.

"Kris, I wanted to ask you something. Every time we make love, you always cover your mouth right when you cum. And other than maybe one 'Oh my god,' you're pretty silent. Why is that?"

"I'm just used to not screaming out loud. When Taylor and I have sex, he's totally silent the whole time."

"Totally?"

"Totally silent. It finally got kind of freaky, so I told him he had to stop. But I guess I became used to not being vocal also."

"Well, nothing turns me on more than knowing that I'm making you feel good. Honestly. I want to hear you scream when you cum, and I want to hear your dirty talk."

We made love again that night. I could feel Kris give way to open abandon as she climaxed. She screamed, "Oh my god, I'm cumming hard! Fuck me, Ryan." I pumped Kris harder in response, and I whispered in her ear that I was going to fill her up with my hot cum. Moments later, we climaxed together.

Before going to sleep, I told Kris that one of my fantasies was to be woken up in the morning by someone, preferably female, giving me a blowjob. She took care of that fantasy the next morning as a warm-up to us making love again. Afterwards, we lounged entangled in bed.

"Wow, we went to 'Portland' three times this trip. So let's see. We had sex once three dates ago. We did it twice last date. This time we did it three times. I'm afraid of our next date," I said with a laugh.

"I know. My cookie is sore."

"Cookie? Is that what you kids call it nowadays?"

"Yup, cookie," Kris giggled, hugging me tightly.

My flight wasn't until noon, so after lounging for a bit, Kris began to collect her things to head home. She didn't want her grandparents to worry. I lay in bed watching her move around the room picking up various pieces of clothing.

"This time, I feel like the sugar baby since you're leaving first, and I'm just lying here in bed," I laughed. "And don't forget my Christmas gift. You still have to email me a few pictures."

"I remember," she smiled.

After she collected her things, she crawled into bed with me for one last hug.

"This was my favorite date," she whispered.

"Why is that?"

"Because we could actually go out, hold hands and walk around. It felt like we were a real couple."

Date 7: January 12

Email from Kris (12/23):
Some things I would've said in my letter: I'm so very glad I met you. You've become my secret best friend. Since that very first night, you've unknowingly challenged me to grow. Some of our talks made me question things I had never even considered before regarding the difference between right and wrong and my own personal morals. While getting to know you, I'm also getting to know myself because I can be completely honest when we're together. I want to thank you for that, and everything else of course. I can't wait to see where this takes us. :)

Email to Kris (12/23):
Thanks Kris. Your electronic "card" means a lot to me. Even if it was just plain text in an email . . . not some fancy "e-card" with lots of graphics of dancing babies . . . man, I love those dancing babies . . . where was I? Oh yeah, your email – I feel the same way. Like I said a couple visits ago – you're really special, and more importantly you're really special to me.

And while I know we both try to maintain a bit of emotional distance, because we know in some part of our hearts that there is a finite window for this relationship (has to be, right?) . . . I'm actually a little hopeful now that doesn't mean there is a finite window to this friendship. The more I think about it, I don't see actually why one has to necessarily imply the other. Anyway, no need to talk about depressing stuff like that right now – but I know we both think about it, so just food for thought.

Speaking of which, you said something else to me this morning that meant a lot to me, and I'm not even sure you caught how special it was. And I just wanted to thank you for saying it. What I am referring to, of course, is you saying that my penis is large. Wow – jackpot! And then you went on to say I was larger than Charles and better proportioned than Stephen, which was icing on the cake. Take THAT Charles (i.e. my Asian competition for Kris's affections) . . . now THAT'S the way you "break the mold," baby!

Okay, last thing I wanted to say, in all seriousness, is that in the same way you said you would never want to be the cause of a wedge between my wife and myself, I don't want to ever be an emotional wedge between you and Taylor. Finding someone you love who loves you back completely is exceedingly rare. So when we were talking at Nobu yesterday, and you said you sometimes discipline yourself to remain a little "cold." I think that's actually right to do (and by "right" I mean "correct," not the opposite of "left"). Regardless of how we each feel about "love" and the definition of "cheating" . . . there is a special place in our hearts for one person, I believe, where if the world comes to an end, that is the person you want to be by your side. That's my wife for me, as you know. And sounds like that may be Taylor for you (or if not, I'm sure you will find that person – jeez, Kris, you're only 19 after all). So anyway, please make sure to throw yourself completely back in when you're in Florida, and I don't expect you to communicate much during that time. If you want to, of course, I'd love your emails – but I mainly don't want to BE something that distracts you, emotionally confuses you, or most importantly, makes you hold back from living in the present while you're there. Just feels like when you left Florida, there were a lot of "untied strings" that need your full attention now.

Okay, off to bed . . . with my, y'know, large penis . . . heh, heh, heh.

Happy holidays, Kris. :)

Email from Kris (12/25):
Merry Christmas to you too! We just opened up all of our presents. :) Do they celebrate Christmas in Shanghai? Like lights, tree, the whole thing? What's the weather like? I wish you could've stuffed me in one of your suitcases.

Tell me what's going on! I need something to distract me. I'm getting really anxious about my trip. I've been packed for two weeks now and have nothing to do but smoke the rest of my weed and start returning for the horrible clothes that my stepmom (erm, Santa) brought me.

I miss you only a little bit.

Email to Kris (12/26):
It's wintertime here, so like high 50s during the day. But pretty decent relative to the summer (which can get unbearably hot and humid).

Christmas is sort of a non-event here. Some modest public lights and decorations, but no one really celebrates Xmas. They do celebrate the New Year, but the biggest holiday (equivalent to Christmas for us) is Chinese New Year, which is based on the lunar calendar, in February. That's when everyone gives gifts and takes the week off. Actually the "gifts" are almost always just red envelopes full of cash (called hong bao) . . . we're a very practical people.

Good luck in Florida. To be 100% honest, I've naturally got mixed emotions. The instinctual, selfish side wants you all to myself. But in truth, the greater emotion comes from the side that really wants you to be happy in a relationship where someone can love you the way you deserve to be loved. (regardless of what that may imply for us going forward) The fact that THAT is honestly the "greater emotion" (at least as honest as I can be with myself) says a lot about our relationship and how I feel about you, btw. :)

Get anything good for Christmas (besides unstylish clothes)? I think your email with MY present must have gotten lost in my spam? Ahh, Kris – killing me.

I miss you only a little bit also.

    Kris finally emailed me a picture a couple of days after Christmas. One grainy iPhone shot of her smiling in the jacket I had given her on our first date. Cute, but to be honest, I was a bit disappointed. I had hoped for a collection of pictures from her past with some narrative around growing up, similar to the pictorial montage that I had given her. This seemed almost an afterthought fired off in order to avoid my constant reminders to send me pictures.
    I started to have mixed emotions at this point. I was in Shanghai over the holidays with my family, and yet I would obsessively check my email account dozens of times a day, hoping for new messages from Kris.
    Nothing.

I acknowledge that I had instructed Kris specifically to not email as often while she was in Florida so that she could fully immerse herself back into her relationship with Taylor, but I guess a part of me didn't actually want that to happen. As the days went by with extended silence from Kris, I began to feel forgotten, hurt and angry.

"She's back with Taylor in Florida, and of course she's forgotten about you, you idiot," I'd berate myself. "She's a nineteen-year-old girl. Why in the world would you delude yourself that you are actually important to her? Just stop it, Ryan. You have to stop this." But I would still check email obsessively.

Email from Kris (1/7):
Hi stranger. When can I see you again?

Email to Kris (1/7):
Ohh, dunno – probably every time you close your eyes. Okay, now that you are done throwing up in your own mouth – save this Thursday if you can.

How's my buddy Charles? I miss him greatly.

Email from Kris (1/9):
Thursday sounds good to me!

I entered the hotel suite and gave Kris a big hug and deep kiss. I put her envelope into her handbag at the beginning of our date, as I always did, and then we sat down to eat dinner and catch up on our respective holidays.

I told her about Shanghai. I let her scroll through some of my holiday pictures on my Blackberry. She paused over the ones of my wife and three kids in particular, including pictures of them sleeping together in Shanghai, playing at the park, and visiting various museums.

Kris filled me in on her trip back to Florida. It had gone well with Taylor. They were still together. They didn't fight during the ten days, which was unusual for them. She added with a laugh that her parents were impressed that Taylor had "bought" her an iPad.

After dinner, we had sex. Then we each called our respective partners to say goodnight and tell our usual cadre of lies to the people whom we supposedly cared about the most.

We had sex once more before we went to sleep and then again in the morning before I left for work.

This relationship had run its course. I had let myself become infatuated with a nineteen-year-old girl probably because of some deep-seated psychoses that I possessed from being romantically rejected growing up. I had now successfully fucked the prom queen.

Congratulations.

I had let myself be swept up in this fantasy that we were in love, but the fact was that she didn't really care. She cared about Taylor, her boyfriend, as she should. Christ, I was paying her thousands of dollars. Of course she would play along with this fantasy of mine.

It was time to get out before I got hurt. It was time to end this.

Date 8: January 24

Email from Kris (1/15):
So much to tell you next time we meet. My parents, grandparents and I sat down and had a pretty serious talk today. It's looking as though you might be flying me in from Florida starting in the next few months. That is, if you're even willing to do that. I'm positive it's more expensive, maybe you could reduce the envelope amount to make up for it? I'm not sure. Lots of things are up in the air right now. When is the next time I can see you?

Email to Kris (1/15):
To quote one of your emails, "I can't even respond to anything else you've said without finding out why . . . So explain!"

Email from Kris (1/15):
My grandparents are moving into an assisted living facility at the end of next month, and my parents have noticed that I'm really just not happy here so they offered to set everything up for me to go back. I love California but I have absolutely no friends. I had hoped that I would make some at school, but frankly most people at a community college are there to get their shit done and go home. It's not like high school where everyone is basically forced to get to know each other. Most of the classes at community college that I need are also already filled up, and even if I wanted to move to Long Beach with my dad, it would be an hour drive to and from school. Of course, other big factors are Taylor and my Grandma. I'm very lonely here and it's starting to wear on me. I've been feeling like my life is literally in two different places.

Email to Kris (1/15):
I could go on and on with a lot of counter-arguments (and I have in my head all day long) – but let me, for just this once, be succinct and say, "I understand."

At the end of the day, I want what is best for you (which I hope you believe by this point), and if you feel that is best – then it would be presumptuous for me to argue otherwise. If you feel that is best, then that is what you should do.

As to "us" – I know it's sort of ridiculous for me to assume the last three months have meant as much to you as I've built up in my own head. But I'm not ashamed to admit that you've somehow and someway left a permanent handprint on my heart, which is both a blessing and a cross to bear.

It's not the easiest thing in the world for me to fully digest immediately, so please just give me a little time, Kris. (great, now I feel like one of those guys on the side of the "Kris" road)

All I know for certain is that I will always be there as a true friend if you ever need me.

Email from Kris (1/16):
I just don't want you to be upset with me. It's not ridiculous at all to assume that my relationship with you, as unconventional as it is, does mean a lot to me. You really have been my only friend here, and I appreciate that more than you know. I don't want it to end, but if it has to, I understand. Take as much time as you need.

Email to Kris (1/17):
Sorry, been a little absent, Kris. First, I'm not upset with you (per your email).

I just really haven't figured out what to say. I'm mostly sad that you have this shot (maybe not high probability, but a real shot if you got honors at community college) to go to UCLA or Berkeley, a couple of the best schools in the country, and break the cycle that we talked about. You'd be fully caught up in terms of your "opportunity set" with all those rich kids from Calabasas, and anything you do from that point would just be based on what you personally achieve.

So that makes me a little sad, because I have so much faith in how smart you are.

But I sympathize with how hard it must be as your own island in CA (and how much you miss Taylor, your Grandma and all your friends).

And that's not to say that you can't still overachieve and "break the cycle" from Florida. But there's just no UCLA or Berkeley equivalent in Florida – so it just makes it harder.

Ha – I bet you thought I've been struggling the last couple days with selfish questions like "How can Kris be leaving me?" or more practically "NOW, how am I going to get laid?"

Nope – getting laid is easy . . . unfortunately. (I sometimes wish I lived back in the 60s when it was a lot harder and opportunities for "cheating" would be limited to sneaking a peek at a Playboy on the magazine rack. I'd be so much of a better boy.)

As to "us" – I haven't been able to figure out how it can work from Florida, honestly. There are a myriad of reasons (none of which have to do with additional cost, btw). It's not worth going into in this email (this email is long enough). But I just don't see it working when you are back in Florida (or at least working well for both of us).

And while a part of me would like to see you again for the finite time you have left here – I know myself, and I think I might be really bad company for the last couple of visits knowing that it's going to end imminently. It's different when you leave Taylor (where it's sad, but you know it's just a matter of time before you see each other again). In this case, when you leave, who knows? (I mean we can be email buddies and such, but who knows when or if we'd see each other again.)

So I think I'd just be bad company for you over the next few weeks, and it wouldn't be "stress free and enjoyable" for either of us. So that makes me a little sad also.

Finally – I meant 100% what I said that I will always be there as a true friend if you ever need me. And no matter what happens or where you are – I want you to please keep that promise as a security blanket. So if you ever reach a low point again (like in Calabasas or last year in Florida) and you need a friend – you'll reach out to me and know that I'll do what I can to help.

Email from Kris (1/17)

So that's it? You're not even going to see me before I go? Not even going to try? I don't think I want a friend like that. I mean it's bad enough that for whatever reason, you think a few extra hours on a plane somehow changes the situation. As if my living arrangements had any effect on you at all. But to not even get to say an unnecessary goodbye is just . . . I can't even find the word. I probably shouldn't be so hurt, but I am. Don't worry – I won't try to email you again. Thanks for everything Ryan.

Email from Kris (1/17)
Look, I'm sorry for my last email. Kind of. I just don't understand your reasoning. I don't want it to end. At least not right now. Not so soon. But I'm not going to beg, and if you think this is the right thing to do then I guess I have to respect that. I'm just going to miss you a lot.

Email to Kris (1/17)
Now Kris – we can't possibly leave it like that, please.

Okay, if you want a more brutally honest explanation, you deserve it. Fair enough. So here you go:

1) The truth is that I was really jealous when you were in Florida and back with Taylor. The thought of you and him sleeping together every night was no fun over the holidays, and the idea of that now being the permanent situation (not the exception) is something I don't think I can deal with in a healthy way. Yes – I fully acknowledge that is totally hypocritical given the situation. But regardless, it's the truth.

2) I might be able to deal with it ("might," but not even sure) – IF I felt like there was a part of you that was really mine. Y'know – that you really cared about me as much as I do you ("DO", mind you, not "did").

But when you came back over the holidays and were so excited about the skateboard you had bought Taylor . . . that you wrapped so carefully, packed in your suitcase so lovingly and even wrote a note to the TSA to "not open" – and I compared that to how you couldn't even bother to email me a few pictures of yourself as my very "modest" Christmas request sometime, ANYTIME over the last month (what would that take . . . like 10 minutes, Kris?), how I wasn't top of mind enough to even bother to email over the holidays, and how I always email you long, cheesy emails – and it takes days sometimes to get a four-line response.

I've been thinking a lot about that imbalance in our relationship over the last couple of days. I know you genuinely care about me. (I do . . .

you don't have to convince me of that . . . I know you're not that good of an actress.) But think about all the above in an objective way . . . from my point of view, please . . .

Not continuing the relationship has nothing to do with the costs (nothing, zippo, zero). It has a little to do with the logistics (think about the delays you've had just trying to fly up to SF – and multiply that by a flight that is FIVE times as long AND has a connection – it will be brutal on you, even if it went smoothly . . . and I travel often enough to know, it often does not go smoothly . . . and when it's brutal on you, Kris – it DOES affect me).

But it mostly has to do with (when I was forced to step back over the last couple of days) – I just felt a little like . . . well, like a "rube." To be clear – I don't blame you at all that there's this imbalance in our relationship. That's just the danger of "falling for Kris." So totally not your fault, and I know it's not malicious or intentional.

But I've been a rube before, growing up in high school (as you know). I don't like it – it hurts. And I even cringe a bit to think that I was so enamored that I did that long "arts and crafts" project for you with a cheesy reprisal of my pictures with silly annotations. And I got one grainy picture in return (finally, after much prodding multiple times).

3) If you want to come up before you go, okay – a part of me would love that. But Kris, you should just expect me to be sad and pensive the entire time. Because I know that would be "goodbye" (given all the above), and that's all I'd be able to think about when I see you.

But okay, if you'd like to come up for us to do that "goodbye" – okay, I can't say "no" to you on that point. You tell me when, and I can arrange it. But think about it first and just make sure you understand what it will be like.

4) You can be mad at me. I don't care how mad you are at me . . . I am your friend and always will be. And we all have dark days in our life, and at some time you may want a friend who really cares about you for you . . . and that will be me. Even if you say cruel things to me like "thanks for everything Ryan." :)

Our first fight! Interesting to see this side of you. Makes me kinda want to spank you. :)

Email from Kris (1/17)
Oh, the irony! Taylor just threw a fit because I called him in tears, upset about your decision. Probably a stupid move on my part but I didn't really know who else to call. It seems as though I have downplayed my feelings for you to a fault. Please let me explain more in the morning. I just got back from the gym for the third time today . . . I'm positive that's not healthy but with all this stress and no cigarettes, I had to try and clear my mind somehow. Anyway, I'm exhausted. But don't give up on me yet.

Email from Kris (1/18):
Cjbwhcjsnskdbele you make me want to rip my hair out!

All the recent photos of me are "grainy" because they've been taken with my phone. Any quality photos either have Taylor in them, or I have some ridiculous haircut/color, and it's embarrassing . . . Although I guess not as embarrassing as your bowl haircut. To be fair I could've tried harder, but I wasn't aware how much it really meant to you. I'm sorry for that.

As far as emailing over the holidays, you basically TOLD me not to contact you on my trip. You were on a trip of your own with your WIFE and CHILDREN. I assumed you were doing something with your family and I didn't want to ... poison that? Again it's hard to type out exactly what I mean.

It hurts you to hear about me and Taylor just as much as it hurts me to see pictures that you took of your wife sleeping with your little kids. Seeing your perfect life from your point of view and knowing that I'll only ever have a small, secret spot in it. And now I can't even have that. Your wife has everything I don't. She has three beautiful children, a huge house, anything and everything she could ever want – and you. Forever. I can't blame anyone for that. It is what it is. It does wear on my mind but the bigger part of me appreciates what I am allowed to have with you. Or rather, had with you.

Anyway, I would like to see you one last time. It's not going to be easy for me either. I have tried very hard to keep you from seeing how attached I've become, and it looks as though my plan to protect myself has backfired on me. Oh well, I guess. There doesn't seem to be anything I can do about it now. So if you want to schedule something in the next two weeks, I'm completely free. Just let me know.

Email to Kris (1/18)
Kris – I don't want to fight. And I don't want us to make each other sad.

Let me look into flights tomorrow for next week. How is next Tuesday?

Email is not good for working through these sorts of things. Too much gets lost in translation. So let's just talk about it when we get together – what we want, what we're each afraid of, what we each could live with. I know in my heart that if we were to try to maintain our current relationship pace – it wouldn't work out well. At least not for me (and I don't think for you either). It would be too much like a true relationship. I'm already in too deep, and I'd spend too much time spinning around what you and Taylor were doing all the time together (hard to fight a million years of evolution). On the other hand, to never see you again . . . to lose one of my friends who knows everything about me "unmasked" would seem equally horrible (heck, I only have two friends in that category . . . And you're better looking than Andrew). I don't know if that means we catch up / visit every few months like old friends throughout the year. I don't know if that's better or worse for me. I don't know if that's better or worse for you. I don't know. I know it's been a few days now since you broke the news, but I'm still working through all this.

So let's not fight over email. If we need to, we can fight about it live next week

Email from Kris (1/18)
Next Tuesday sounds good to me.

Email from Kris (1/19)
My dad just called to tell me he's running my car through a bunch of tests "early sometime next week, like Monday or Tuesday" but I'm trying to convince him to do it Wednesday. If not I can take a cab to and from the airport. Did I mention I'm driving to Florida?

Email to Kris (1/19)
Chatsworth, CA to Naples, FL = 2,716 miles / 38 hours. That's even before building in the fact that you have a terrible sense of direction (GPS or no GPS) – apparently only surpassed by my own lack of navigational skills.

No, Kris, you did not tell me that. And no, I am not okay with that. Is anyone else driving with you? Can Taylor fly out and drive back with you? Do you have friends or relatives that you can stay with along the way at night?

Otherwise, that's probably 4 days of driving and 2 – 3 nights in some random motels in the middle of nowhere.

Just – no. Here's what you're going to do instead. You're going to pack up your car, bid adieu to your grandparents, drop off your car to be shipped in LA, take a taxi to LAX, fly to Florida, and then hang out in some local Naples hotel until your car arrives and you can credibly pretend to have driven cross-country.

I'll cover it . . . mainly because I don't think I can deal with the thought of you driving cross-country alone (i.e. 19 year old, attractive girl, with a terrible sense of direction, likely "high" some portion of the drive, staying at random motels at night – just no).

Plus you can get to Naples sooner, and you can have a mini-vacation with Taylor for a few days to welcome you back (I really do want you guys to be happy together, btw. I hope you didn't take anything otherwise from my prior emails . . . I just can't emotionally deal with being the "third wheel" in that relationship . . . though, in truth, I have fantasized about a menage-a-trois with you . . . but that's got the wrong, y'know, ratio.)

Anyway, we can talk about it on Tuesday – but no. Seriously.

Email from Kris (1/19)

Oh, Ryan. You make me laugh. I wasn't aware I asked for your permission! I do love how protective you are, though.

Here's the real plan. My dad and I are driving to Nevada together. Figure it'll give us a little time for last-minute bonding. He's flying back home, and I'm staying the night with my mom. I'm also stopping to see the few childhood friends I still keep in contact with.

From Nevada, I'm driving 13 hours to Lubbock, Texas. I'm staying with my good friend Serena, and, if all goes well, she'll be making the 24 hour stretch to Naples with me. We're still looking into flights home for her.

I appreciate your offer but this is something I want to do. I might even go as far as to say I need it. And I'm almost 20 years old, dammit. I'll be fine.

AND I'll have you know I haven't been high since my trip to Florida. So there!

Email to Kris (1/19)
Oh I see how it is . . . You move 3,000 miles away and suddenly feel like you can develop an attitude with me. (or 'tude as us cool kids say)

Sigh . . . I'm going to miss you, Kris.

Okay, your plan is okay . . . Don't love it . . . But I'm okay with it (even if you didn't ask my permission).

Email from Kris (1/20)
Is it just me or are the days leading up to Tuesday going by painfully slow?

I'm so not looking forward to reactivating my profile on the sugar baby site. :(

Email to Kris (1/20)
Not just you. You are trying to kill me, I know.

Email from Kris (1/20)
Just think! Poor little innocent me is probably going to have to sleep with some savage beast who doesn't give a shit about me just to be able to make rent every month . . .

Because you're abandoning me! But I don't want you to feel bad or anything. I understand. ;)

Email to Kris (1/20)
First (and most importantly) – I'm NOT a "savage beast"??? I'm offended. I like to think of myself as quite the overpowering masculine type.

JESUS, Kris (a.k.a. Isabelle) . . . let's talk about everything on Tuesday. Tell me about working out, how packing is going, the LA weather, how you bought another skateboard for Taylor . . . whatever.

But I told you that I didn't want to do this over email.

Egads, I have to go into a meeting now, and now I can't concentrate . . . or actually, even worse, I've got some crazy image of some gorilla (like Ronny from Jersey Shore, but really hairy) crawling all over you.

Wipe that grin off your face, I know you are enjoying this . . . but it's hard on me, my dear . . .

Email from Kris (1/20)
Now, now. I didn't say I was going to find ANOTHER savage beast. And good news – the Naples strip club is taking applications! Maybe I don't need you after all.

I really am enjoying this. :) Hope your meeting goes well.

Email to Kris (1/20)
Spanking. Tuesday. Hard.

Oh and by the way, one of the things on my "list" for Tuesday is that we are going to go through your iPhone pictures together, and I get to choose FIVE that you have to email to me right then and there.

I'll make sure to bring plenty of Smirnoff Ice for us to drown our sorrows. I swear, if you keep making me drink those, my penis is going to disappear – and there's not a lot to start with . . .

Also, if we get drunk enough on Smirnoff Ice (basically to the point where my penis is really, really tiny . . . y'know, like basically the size of Charles's) – we might take a picture of both of us, email it to both of our secret email accounts, and then delete it off your phone.

But hopefully we don't get that drunk.

Email from Kris (1/21)
I hope you know I'm going to be stubborn about the pictures if you're gonna use them to remember me by because, ya know, you could always have the real thing . . . But we'll see. If we do take a picture together it should probably be as soon as you walk in the door. As embarrassing as it is to admit, the past few nights have been plagued with waterworks – no, I'm not talking about wetting the bed. Unfortunately I'm sure they will surface again when I see you.

As far as the spanking goes, I would've been making you mad this whole time if I knew that would be your reaction . . .

I'm really getting nervous thinking about seeing you on Tuesday.

Email to Kris (1/21)

Ironically, Tues is three months to the day from when we first met on October 22nd. I went back and looked.

Don't be nervous, please. Tuesday won't be a goodbye forever, I'm sure of it – it will just have to be a sort of relationship going forward. I'm not sure what that means exactly, but I'm sure we'll figure it out along the way. Frankly, I also want to spend some of Tuesday understanding your plans in Florida, community college, and university goals – as unsentimental as that may be. I can clearly envision you and Taylor in ten years, both with professional careers, a bunch of screaming kids and a beautiful life – so you can't, can't, can't get caught up in less important things along the way (yes, like us – painful as it is for me to say it).

Email from Kris (1/22)

Only three months? Wow. Feels like we've known each other for much longer than that, yet still not long enough.

You're making me really sad and it's not fair. I've always been overly sentimental, so it's things like that will cause me to cry myself to sleep and then I'll have nightmares. No, no, no, no, and no. Please.

You know, sometimes the selfish part of me wishes you weren't married, and I had your actual phone number just to call and say goodnight.

But this is reality. So sweet dreams, Ryan. See you soon.

Email to Kris (1/23)

If I weren't married, everything would be different. Of course, if I weren't married, I'd probably also be some 38-year-old guy who surfed porn and munched on cheese popcorn all day and had bad hygiene. But this is reality, as you say. :(

Sorry, in my email, I meant to say "a different sort of relationship" NOT a "sort of relationship." I'm still not sure what that exactly means, but "a sort of relationship" sounds pejorative for some reason, and I didn't mean to imply that. Let's talk about everything on Tuesday, please (oh Kris . . . you keep dragging me back in over email).

Also, JESUS, I've spent the last couple nights trying to figure out what "waterworks" means. My god, the videos that come up when I search for that term . . . you know how there are stories of some people going blind when they see something too horrific to comprehend? Kinda like that . . . you want to talk about giving ME nightmares . . .

Yes, see you tomrorow, Kris . . .

Email from Kris (1/23)
BTW, I wrote you a letter so please don't let me forget to give it to you. Also, don't bring an envelope. If you do I will use it to tip room service.

"Don't bring an envelope." I replayed these words in my head as I drove to the hotel to meet Kris. I remember warning myself, in the early days of our relationship, that if the day came when we met and no money was exchanged, we would be crossing some dangerous emotional line.

I had always been able to purposefully retain some small doubt about the veracity of Kris's feelings towards me because I was paying her money. Far from being disturbed by this small doubt, I clung to it like an emotional fig leaf of protection. "Don't forget, she is hanging out with you because you are paying her!" I would tell myself over and over again as I sensed myself spiraling ever deeper into our relationship.

"Don't bring an envelope."

With those words, the fig leaf dropped away. There was no more pretense that this was just a fantasy relationship with fantasy emotions. Those words were an official acknowledgement that we had crossed that dangerous emotional line.

The truth is, of course, we had crossed that line a long time ago.

I walked into the suite, and saw Kris sitting on the couch in the living room. She gave me a sad smile, and then she walked over and gave me a hug. She had dark circles under her eyes and looked tired.

I gave her a deep kiss. We ordered room service and sat down at the dining table.

We sat silent for a few minutes, not sure where to start. Finally, she looked up at me.

"I'm really mad at you," she said softly, tears running down her cheeks. "It's like you can have your wife, but you can't handle me having another relationship with Taylor. And you hold all the power, and you get to decide that this ends. It's not fair."

"I know Kris. I'm not going to try to justify that. Emotions are emotions, and it was really hard for me over the holidays thinking about you and Taylor together in Florida. I think if I had to live with that now as the constant, it would destroy me."

"So we'll never see each other again?" she asked.

"Of course we will. You're one of my closest friends – one of the only friends I'm completely maskless with. We just won't see each other every couple of weeks. Leaving emotions aside, even if we wanted to maintain that pace, it would be logistically impossible. I know you said it doesn't matter, but think about flying cross-country with a connection every couple of weeks to see me for just one evening. You would get tired of that quickly. So maybe we try to get together every two or three months to catch up on each other's lives," I offered tentatively. "I travel a lot to the East Coast, New York in particular, so we could meet there."

"So we're only going to see each other a few times a year?" she asked with hurt in her voice.

"I don't know, Kris. It's not like I've done this before, so I don't know how it works. I just thought we could try that as an in-between. I don't want to say goodbye any more than you do, but I can't lose myself in the process either."

Kris sat silent for a few minutes. Then she wiped away her tears and seemed to brighten up. Maybe it was the recognition that we could see each other once in a while and that this wasn't a final goodbye. In retrospect, I think it may have been her belief that she would be able to convince me to see her more than a few times a year.

"Oh, here is the letter I wrote you," she said. She handed me a piece of loose-leaf notebook paper. It was folded several times into a small rectangle. It reminded me of a high school note passed in study hall.

"Should I read it now?"

"No," she said with an embarrassed smile. "When I think about what I wrote, I feel like a fourteen-year-old."

"As opposed to a nineteen-year-old?" I smiled. "I have something for you also."

I handed Kris a Tiffany's bag that had a small box and an envelope inside.

"First, I know you said not to give you any money, which I appreciate. But I like taking care of you. I want to make sure you have some money to help with your move. Three thousand dollars. Second, I bought you Tiffany's earrings that match the original teardrop pendant that I gave you on our first date. I thought they were a nice way to celebrate how our relationship has come full circle."

"Thank you," she said softly as tears welled up in her eyes again.

"Okay, no more crying, please. Let's enjoy the time we have to be together tonight."

She wiped away her tears again and nodded. The room service food came, and we talked as we ate.

"Katy called me wasted last night and started crying when I told her that I was coming back to Florida. It reassured me that I was making the right decision because I've honestly been struggling with it – especially after your reaction. I have to admit I never saw that coming. If I had, who knows if I would still be going through with it. You know what they say about hindsight, though."

I nodded, refusing to take the bait. "Katy sounds pretty unique. I've always wondered, though, why you're still friends with her. I mean, I've never met her, but I would have thought after she pushed you to sleep with your boss and to meet Max in Vegas so that you could pay rent, you might resent her, given how unpleasant those two experiences were."

"Oh Katy is just Katy! I love her," Kris said with a laugh.

We caught up on the rest of Kris's plans. She was going to drive cross-country next week with a first stop in Henderson, Nevada to visit her mom and some old friends. "When I was living in Henderson in elementary and middle school, I went to this magnet school for gifted kids. I remember just loving it. I loved being challenged in school and studying new things."

"You still keep in touch with those friends? That was a long time ago."

"Not actively, but we're all connected on Facebook and Instagram. So we stay updated on our lives in that way. It will be good to see my old Nevada friends."

"Seeing any ex-boyfriends while you are there?" I asked with a twinge of jealousy.

"No. But there is this boy, Kevin, who I used to have a big crush on in elementary school. He always liked my friend, Jennifer, though, so nothing ever happened between us. Recently though, he started 'Liking' all my Facebook pictures and posting comments like, 'You're so beautiful!' I guess the tables have turned. Now that I think about it, he was half-Asian. I think I might just have a thing for Asians," she said with a smile.

"Maybe," I laughed.

From Henderson, Kris was going to drive to Lubbock, Texas to visit her friends Rebecca and Serena. Then Serena was going to make the final leg of the drive with Kris from Lubbock to Naples, Florida.

She had rented a one-bedroom apartment in Florida, and Taylor and she would basically live together. He was excited about that, particularly because he was crashing with various friends right now. She planned to attend community college in the fall, and then move with Taylor after he graduated high school to wherever he went to university.

"It would be funny if he got into Berkeley, and we moved to the Bay area," she said. "Maybe we could double-date with your wife."

I laughed at the image.

After dinner, we took a bubble bath and made love. True to my word, I spanked her hard as I fucked her from behind. I could tell she was excited by it, and she came quickly and loudly. I came inside her, of course.

We lay in bed afterwards, holding each other.

"Okay," I said. "No more hiding. Pull out your iPhone, and I'm going to pick five pictures that you have to email to me right now."

She smiled, and we snuggled closer as she picked up her iPhone. As she tapped to bring up pictures, a search screen displaying her previous searches inadvertently popped up.

Definition pejorative

Sandy Lee

Ryan Lee home

I burst out laughing. I immediately recognized "pejorative" from my recent email. I found it cute that she had cared enough to look up the definition. I then asked playfully, "Doing searches on my wife and my home?"

"Well, I couldn't find her Facebook page, and she has a Pinterest page with nothing pinned," she said defensively and a little embarrassedly.

I know that I should have been horrified that Kris was stalking my wife online now, but I was more amused that we were both similarly obsessed with each other.

"Don't worry, I stalk you online also. I stalk Taylor too. I've read all your Facebook Timeline posts and comments," I said with a smile.

"I also changed all my passwords to your full name," she said with a laugh. "Ryanlee. Taylor is always trying to log into my email and Facebook accounts, and he would never guess that. By the way, did you find my Tumblr page when you were stalking me online?"

"No, you have a Tumblr blog? What's the website address?"

"Nope, I don't think I'll tell you. I know how jealous you get about Taylor, so you probably don't need to see all the stuff I've posted. I challenge you to find it, though. I keep it pretty well hidden."

"Oh, I'll find it," I said confidently. "Is there anything about me on the blog?"

"Not directly. Sometimes I post things like poems or pictures with you in mind, but everyone just assumes they are meant for Taylor. Even Taylor thinks they are meant for him."

"Interesting – makes me extra-motivated to find your blog. Okay, now show me those pictures."

She smiled as she turned the phone slightly away from me as she tapped a few times more, so that I would not see anything else inadvertently. Then she turned the phone screen back towards me, and we started to scroll through her pictures.

She showed me pictures of Taylor, her dad, her mom, her dog, her prom pictures. It was fun to have a pictorial window into her life, which I had heard so much about over the last few months. I was so engaged as we flipped through her pictures that I forgot to actually make her email pictures to me.

We started to watch the movie *Ted*, but as usual, we only made it partway through before giving way to temptation and making love again. As I licked her pussy and fucked her with my middle finger, she moaned, "Oh Ryan, I love the way you touch me." I made her cum twice before I filled her up again.

As we cuddled afterwards, I said, "You told me when we met that you were equally attracted to girls and boys. I was wondering if you are still attracted to girls."

"What do you mean?"

"I was just thinking about all of your sexual experiences, and how none of them actually sounded that good. Stephen was your first, and he was uncircumcised and too long so it hurt. Derek was a virgin, so that was probably terrible. Warren was meaningless sex while high on cocaine. Taylor was a virgin and is eerily silent when he has sex. Charles was pretty good technique-wise, but he had a small penis. So he is, y'know, structurally limited. Sorry, I couldn't resist. Your boss, Bill, was disgusting, and then the threesome with Evan and Heather got cut short before anyone finished. So I was kinda hoping that if I could just fuck you well enough, I might... I don't know... be able to fuck the lesbian out of you," I said with a slightly embarrassed smile.

Kris laughed lightly and turned her head to give me a light kiss. "You're cute."

We went to sleep after that. We made love again in the morning, and then it was time to say goodbye.

"Kris, good luck with the move, and let me know if I can do anything to help. Please keep me updated as you drive cross-country. I can't help worrying about you," I said as I gathered up my clothes.

Kris just sat in bed with tears streaming down her face. We kissed passionately and sadly a few more times, and then I waved goodbye and walked out the door.

Date 9: January 31

I sat in my car in the hotel parking lot, emotionally spent from our goodbye. Then I unfolded Kris's loose-leaf note. I admired the overall gestalt of her looping handwriting on the page for a few moments before starting to read.

Dearest ▮

    I can't even remember the last time I sat down to write a real letter. But I need to make sure you know how I feel about you if this really is the last time we'll be seeing each other. Of course, I keep hoping you'll change your mind. This is a very strange feeling for me. I've never really had anyone leave me before. I've always been the one to leave, and I suppose in the literal sense I'm continuing the tradition. Emotionally, this is new to me. Never in a million years did I expect it to hurt so bad. Maybe this is payback for all the hearts I've broken over the years. Regardless, I don't think either of us could've predicted the feelings that have developed over the past few months. You have been my rock – one of my only constants. You've supported me – financially, yes – but in so many other ways I'll never be able to repay you. Funny thing is, I know you don't expect me to

> I also know that eventually you will find someone to take my place. As painful as it is to think about, I don't blame you one bit. I just hope she appreciates what an amazing man you are. I hope she realizes how lucky she is. You've always done such a great job of making me feel 100% comfortable. And like I said before, I don't think I've ever met someone so thoughtful. I'm just sorry I didn't give you a reason to be able to say the same about me. Even if we never speak again, know that I will never forget you. I couldn't if I tried. I will forever remember the way you looked at me, the way you listened to me, the way you touched me. Like I was a princess. Like I was worth something. I can only pray that the man I end up marrying has half the heart that you do. In whatever strange, limited way I'm allowed to, I love you ▬
> Please don't forget about me. Always,
> ▬

My heart ached. It ached because of our breakup. But it ached even more that this girl, whom I had fallen in love with, could write, "Like I was worth something." It was as if she didn't realize how special she was.

I drove to work and emailed her when I got to my desk.

Email to Kris (1/25)
Home safe?

Thank you for the letter, Kris. It meant a lot to me that you cared so much to write it, and it made me feel both happy and a little sad to know that we've been in synch all the way through this relationship.

Have you ever heard of Chaos theory – sometimes referenced to as the "butterfly effect"? Basically a branch of mathematics that says because of the interplay of one factor impacting another which impacts another and another, etc. . . . in theory, a butterfly flapping its wings in Florida could eventually cause a tsunami in Shanghai (just to pick two random places).

Anyway, I've been thinking about you and the millions of decisions (both big and small) and life experiences (both the good and the very painful) that you've had in your young life – and I'm so thankful that somehow this confluence of a million decisions and experiences created this beautiful masterpiece of a soul that I was able to consider at least partially mine over the last few months. And I'm even more thankful that this serendipitous path of your decisions and experiences finally led you to log onto the sugar baby site one random night and decide to respond to my message . . . basically, this serendipitous path of your decisions and experiences finally led you to me. And that simple response to my message just three months ago has had its own "butterfly effect" on my life – in ways that I'm still trying to figure out.

I don't know what you mean in your letter by "like I was worth something." I have so much admiration for who you are even at the tender age of 19 (fine, almost 20). And I want you to promise that you'll achieve everything that I know you can in this life. That will make me really happy.

Anyway, I had this fantasy (which I've told you about) of taking you to a Broadway show in NY at some point (not sure how or when) . . . and one of my favorite shows is *Wicked*. I won't ruin the entire plot, but one of my favorite songs is from the end when two best friends have to say goodbye and they are trying to express the impact they've had on each other. The song (titled "For Good") reminds me of us – cheesy, I know . . . but you wrote me that letter already, so I don't feel so bad now (you'll recognize the "handprint" lyric, maybe):

http://www.youtube.com/watch?v=uzrGFQysfYU

Let's see how all this evolves, please. And let's not say goodbye . . . or at least, not like we're never going to see each other again. Regardless of how episodically we get together from this point forward – I'm a permanent part of your life in the same way you are of mine.

Ryan

Email from Kris (1/25)

And you say I pull you back in! After you left, I threw a tantrum, ran out to the balcony to try and catch one last glimpse of you walking to your car, splashed around in the bath tub until I wore myself out, and maybe subconsciously on purpose came the closest I'd ever come to missing my plane. Seriously. The doors were closed and they had to re-open them for me. I slept through the entire flight. Then after obsessively checking my email every 5 minutes until I got home I started to process the thought of letting you go, so for the past few hours I've forced myself not to check my email. Now when I give in, you've sent me the most beautiful email ever composed. You don't play fair.

I guess I'm not sure what happens next. I mean, I've accepted the fact that I'm not going to see you often. But how often will we talk? If I wrote to you every time you came to mind, you would get sick of me. I also don't want it to hurt when we talk to each other. I don't know, I'll let you set the pace.

Don't worry about my future. Trust me, I've got it. I'm going to make you proud.

Looking forward to NY. :)

So that was it. We had our goodbye date, and we had survived. The date had been tear-filled and heartbreaking in parts. And the last masks had been stripped away. But I felt good about where we had left it, and we had our plan of seeing each other a few times a year, hopefully.

But I missed her already.

Email from Kris (1/27)
Missing you.

Email to Kris (1/27)
That's so spooky. I'm in a car right now going to meet my buddies for a "guys' night." So an hour ago when I was getting ready at home, I looked in the mirror and concentrated on you and "sent" you a psychic message asking you to email me. And I asked you to just email me "I miss you." And I told myself if you actually did it, I'd take it as a sign that we should see each other one more time before you left for Florida. And then you just emailed! (Got the message a little wrong, but close enough.) Will "drunk email" you later – but I'm a little spooked out right now. Miss you too.

Email from Kris (1/27)
Well there's your sign! I love the drunk emails – don't skimp on the mushy stuff either. In the meantime, have a fun night with the guys. :)

Email to Kris (1/28)
Drunk. Should have stuck with the Smirnoff Ice tonight – but no such luck when hanging out with a bunch of Koreans.

I'm still a little astounded by your receipt of my psychic message tonight. Coincidences happen, I know – but the timing and the message were uncanny. Who am I to fight such a clear cosmic sign? Would you like to come up again before you leave? A part of me knows I don't deserve it, given how I've already hurt you, and I also know how hard it was the last time when we said goodbye. But I'm drunk right now, so I will be a little selfish and just say I really miss you. That and I really, really need to know what waterworks are (I forgot to ask you last time)!

Will leave the decision to visit again before you leave for Florida up to you.

Gotta get some rest now as my legs and liver are about to collapse. But I will now send you a psychic kiss . . . Ooh that feels nice . . . Okay, and now, I'm applying some psychic lube on you . . . Yeah baby . . . And now I'm going to psychically fu . . . Oops gotta run . . .

Night Kris.

Email from Kris (1/28)
Good morning! Man, your Friday night was a lot more exciting than mine.

I think coincidences like that happen to me more often than they happen to the average person. I like it though. It's comforting.

I really would like to come up again if you have the time. I think I got all the tears out, so we can just have some fun on this visit. NO, that doesn't include waterworks!

Dirty, dirty old man . . .

Email to Kris (1/30)
Random question – have you ever seen the movie *The Wizard of Oz*? No, not going to make you watch it tomorrow, but shoot me a quick email (yes or no) and I'll explain tomorrow.

Email from Kris (1/30)
Yes! I took a film class in high school. Looking forward to your explanation tomorrow.

"Hi Kris," I said as I walked into the hotel suite. "This is ridiculous, you know."

"Of course," she said brightly. "It's all ridiculous." I was glad that she didn't look as emotionally worn as on our last date.

"Let's eat," I said as I unpacked the Italian food that I had brought. "We have to leave in about an hour."

"Okay, so where are we going and what's all this about the Wizard of Oz?"

"Well, do you remember in my email I said that someday I wanted to take you to go see a Broadway show and that my favorite show was *Wicked*? We're going to see it tonight."

Kris gave me an excited smile. "I've never seen a show before."

"Great. I'm glad that I'm the one to take your Broadway show virginity. *Wicked* is a musical based on *The Wizard of Oz*, but it focuses on the story of the Wicked Witch of the West and how she's a misunderstood and somewhat tragic character. That YouTube song I sent you, 'For Good,' is from the end when two lifelong friends have to say goodbye. I thought it was apropos."

After eating quickly, Kris put on a cute summer dress. In contrast, I donned a nondescript sweatshirt and wore a baseball hat low. I knew there was some risk of someone recognizing me, since Kris and I were going out in my hometown. Oddly, I wasn't nervous. Still, it was best for me to dress inconspicuously.

We made it to the theater with fifteen minutes to spare. We walked into the theater close together, but not holding hands. Kris sat down first, and I playfully stood next to the empty seat to her left and said, "Is this seat taken?"

She shook her head, so I sat down.

"Here alone?" she asked with innocent eyes.

"Not anymore."

We both chuckled.

During the show, I remember the electricity coursing through my body as she held my right hand in one of her own and lightly stroked the inside of my forearm with the other. I remember glancing over and watching her laugh and smile, lost in the musical. I remember wanting to take a picture of her look of unburdened happiness in that moment. That this girl, who had experienced so much pain in her life, could still be possessed of such an unbroken spirit was a miracle to me.

I have talked about the dangers of sugar daddies falling prey to the "hero complex." Obviously, there was some of that within my obsession with Kris. But recognizing my neurosis didn't necessarily make it any easier to deal with. I wanted to protect Kris and show her that life could be so much more beautiful than what she had experienced. I wanted to prove to her that some people would always care for her, never abandon her, and never hurt her. The irony, of course, was that I wanted to be the one to show her all this. And yet I was an obviously deeply flawed individual who could never fully be with her. A cheater. Just like her dad.

I leaned my cheek into hers and held her close as the musical neared its finale. For those who have never seen *Wicked*, the climax is a bittersweet moment when two best friends have to say goodbye forever. The climactic duet is called "For Good." The song basically describes how two friends have impacted each other's lives so fundamentally that they will always carry the other person in their hearts. Given the parallel to our own final goodbye this night, I braced myself for a flood of emotions as the climactic song began. I've always been cheesy like that.

And then the fire alarm went off in the theater.

As is typical in these situations, the first reaction was for everyone in the theater to look around in order to figure out if it was a false alarm. For the most part, everyone stayed seated. There was no discernible smoke or fire. In a testament to the old saying, "The show must go on," the actresses on stage continued their duet, but the poignancy of the moment was ruined with the constant beeping of the fire alarm in the background.

After a minute, I took Kris's hand, and we walked down the aisle and out the double doors in the back of the theater. Better safe than sorry, I figured. Out in the atrium, a guard informed us that it was a false alarm, so we went back into the theater. By that point, the finale song was almost over, and so we just stood against the back wall. Kris stood in front of me, leaning against my chest. I wrapped my arms around her waist as I gave her gentle kisses from behind on her neck, her ears, and her cheek. We laughed quietly at the absurdity of the situation and the inopportune timing of the fire alarm exactly at the climax of the musical.

After the play, we walked holding hands through the streets of San Francisco for a few blocks to my car. In my nondescript outfit and with baseball hat pulled down, I figured the risk of someone recognizing me was low. And I just wanted to hold Kris's hand.

We passed some teenage boys doing skateboard tricks in a small public park.

"Everywhere I look, I'm reminded of Taylor," Kris said as she pointed to a closed Ann Taylor store. "It's always been that way. We've broken up so many times, but then something would always draw me back."

"Taylor must be excited you're moving back."

"He is. He sent me a text begging me to move back. I miss him a lot, but I don't know."

"Don't know what?"

Kris just turned and gave me a soft kiss, and then she snuggled closer under my arm as we walked.

On the drive back, Kris was silent for a while, staring out the window. Then she said, "That was really fun." She said it not as a throwaway comment, nor as a courtesy thank you. She said it like she was simply happy, as if she was just saying it to herself.

"I'm glad, Kris. I'm only sorry that the finale 'goodbye' song was ruined by that fire alarm."

"It's okay," Kris said with a smile. "I think I would have been too emotional thinking about us also saying goodbye tonight. I almost prefer that it became a funny moment for us instead."

When we got back to the hotel, I cleaned up the take-out food that we had left on the dining table. Kris went into the bedroom. A few minutes later, I looked over and saw her through the open bedroom doorway standing with her side towards me as she fixed her hair in front of a wall mirror. She had changed into a black lace teddy that showed off her perfect form. I was enthralled.

My breath quickened as I walked into the bedroom and encircled her waist in my arms. We kissed deeply, and I pushed my tongue into her excited mouth slowly and rhythmically. I sat her on the bed facing me and then gently guided her to lie down with her legs hanging off the bed. I tantalized her a few minutes with licks up and down her thighs and my hot breath on her swollen pussy. Finally, I pushed my tongue onto her pussy, and she gasped as she grabbed the top of my head with both hands. I gently worked her clit with my tongue as I fucked her with my middle finger, simultaneously rubbing her special spot inside. As I felt her body squirm against my tongue, I knew she was nearing climax. So I pulled my head away and stood up. I took both her arms and pulled her up.

"Come here," I moaned in her ear as I turned her around and placed both of her hands on either side of a full-length wall mirror. I pulled her hips out towards me so that she was bent over with her perfect ass sticking out. I crouched down behind her and began to lick her pussy again from behind. She tasted tangy sweet tonight, and I couldn't get enough.

Then I stood up, gave her pussy a few gentle rubs with my finger, and then I pushed my stiff cock inside of her.

"Oh my god, Ryan," she moaned.

As I fucked her from behind, I watched both of us in the full-length mirror. Her head was bent forward and her eyes were closed in ecstasy.

"Kris," I whispered into her ear from behind. "Look up, baby. Look at how beautiful you are."

She looked into the mirror. At me. At herself. At us. Then I saw tears streaming down from her eyes.

Jesus. I turned her around and kissed her. Then I lay her back down on the bed, and we bathed in the sensuality of my body covering hers as I fucked her. She came on my cock even as tears continued down her face, and I came inside her a few seconds later. We lay entangled in each other and didn't speak for a long time.

Finally, I said, "So what the heck are waterworks? You said in an email that you had waterworks for several nights. When I googled the term, it pulled up a bunch of horrific videos of people peeing on each other. And by 'horrific,' I mean fascinating, of course."

"Jesus, Ryan. I just meant that I've been crying a lot. Not that I've been peeing on a bunch of people," she said with a small laugh as she shook her head derisively at me. "Did I ever mention that I had a guy from the site offer me a ridiculous amount of money to kick him in the balls with heels on? And then there was another guy who wanted me to poop on him. You really have no idea how thankful I am for your normalcy."

I laughed. "Normalcy is all relative, I guess. I'm not sure this qualifies as normal. Anyway, who am I to judge? Different strokes for different folks."

"No," Kris said, still smiling. "Some of that stuff should be illegal."

We made love again in the morning. Our typical "Good Morning," Kris joked. Then I drove her to the airport, we kissed again, and she was gone.

Date 10: February 7

Email to Kris (2/1)
Text me when you get home so I know you got there safely . . . please.

I can't find your Tumblr and wasted an hour already at work searching for it. Oh well, I give up. You win . . . no pictures, no Tumblr, no Facebook . . . but you do realize I'm going to forget what you look like. I think I've told you this before, every time I see you, I am surprised by how stunning you are relative to my fading, geriatric memory of you. Especially this time . . .

Email from Kris (2/1)
YOU DON'T HAVE TO FORGET. Just quit your job and run away with me. People do it all the time! We can have really good mornings until you can't have good mornings anymore!

Email to Kris (2/1)
Wow – so we can have "really good mornings" for like . . . I dunno, at least three months.

Didn't you learn anything from *Wicked* yesterday, Kris? Beautiful people can't be with ugly people for the long run . . . otherwise they get turned into, y'know, scarecrows. And I just couldn't do that to you . . .

Good luck packing and with the trip. And drop me quick emails when you get to Nevada, Texas, and then eventually Florida, please. I'm actually going to be in Las Vegas again for work next week, so not too far from Henderson. But sadly, you'll have already left for Texas by the time I get there.

Email from Kris (2/1)
You have no idea what a beautiful person you are. I'll keep in touch. :)

Email from Kris (2/2)

Well, no time left for cold feet. Leaving now with my dad to drive to Nevada. He's going to fly back from there, and I'm going to stay a few days with my mom before continuing my road trip. Wish me luck. Miss you already.

Email to Kris (2/2)

Okay, in the spirit of us always being TOO honest with each other – to give you a flavor of what I've been up to during the last 36 hours since you left . . . here it is, in all its pathetic glory:

- Wasted an inordinate amount of time trying to find your Tumblr page to retain some link to "my Kris." Course, it was easy to find some random references to your old one (thewisdomtoknowbetter), but you've been good at hiding your current one

- Tried to log into your Gmail account thinking I could find it there (btw, I fully recognize that is both highly unethical and also borderline illegal. I'm glad you changed the password to save me from myself)

- Surfed the sugar baby site, but realized that just made me feel worse. Maybe next week, next month or next year. But not now – not so soon

- Bought your birthday present one and a half months ahead of time. Will send it once you settle in, and you have an address

Did you ever see *Brokeback Mountain* – y'know, the movie about two gay cowboys? (No, this is not the moment I tell you I'm gay . . .)

Aaaaanyway, there's this scene in the movie when Jack Twist is heartbroken and turns to Ennis and says, "I wish I could quit you."

I feel a little like that right now towards you (minus the desire for anal sex). It's been a long time since I've felt like this. Anyway, "time dulls all wounds" (I think "heals" is not the right word), but honestly it just kinda sucks right now.

I can feel the miles taking you away. (And I don't mean the physical distance.)

Okay – enough adolescent drivel on my part . . .

Hope your drive with pops is good and you guys made up. You should tell him you love him at some point, btw, despite all the water under the bridge.

Take lots of breaks if you need them, and don't be a hero. Wake up your dad when you get tired. Just shoot me a one-word text "here" when you get to your mom's so that I know you're safe.

Email from Kris (2/3)
I drove the entire way from Burbank and Waze navigation killed my battery. I definitely should've invested in a car charger.

In response to your email,

- That was my post-rehab Tumblr. It's actually "thewisdomtoknowthedifference." It's part of the serenity prayer. I'm sure you've heard it: "God, grant me the serenity to accept the things I cannot change, the courage to change the things I can, and the wisdom to know the difference." It stuck with me I guess. I'm actually really proud that I hid it so well! It's comforting that I can keep at least one thing private on the Internet.

- OH MY GOD. I can't even respond to that except to tell you that your name alone is too short. Hahah, short.

- I did too. And I felt the same way.

- Nope, never gonna give you an address! You have to hand-deliver it. ;)

- If you wanted to put it in my butt all you had to do was ask . . . and double up on the AstroGlide.

I actually waited for your text as long as I could before we crossed over state lines. But you emailed me right after we stopped for gas, and I didn't stop again before I got to Henderson. The moon over the highway was the biggest moon I've ever seen. It looked like we were going to drive right up into it. Then there was either a mini meteor shower, or I saw a UFO. Either way I thought of you the whole time.

My dad and I said goodbye on better terms.

You know, I have this strange feeling my car is going to break down in Nevada and I'm going to have to stay a few extra days (that just happen to overlap with your business trip to Las Vegas). As a Pisces, I have very strong intuition.

Email to Kris (2/3)
Stop emailing and go spend time with your mom . . . or the "magnet-school-half-asian-who-you-used-to-have-a-crush-on-but-now-the-tables-are-turned" guy.

You're not serious about Tuesday, are you? I thought you were leaving for TX on Sunday? I get into Las Vegas on Tuesday night around 10PM (for Wed meetings). But if you were serious, I could try to move my flight earlier to land at around 6PM, and you could stay overnight Tues and leave Wed morning . . .

But you are joking? Right? I mean, you shouldn't make anal sex promises to a guy and then joke about seeing him again. That's just cruel. Plus I really don't know how we keep having these multiple "goodbye" meetings . . .

Email from Kris (2/3)
Mom's at the bar and I'm watching Dr. Phil. She actually wants me to stay until Monday morning, and she wants all of that time to herself. I guess we're going to lunch with my hippie grandpa tomorrow – did I ever tell you about him? If she wants now through Monday morning to herself, I'm thinking I'll spend the night at my friend Jennifer's Monday night and smoke with half my 3rd grade class on Tuesday afternoon before I leave. But after all that smoking, I'll probably be tired and, ya know, it would be dangerous to leave for Texas . . . Just a thought. Plus I asked for sushi last time, and you didn't bring sushi! Very, very angry about that.

Seriously though, you don't have to if you don't want to. If you do, I'm very adamant about you not bringing an envelope. You ignored my wishes at the first "goodbye," and I didn't say anything. At this point I have plenty of your cash. I just want one more night of your time. I think it would be fun to run around in the desert together. I really do love it here. But if it's messing with your emotions then I completely understand. Just let me know.

Email to Kris (2/3)

Ha, ha – messing with my emotions. That's funny. Y'see – one other thing I forgot to mention doing in my "36-hour confessional" email was that I also emailed myself what I could remember from all nine of our dates (like a mini-diary). Mainly because I didn't want to forget some of the touching details when I'm an old Chinese man (i.e. in six months). For example, here's one excerpt:

- Date #2 – Kris's shuttle got delayed from airport taking backroads, massive amount of sushi, no sex (my assertion), Kris was surprised (I guess) that I wasn't out of shape when I took my shirt off for the first time, I did NOT fart in car on way to airport despite Kris's accusation . . . etc.

You get the idea.

Anyway, an excerpt from my entry from Date #1:

- Question: Have you ever dated an Asian guy?

- Kris: Yes, in Florida. His name was Charles.

- Question: Was he valedictorian of the school?

- Kris: No – he was a drug dealer. Breaking the mold!

- (that's the moment that I knew I was in trouble)

My point being that if I wanted to avoid you "messing with my emotions," I should have gotten up and left right after that moment on the very first date. Because that's the exact moment that I knew this was going to be something very (maybe too) real. And I even texted you something to that effect that night.

So to summarize (btw, nice to see that I haven't lost any of my verbosity over the last three months) – yes, I'd love to see you on Tues. (I suppose a simple "yes" would have sufficed.) Let me try to move my flight to land earlier (early evening), and we can figure things out from there. If we end up going out again, I'll probably need to wear my crazy spy costume again.

I can't wait to hear about your hippie grandpa. Don't think you ever told me about him.

Finally, keep your "short" jokes for . . . well, we all know who. Remember, no takebacks on compliments about each other's anatomy. (I cannot stress enough how important this rule is.)

Email from Kris (2/3)
Too real, indeed. But I'm not ready to quit you yet.

Email me the details when you figure everything out so I know when to leave to pick you up from the Las Vegas airport. As usual, I can't wait to see you. And kiss you. And, um, cuddle – which you definitely do.

Email from Kris (2/5)
Today my mom made me take cheesy pictures in front of my 2nd of 4 elementary schools. Consider this picture a prelude to the album I've put together to share with you on Tuesday night after the aquarium. We're also smoking a blunt. You can't mess up smoking a blunt. Missing you always.

Email to Kris (2/6)
What a perfect surprise – I love cheesy pictures, especially of you. I spent the first thirty seconds just appreciating how pretty you look in the picture. I spent the next thirty seconds nostalgically imagining an elementary-aged "little Kris" walking in a single-file line with her class into that blue door in the background. (Whether true or not, the image I conjured up was of a really happy kid). I spent the last thirty seconds staring to see if I could glimpse your panties (given the semi-exposed way you are sitting).

Sigh . . . I'm not sure how this "being completely honest with our thoughts to each other" is working out. I mean, I believe in some states they arrest people for having those sorts of incongruous thoughts all at the same time (especially the last two).

Long day . . . off to bed. Thank you for the picture – I honestly love it. Can't wait to see you Tues. We'll see about the blunt – I'm sure I'll still mess it up.

I had my assistant cancel my car service from the airport to the hotel. I told her that I was having dinner with an old college friend who would pick me up from the airport.

When I landed in Las Vegas, I made my way to Arrivals and texted Kris. A few minutes later, she pulled up in her old Toyota Camry. Both the trunk and the backseat were so overstuffed with her clothes and bags that I could barely find room in the car to fit my overnight bag. It looked like she had just grabbed everything in her room and thrown it haphazardly into the car, which I'm guessing is exactly what she did.

I hopped into the passenger seat, leaned over and gave her a kiss. I knew she loved aquariums, so I had suggested that we visit a small aquarium just outside of Las Vegas for our "goodbye" date tonight. It was about a twenty-minute drive.

"I got a puppy!" Kris said brightly as she drove.

"A new one? Where is it?" I asked as I craned my neck to look in the backseat.

"She's a husky. I named her 'Veda.' She's perfect. I picked her up in Henderson. My mom is watching her now, so I'll drive back tomorrow morning to pick her up before leaving for Texas."

"Cool," I said, though I had doubts internally about the wisdom of a girl who had trouble supporting herself taking on an additional responsibility. "What was the catalyst for that?"

"Well, I had to leave my other puppy in California with my dad, and I don't know . . . I just need something to love on. I posted a picture of her on Instagram," she said as she held up her phone for me to see. "Taylor is really excited. He commented on Instagram, 'Ours, ours?' and I was like 'Nope, mine.'"

"Your Florida friends must be excited the Queen Bee is coming back. Especially all your ex-boyfriends. They're probably already circling in excitement."

She laughed. "Charles has been trying hard. He actually wanted to fly out and drive cross-country with me. Y'know, for my safety."

"Yeah, I bet. I thought he had another girlfriend now?"

"Apparently not stopping him. Plus he suddenly started calling me Kris. Of all my friends, you're the only one who calls me Kris, not Kristina. You and my grandma."

"Do you want me to call you Kristina?"

"No," she laughed. "That would sound weird now. It would sound like you're mad at me or something. Anyway, I can tell that Charles is trying to sleep with me again."

"Aaah, this is not going to be easy on me when you move back, Kris," I said wryly. "By the way, you do realize this is our third 'goodbye' date. I'm not sure we can call them 'goodbye' dates if we keep having them. I can't believe you actually delayed your road trip to see me again."

"I know. I guess I'm just addicted to you."

We got lost driving to the aquarium, as we seemed to do every time Kris was at the wheel and I was navigating. We just laughed about it and spent the time telling more stories from our past and listening to music. I picked up a CD jewel case from the floor. The cover had a hand-drawn doodle of two people, I assume Taylor and Kris, holding hands.

"It's a mix from Taylor," Kris said with an embarrassed smile. "Don't judge."

"It's sweet. Reminds me of the mix tapes I used to make when I was in high school in order to woo girls . . . unsuccessfully, of course. I remember how much thought I would put into each song so that the overall romantic message of the mix was clear. Making mixes is really a lost art in today's day and age with on-line services like Spotify. Nowadays, you can just pick any song you want at any time and just play it. I kind of feel the same about letter writing. Now everyone Twitters or posts Facebook notes. I think that's why I like writing emails to you. It feels more thoughtful and romantic."

"Well, you basically took my email virginity," she smiled and leaned over to give me a kiss.

We stopped at a McDonald's to ask directions to the aquarium and get a snack. We ate in her car. Kris ordered fries, and she ate them with ketchup mixed in ranch.

"You must be looking forward to being with Taylor again," I said with an internal grimace.

"I guess. This whole relationship with you has impacted my perspective on things. I mean, I always used to worry that when Taylor and I got married, he might cheat on me. I feel like he hasn't dated enough girls. That's my biggest fear. But now I feel like I might be more likely to cheat on him. It's kind of hard to explain. I mean, I practically raised him, and Taylor is like family to me. But he doesn't challenge me," she said thoughtfully. After a few moments, she added, "But still, I'm not ready to give that up."

I wanted to tell her that she shouldn't settle. That she should be with someone she feels passionate about. But I recognized that would appear to be just a self-serving comment. I also noted, ironically, that I should hardly be giving marriage advice. So I just nodded.

We finally made it to the aquarium a few minutes before 8 P.M. I hopped out of the car and ran to the ticket counter to see if they were still open. They closed at 9 P.M. Plenty of time.

The aquarium was spread out across a few different "houses." There was the "Predators" house, the "Coral Reef" house, the "Wild and Open Sea" house, etc. We walked along an outdoor path holding hands and visited each aquatic house. In the "Coral Reef" house there was a petting pool where we were able to touch starfish and sea snails. We'd stop for a few minutes in front of some of the more exotic displays. I remember holding Kris in front of me as we stared at the moray eels display. We just watched them open their gaping mouths as they extended from and retracted into their hiding holes. I placed my hand gently on Kris's bare stomach under her shirt.

"Feel that?" she asked.

"What?"

"The baby."

"Jesus, Kris. Not funny," I said with a grin. "Course, I'd worry more that you were trying to trap me by getting pregnant if you didn't keep reminding me to pull out before I cum."

"And, of course, you never do."

"Can't help it," I laughed. "Just remember to take your pills."

As I pulled my hand out from under her shirt, I suddenly panicked.

"What is it?" Kris asked.

"My wedding ring. It's gone. I might have dropped it in the petting pool!"

I scanned the ground hopelessly, and then, with relief, finally located my wedding ring in my front pants pocket. But the magic of our bubble was burst, and Kris was quiet as we finished walking through the rest of the aquarium.

On the way to the hotel, we stopped at a couple of sushi restaurants, but they were all closed. So we decided to just head back to my hotel and order room service.

As we drove, Kris remained quiet. I was lost in my own thoughts as this was, in all likelihood, our final "goodbye" date. I know we joked about our multiple goodbye dates. But she was now actually on her way to Florida, and I had no idea when I would see her next.

"Kris," I started. "I want you to know if you ever reach a point where you feel hopeless like you did when you tried to commit suicide, I'll always be there to help. But help me understand why you tried to commit suicide before. You have so much going for you – smart, pretty, funny. You told me that you were lonely in Calabasas, and that led to the suicide attempt. But what specifically happened that day, or those couple of days, that led you there?"

"It was in my senior year. I was lonely. I didn't have that many friends as the new kid in town. I mean, I knew a lot of people, but as I told you, sometimes I think they just liked me because I'm pretty. Anyway, that Halloween, I dressed up like Tinker Bell because I had short blonde hair back then. I had two guy friends, Gavin and Rob, who I hung out with quite a bit. They were both recovering heroin addicts, which was really tough to watch. Sometimes Gavin would suddenly take off running down the street acting crazy, because he had to fight the urge and burn off energy. We were basically hopping from party to party that Halloween night, and at one party, I snuck away to do some cocaine. I was in the bathroom alone, when I suddenly heard Gavin screaming outside, 'Where's Kristina! Where the fuck is Kristina!' And then he's pounding on the bathroom door. When I open the door, he sees the cocaine, and he starts screaming, 'You don't know what the fuck you are doing!' So I followed him out of the bathroom, and I just threw all the cocaine on the floor. It was probably a hundred dollars' worth of cocaine. Gavin gave me a huge hug, and just kept saying, 'Thank you,' over and over. I told him, 'It's just cocaine. It's not worth our friendship.' That night, we stayed at Rob's house, which we often did because it had like nine bedrooms. Gavin and I just hung out that entire night."

"Did you guys hook up?"

"We kissed, but we didn't have sex. But have you ever had the feeling that someone else was so above you?"

I was silent. I honestly had never had that experience before.

"I don't know why I felt that. I mean, it's not like Gavin was so accomplished. He was a heroin addict. But I just had this overwhelming feeling that his heart was so much greater than mine. The next day, I tried to commit suicide."

I can't say that I honestly understood her pathway to suicide from her seemingly unrelated story. I've replayed it dozens of times in my head. The best that I can guess, it was almost as if she was so lonely in Calabasas that the moment someone showed her true care and love, she couldn't accept it. Maybe she couldn't believe it, or she was too scared to.

"Kris, it doesn't matter if we don't talk for weeks or months or years in the future. If you ever need me, I'll be there."

"I know. Thank you," she said softly.

When we arrived at my hotel, she parked in the furthest corner of the parking lot away from the entrance. With mischievous eyes, she pulled out a blunt.

"Okay, I told you that you are smoking a blunt, but I think it's a better idea if we just shotgun it. That way, for sure you can't mess it up."

"What does shotgun mean?"

"It means I smoke the blunt and then breathe the smoke into your mouth."

"I like the sound of that," I said with a smile.

So, we smoked for a while in the car. When she would shotgun the smoke into my mouth, I would use the opportunity to hold her face in both my hands and kiss her passionately. It was wonderful. And for the first time out of the few times that I've smoked pot, I actually felt high. Really high.

We eventually made our way up to my hotel room. We ordered room service. We made love before and after the food arrived. I remember noting the odd sensation of fucking Kris while I was so high. For some strange reason, it felt like I was fucking someone else other than Kris. Or maybe it felt like I was someone else who was fucking Kris. I didn't like it. I didn't dislike it either, but I preferred to not be in an altered mental state. Making love to Kris was always an intensely passionate act, and I didn't want to dull any of that.

Afterwards, I pulled out two small envelopes, and we sat cross-legged on the bed facing each other.

"I want to make sure you are okay in Florida and that you never have to do anything you don't want to do in order to make rent," I said as I handed her a thick envelope containing eight thousand dollars. "This should cover your first year's rent."

"I can't take this."

"Take it. Consider it a down payment on our future dates. I know we'll only see each other irregularly now, but I'd also prefer to not carry a lot of cash with me in the future when I see you. Now, I know you keep telling me not to give you money anymore . . ."

"Right, I keep telling you that . . ."

"And I keep giving you even MORE money," I laughed.

"Right, it's like some weird reverse psychology."

"Well played, Ms. Strauss. Now, this second envelope is your early birthday gift. I looked online and saw there is a professional theater near Naples. And what do you suppose is playing during your birthday weekend but my other favorite Broadway show, *The Phantom of the Opera*."

"Are you going to come with me?" she asked with an excited look.

"No," I said with a smile. "I'm not sure how that would work. It's for you and Taylor. Or for you and your grandma. There's a note in there from me, but don't read it now."

"Thank you," she said softly.

We slept in each other's arms again that night. We made love again in the morning. Kris left the hotel room before I did. She had to pick up her new puppy in Henderson, and then she would continue her cross-country journey to Lubbock, Texas and eventually to Naples, Florida. Her new, old home.

Date 11: March 14

Birthday letter to Kris accompanying *The Phantom of the Opera* tickets.

Dear Kris,

*You mentioned a theater near Naples – so I looked online. And what do you think just happens to be playing during your birthday weekend, but my SECOND favorite musical (*The Phantom of the Opera*). How serendipitous . . .*

Hopefully you and Taylor can carve out the time to make this work (but if for whatever reason schedules don't work, just sell the tickets on Craigslist). Please don't tell him I bought the tickets, though. I don't want to make him feel bad (and I figure, he must be pretty special to have stolen your heart so completely). Just say you bought them after he said he wished he could go to the theater with you. (Of course, I remember that.)

Selfishly, I wish that I could be there to escort you and make you happy myself. But destiny is a funny thing (and cuts both ways) – so, my dearest Kris, we will have to leave that for another lifetime.

All my love,
Ryan

> Text from Kris (2/9)
> I'm sorry I haven't emailed. I'm in Lubbock now with my friend Rebecca in her college dorm room with her friends. I'm fine but I'm really mad at Taylor. A lot is going on. I miss you. I told her about you, and she signed up for the sugar baby site. LOL

Text to Kris (2/9)
Have fun at the dorms . . . I'm sure all the guys are thinking, "Who's Rebecca's hot friend?"

Text from Kris (2/9)
Drunk. Miss you. Wish you could call but it's totally not an emergency. Miss you. You're a nice man.

Text to Kris (2/9)
Heh, heh. My first drunk message from you! They say when you are drunk, you tell people how you really feel about them. Which, in my case, is apparently that you think I'm a "nice man." I've definitely heard worse, so I'll take it! Have fun and blow off steam tonight – you deserve it. My only request is just stay close to your friends tonight, please. Lots of shady guys out there who would love to take advantage of "my drunk Kris" (and I'm the only shady guy allowed to do that).

Text from Kris (2/9)
Nicest man. The best. Come take advantage of me yourself. I like college. My dog is literally perfect.

Text to Kris (2/9)
Ahhh, if only I was twenty years younger and could come party with you and your friends – that would be fun. Course we both know what I looked like twenty years ago. So who am I kidding. I'd probably be at the library right now since I didn't get invited to the cool party. (Sigh . . . even in my dreams, I get ostracized.) Night, night Kris. :) Let me know when you get to Naples.

Text from Kris (2/11)
Serena and I drove straight through! Here safe.

Text to Kris (2/11)
A tad bittersweet, but I'm glad you are there safely. Good luck settling in, Kris.

Text from Kris (2/11)
Don't think I've forgotten about you yet. I just can't really describe how I feel right now, but I guess bittersweet is as close as I'm gonna get. As

happy as I am to be here, there's this dull stinging that's making me anxious about being so far away from you. Maybe I should sleep on it. I am exhausted and I probably sound delirious. I'll catch you up on all of the fun details from my trip tomorrow.

Text to Kris (2/11)
Sure Kris – I feel the same. (btw, tell Charles he's not allowed to call you "Kris" – only one Asian guy gets to do that.) Go get some rest. You'll feel better after you have time to settle in and catch up with all your friends over the next few days / weeks. Have fun at your slumber party with Serena tonight. I will picture you two doing some kinky stuff as I have my one-person party later tonight . . . Kidding . . . Sort of . . .

Text from Kris (2/12)
Could've been a three-person party but for some reason you won't abandon your current life and run away with me . . . Turns out buying a bed is easy, finding someone with a truck is hard. Training a husky puppy is even harder. She's so high-maintenance that I feel like I adopted a child. Still no solid poops.

Email from Kris (2/14)
Be my Valentine?

Email to Kris (2/14)
When I was in middle school (y'know, approximately five or six years before you were born – egads), we had this tradition where you could send "Be My Valentine" carnations to other students. I think they were $1 each. A red carnation meant, "I love you." A pink carnation meant, "I like you." And a white carnation meant, "I want to be friends." So I would dread going to school on Valentine's Day. The class royalty (that would be you) would get a multitude of red and pink roses delivered throughout the day that would pile up on their desks sent from various admirers. The popular (but less beautiful) kids would get a mix of pink and white carnations piled on their desks. And the lonely souls would get none (that would be me). And the worst part of it was that it was such an embarrassing public "labeling" of the social castes (since they were delivered in front of the entire classroom). I actually think I got one white carnation once . . . from the teacher . . . who sent one to every student that year.

So . . . before I accept your Valentine, I need to know what metaphorical color carnation you are sending. (Course, really, I'll take anything at this point.)

I went through a period in late high-school / early college where I read a lot of what I'd call "pseudo-philosophy" books: *Zen and the Art of Motorcycle Maintenance*, Ayn Rand books, *A Prayer for Owen Meany*, etc. Y'know, back when I had silly illusions of being a "deep thinker." Anyway, one of my favorites was this book called *The Tao of Pooh*. There's a genius in the innocence of a simple mind that I love. So for today, consider the following my Valentine's Day card to you (which I would have sent to you if you actually gave me your mailing address):

Piglet sidled up to Pooh from behind. "Pooh?" he whispered.

"Yes, Piglet?"

"Nothing," said Piglet, taking Pooh's hand. "I just wanted to be sure of you."

 - A.A. Milne, *Winnie-the-Pooh*

Ryan

Email from Kris (2/14)

I would send you 1,300 red carnations.

Got a bed. I also bought a couch and it gets delivered on Thursday. This is my sworn word that once everything is all set up, I'll send you pictures. I wish you could just come over! I miss ya a whole bunch and wore your jacket tonight when I went out to walk Veda. I swear she gets bigger every day. Solid poops now, too.

I took my second cousin (?) – one of my aunt's granddaughters that she takes care of – to the thrift store today. She found me the coolest little E.T. figurine. Anyway, we started talking about Selena Gomez, and Zoey asked if I was as old as Selena. When I told her I thought I was older because I'm about to be 20, she gasped and called me old. I have to admit it stung a little.

Grandma got her Coach bag and wallet and had a little extra left, so of course she got me a wallet too. She can never completely spoil herself.

In case you've been wondering, absolutely no cigarette smoking since I've been back. Minimal weed smoking as well.

. . . Okay, maybe a little more than minimal.

Tell me what you've been doing. I feel far away from you and not just in a physical sense.

Email to Kris (2/17)
First of all, you can inform your cousin that Selena Gomez was born July 22, 1992. So nearly a year older than you, my dear. Second, you can tell her that Selena has got the body of a twelve-year-old boy, while you are "so cuh-vee" (said with my best Asian manicurist accent). Kristina Strauss 2, Selena Gomez 0.

Glad to hear you are settling in. Your grandma seems like she's got a heart of gold – and I'm glad she wants to spoil you as much as you want to spoil her.

I miss you also, but life's funny. I'm sure it will have more twists and turns for us.

And I'm pretty confident that once you re-establish yourself at the top of the Naples scene, I'll be a comfortable memory (instead of one that's maybe a bit of a dull ache right now).

Anyway, right now I have a work trip scheduled to NY on 3/14. I know it's your birthday week (so your friends / relatives might have stuff scheduled) – but if you're free for the night . . . just a thought . . .

Night, night.

Text from Kris (2/24)
The 14th is really far away. :(I can't wait to see you!

Text from Kris (2/27)
Okay . . . So I'm NOT dying. But it sure feels like I am. My house got broken into today but I'm fine. I'll give you the details tomorrow.

Jesus. I grabbed my cell phone from my office desk and made my way to the parking lot to call Kris from the privacy of my car.

"I got your email, Kris. What happened?"

"This morning, Taylor had just left the apartment to go pick up some groceries, and I was napping on the couch naked. The door was unlocked and within ten minutes of Taylor leaving, three guys broke in and robbed me."

"Jesus. Are you okay? Did they assault you?"

"One guy wrestled me into the kitchen and was banging my face into the ground. I have a black eye and a bunch of bruises, but otherwise, I'm okay."

"Did they do anything else? I mean did they sexually attack you?"

"No. It's kind of weird. They barely stole anything. There was about three hundred dollars in cash sitting on my entertainment center that they stole, but they didn't take anything else. Then they all ran out."

"And you were naked? What the heck were you doing naked?"

"You know that I like to sleep naked."

"Right," I said, and then paused, not sure what to say next.

Finally, I said, "So, were you insulted then that they didn't try anything sexually? You being, y'know, naked and all."

"Totally insulted. When they ran out, I was like, 'You don't know what you're missing. You should talk to Ryan Lee,'" she laughed.

"Holy cow, they have no idea what they are missing," I laughed along with her. "Seriously, Kris, that's horrible, but I'm relieved that you are okay. Maybe you should consider moving to a safer neighborhood."

"I signed a lease, and I really don't want to break it. I like my apartment, and I was just starting to settle in. Plus Veda would be really confused, and I don't want to mess with her puppy emotions. But don't worry, dad, I'll be okay."

We chatted a little while longer. Kris seemed emotionally okay. Actually, she sounded normal, as if we were just catching up on any ordinary day.

Maybe it was the fact that she had been through so much in life already. She just seemed to accept the fact that three strangers had broken into her home, and she had gotten physically assaulted and robbed. Far from putting up a façade of bravery in the face of this emotional violation, she just seemed to accept it as part of life. Part of her life.

I offered to help pay for relocating to a better neighborhood, but she demurred. We told each other how much we were looking forward to seeing each other in a couple of weeks in New York. Kris promised to keep me updated on the police investigation, and then we hung up. I sat in my car for a while, thinking about how odd life was: all the prior steps in my life had led me to this specific moment, when I was hiding in my car in the parking lot of my company talking to my nineteen-year-old mistress who lived three thousand miles away. I knew that I should have felt disdain at the pathetic image. But mostly, I just felt a little surprised at the randomness of life.

Kris disappeared into her life in Florida, and I didn't hear from her for about a week. I know that doesn't sound like a long time, but after becoming accustomed to texting or emailing multiple times a day, each passing hour with no message from Kris seemed to stretch longer and longer.

I began to feel my jealousy grow. I imagined her happy with Taylor, or fucking one of her ex-boyfriends in Florida. I imagined her gradually forgetting me.

I finally found her Tumblr page. Her online blog went back almost a year and it contained various re-blogged pictures and episodic personal notes. I could see that recently Kris had re-posted some poems about how much she missed her lover and some pictures of people in the throes of passionate lovemaking. I liked to think they were posted with me in mind. Her personally written notes were the expected musings of an angst-filled teenage girl as she vacillated in her relationship with her boyfriend over time.

I read through her blog repeatedly as the days passed with no message from her.

As my jealousy grew, I found myself back on the sugar baby site. I didn't know what Kris expected from our relationship at this point, given the unpredictable and lengthy periods between our visits now. But if she was going to be radio silent, she couldn't expect me to just wait around for her.

I exchanged messages with a girl named Marianne who lived in Los Angeles. We arranged to have dinner that Thursday. She was half-Asian and half-white, and she was blessed to get the best physical characteristics of each race.

I flew Marianne up and we had a nice dinner. She was a model and had lived on her own since she was sixteen. She was excited about starting her own clothing line, and we talked quite a bit about the excitement and challenges of starting a new business, which I also wanted to do at some point in my life. She was new to the sugar baby site. She had joined along with a couple of friends just to "see what it was all about." Thus far, she and her friends had only met creepy guys from the site.

As I drove Marianne to the airport after dinner, I asked her what she was going to tell her friends about our date tonight. Another creep?

"I'm going to tell them, there's hope," she said with a smile.

We agreed to try to see each other again in a couple of weeks. When we arrived at the airport, she gave me a light kiss on the lips and hopped out of the car.

Email from Kris (3/4)
I feel like I haven't talked to you in forever! There's been a lot going on over here. On top of everything with the police investigation, I'm flying up to Pennsylvania on Monday. My cousin Xavier is going through another round of chemo, and since I'm not working yet, it makes the most sense for me to be the one who takes care of him this time. I'm staying for a week, flying back next Monday, coming home for a day and then flying back up to see you, if that's still the plan. Have you bought my ticket yet? Only about a week and a half now. :)

Email to Kris (3/4)
Yes, been awhile – much going on here too. I started writing you a long email yesterday – but let's just catch up on each other's lives in NY, shall we? Your flight has been booked for some time now, and I will forward you the flight info.

Thoughts and good wishes for Xavier and you in PA. I know that won't be easy, and I'm sure he's so grateful for having your love and care.

Email from Kris (3/6)
I miss you! I miss you! I miss you!

I made it to Pennsylvania. Xavier looks awful. They still haven't caught the guys who broke into the house. I'm having separation anxiety being so far from Veda. It's freezing. I'm high. But most importantly I really miss you.

Email to Kris (3/7)
I miss you also, Kris . . . and I'm not even high!

Hard to believe that our intense emotional "farewell tour" that spanned several weeks (and several cities, I might add) was over a month ago. Honestly, it's been a little strange adjusting to not seeing you every couple of weeks (at a minimum) and the increasingly sporadic communications over time. But I know it's to be expected, and I've been comforted by my imaginings of my friend adjusting back to her life in Florida, going out, seeing old friends, just being young again and having fun (well, except for getting assaulted – I'm guessing you could have done without that). When I think about it now (and though I know I tried to convince you otherwise in the past), it feels right and healthy for you to be back with your boyfriend and friends (and numerous admirers!) rather than living emotionally alone in CA with your only friend a morally bereft, fortyish Asian pervert (if it sounds weird reading that, imagine how I feel typing that!). :)

Anyway, lots to catch up on when we see each other – too much for email (and it's late, so I don't want to text and wake you). Plus you've got a big emotional burden to carry this week and more important things to focus on. I'm sorry Xavier is in so much pain. I know I don't know him – but maybe he'd enjoy you reading to him? I think if I was sick, just hearing your voice would make me feel a little better.

Email from Kris (3/7)

Still miss you, not high anymore. I'm actually sitting in the hospital room with Xavier and it's snowing outside! Very pretty.

They caught one of the guys that broke into my house last night. I guess the other one drove to Ohio, and they're working on bringing him in. The one in custody is charged with burglary, battery and grand theft of the third degree. The other guy will have the same charges plus intimidating a witness since he's been texting me about how he plans on cutting my tongue out. But please don't worry.

I feel like I've just been giving you the bare minimum but maybe that's because I get so caught up in the details, especially when I'm telling a story. Then when I try to write it down or type it out, I don't know where to start, what to omit, what to include . . . That actually happens to be the reason I always feel like a babbling idiot around you. Anyway, I promise to give you all the details of all the drama when I see you – like it or not.

P.S. You're by far my favorite Asian pervert.

I started to feel guilty about seeing Marianne without telling Kris. I found it ironic that I would feel guilty about cheating on my sugar baby, but not my wife. I couldn't even begin to untangle that emotional paradox.

I justified not informing Kris about Marianne by telling myself that Kris was already dealing with too much between the robbery and assault, the subsequent police investigation, and then caring for her sick cousin who had cancer. But in reality, I think I was just scared Kris would get mad and cancel her trip to NY to see me.

Finally, the day of my New York trip arrived. I was full of nervous energy during the cross-country plane ride as I debated whether to tell Kris about Marianne, and if so, how.

When I finally got to the hotel, I walked through the lobby and saw Kris sitting on a bench sipping a Jamba Juice. We glanced at each other, and then I took the elevator up to the room. I texted Kris the room number, and a few minutes later there was a knock on the door. It had been almost a month since we had last seen each other.

She walked into the room and immediately wrapped her arms around me and gave me a deep kiss. We lay down on the sofa, and I held her in my arms from behind.

I asked how her cousin was doing after chemo. She caught me up on the police investigation. The U.S. Marshall had picked up a second suspect in Ohio. Before he got arrested, he had been sending Kris all sort of threatening texts mixed in with odd texts like, "You shouldn't be dating Taylor. You should be dating me." The fact that he somehow had her cell number and knew about Taylor seemed to indicate the robbery may have been targeted at her specifically for some reason. Kris seemed to just shrug it off.

She asked what I had been up to with a tentative tone in her voice.

I took a deep breath and dove in.

"Kris, we've always been completely honest with each other. And since I don't want that part of our relationship to ever change . . . there are a few things I should share. I will try my best to not make this overly dramatic.

"Since you've moved back to Florida, I have been able to feel you progressively settling back into your life there – with Taylor, with all your friends, with various guys chasing after you – and I can feel me, as part of your life, being distanced in subtle but important ways. And while I would be lying to say that there aren't flashes of obsession or jealousy, I've tried to step back way back, and ask myself, 'Well, Ryan, what do you want for Kris? Do you want her to be torn up, constantly missing you and thinking about you compulsively in a way that she can't be happy in Florida?' While the primal, instinctual part of my human nature answers, 'Yes,' the greater part of me that cares for you as my friend says, 'Of course not – that's just selfish and silly.' I want you to be happy – and so I know this 'settling' process, as grating as it is sometimes, is necessary.

"So anyway, you should know that I'm good with everything. I'm good with you living with Taylor, or dating Charles, or whoever – whatever choices you make that will make you the happiest. 'Good' is maybe the wrong word, but you know what I mean. And I'm going to stop being a 'dad' and stop mentioning weed, or smoking, or school grades, or safer apartments. Unless you ask for my opinion on those matters, those aren't decisions I have a prerogative to opine on. And, of course, I'll always be there as your friend.

"So why am I saying all this? Well, it's an overly verbose lead-in to just let you know that I went on my first dinner-date with someone from the sugar baby site recently. A figurative dipping my toe back in the water. Not a big deal, we didn't hook up, and it's obviously early, so we'll see how it progresses.

"But before we go too far on our date today, I just wanted to let you know up front. So that you don't feel like I was hiding something."

Kris just lay still in my arms for a few minutes. I was afraid to break her silence. Finally, when she spoke, her voice quivered with obvious hurt, but she tried her best to be polite. She asked me the girl's name, what she did, and whether I really liked her. I told her it was early with Marianne, but we got along well. I also told Kris there wasn't that initial spark that I had had with her. But I could tell that only hurt her more.

After a while, we started to kiss, and then migrated to the bedroom where we made love. But there was a distance that I had never sensed before, and afterwards, Kris was unusually quiet.

We got dressed to go to dinner. I had made dinner reservations at a sushi restaurant within walking distance. We were meeting my friend, Andrew, whom I had told Kris a lot about.

I have a lot of friends in this world, and they cover the full spectrum from ultra-conservative Christians on one end to licentious, extreme partygoers on the other. But Andrew was the only friend whom I told everything to. With him, I didn't need to be apologetic or embarrassed by my own moral failings, whether those were my experiences with escorts or my affair with Kris. Andrew and I were on a common wavelength in that respect. We both shared the perspective that life was a summation of our experiences and that we each had a limited time on this earth to maximize those experiences. Not that we should be hedonistic for the sake of hedonism, but rather, we had a basic belief that experiencing how exciting and unpredictable life could be was a worthwhile goal. Anyway, mostly we shared a belief that we didn't want to struggle over our respective moral failings. In our view, the choice was to either "do it" or "don't do it." But certainly not "do it and struggle over it." If you're going to "do it," then embrace it completely.

We had a nice dinner. Kris enjoyed finally meeting Andrew after hearing all my stories about him. They shared a smoke outside the restaurant while I paid the bill, and then Kris and I walked back to the hotel room.

I held Kris in my arms with her back against me as we lay on the bed. I made a few random jokes. She was quiet. I then heard the dull tapping sound of tears falling on the sheets. I craned my neck around her head and kissed away some of the tears.

"I just feel really heavy," Kris whispered as she stared straight ahead.

"I don't know what you want me to say, Kris," I said quietly.

Suddenly, she sat up on the bed and jerked away from me. "Well, you could have told me about Marianne before I fucking came up to New York!"

"Kris, please," I said calmly. "I just knew you had so much going on with the assault and your cousin. I didn't feel right laying this on you over email. Plus, to be honest, I didn't know if you would still come to New York if I told you, and I wanted to see you. Honestly, would you have still come up?"

"I don't know. But you should have told me."

"Look, Kris," I said, feeling my own defensive anger rising out of my guilt. I knew that I should have told her beforehand. "I told you right when you walked in the room before we made love. It's not like I held this information back just so that I could fuck you. Plus, you moved away from me, remember?"

"How could I have stayed in California? My grandparents were moving into a rest home. Where would I live?"

"Kris, with the money I was giving you, you could have gotten an apartment and stayed. You could have gone to college in California."

"Live on my own. No way! I can't fucking believe you're blaming this on me now! Like I did something wrong," Kris screamed as she got up and quickly gathered her things.

"Kris, don't do this. Where are you going?"

She ignored me as she put on her shoes.

"Kris, where are you going? You can't just wander around New York City at night. Kris, you chose to move back to Florida, not me."

"Oh, you chose this!" she hissed as she walked out the door and slammed it behind her.

Stunned, I sat on the bed for maybe thirty seconds, and then ran after her into the hallway. But she had already gone down the elevators.

I ran back into the room and started to text her desperately.

Text to Kris (3/14)
Kris – come back please. I won't say anything more – we don't have to talk anymore. Just come back please.

Text from Kris (3/14)
No thank you. Sorry for being such a disappointment!

Text to Kris (3/14)
Okay, I get it. I fucked up. I'm sorry. But come back please. We'll say goodbye after this trip – okay. And yes, I'm worried about you. Please. And yes, I'm begging. If you've ever cared about me – I'm asking this one last favor. Okay, this one last favor. I won't talk anymore. Come back – or tell me where you are and I'll come get you. Please.

I waited five minutes. When no reply came, I put on my coat and shoes and wandered around the streets of New York hoping to find her, but knowing it was impossible at this point. I kept imagining Kris wandering the streets on this cold night, getting lost, getting mugged. Finally, I went back to the hotel, hoping she had made her way back.

I rode the elevator back up to my room, and when the elevator doors opened, Kris was standing there. Apparently she was about to go back downstairs. I held her by her shoulders, and I just said, "I'm sorry. I'm sorry. Please come back inside."

She nodded morosely and followed me back into the room. Apparently, she had thought about taking a cab to Queens, where one of her cousins lived, but she didn't have his contact information. Then she had come back to the room. But when no one answered the doorbell, she figured that I was mad at her and wouldn't let her in, and so she was leaving again when I had intercepted her in front of the elevator.

True to my word, I didn't restart any conversation. I was too afraid of saying something that would set her off again. We just lay on the sofa together, and this time, somehow, Kris was the one holding me from behind with my back against her chest. I felt queasy at the thought that I had barely caught her as she was heading back downstairs. If I had been twenty seconds later coming back, she would have been gone for good. I felt so much pain from the realization that I had hurt Kris so deeply, I started to cry.

Somehow, this seemed to break through her anger, and she craned around to kiss my tears away. "Finally," she said. "Mr. Lee shows some emotion."

"I miss you, Kris."

"Me too."

We made love again. I mainly remember this vision of Kris mounting me as I lay on my back, and then slowly impaling herself on my cock, over and over again as she arched backwards. She was a goddess. My goddess. She increased the pace and started riding me hard as she neared climax, and I moaned as I desperately tried to hold on. After a few aching minutes, she cried, "I'm cumming hard!" As she came, she suddenly moved to dismount me as her climax was too intense, but I grabbed her hips and drove my cock back deep inside her. She screamed. A few seconds later, I burst inside her. She collapsed onto my chest.

For several long moments, we just held each other as we caught our breath.

"Let's see Marianne do that!" she finally said with a small laugh and a hint of sadness.

I turned her over and gave her a massage.

"I don't know where our relationship goes from here. But I have a request."

"What?"

"I know you hate this scar on your back, but I love it. It reminds me of all the things you've overcome in your life. So I'd like to have it. I want to own this little piece of you. Forever."

"Sure, it's yours," she murmured.

"By the way, I finally found your Tumblr account," I said as I paused the massage and leaned down to give her scar a kiss. She giggled.

As usual, we slept entangled in each other that night, and we made love in the morning before I left for my meetings. It was rougher this time. I bent her over the bed and ate her out from behind. I then held both her arms down tightly against the bed, and I pounded her from behind until she came on my cock. Afterwards, I noticed her looking at her arms.

"What is it?" I asked.

"Look at these bruises," she said. I could see my handprints on her upper arms where I had held her down.

"Oh my god, Kris. Did I do that? I'm sorry," I said with a sinking feeling in my stomach.

"No, it's okay. I bruise easily because I'm anemic. Don't worry, it felt wonderful."

After the drama of the night before, Kris seemed to be in good spirits, and our relationship appeared to be back to normal.

But of course, appearances can be deceiving.

Date 12: May 2

Email to Kris (3/17)
Happy birthday, Kris!

Though I can't be there to celebrate with you – you should know that I'll be thinking of you:

For your birthday – THREE Pooh quotes! (groan)

Pooh quote #1:

"What day is it?" asked Pooh.

"It's today," squeaked Piglet.

"My favorite day," said Pooh.

I like to imagine that exactly twenty years ago, as I was walking around my college campus, there was a moment when I felt my heart skip a beat as you were brought into this world, and a higher power tied an inevitable thread between you and me. And we would both unknowingly wind this thread around the experiences of our lives until it finally brought us face to face last October.

Pooh quote #2:

"As soon as I saw you, I knew an adventure was going to happen."

And for that . . . and all that has happened and will happen since then . . . I'm just so thankful. (Unfortunately, on your side of the equation, I imagine that I'm probably more the metaphorical cross you must bear.)

Pooh quote #3:

"If you live to be 100, I hope I live to be 100 minus 1 day, so I never have to live without you."

Hope you have fun celebrating with friends this weekend. (And to think, you're not even at your peak yet . . .)

Always,

Ryan

Text from Kris (3/17)
Your nice words were too nice and made me cry, per usual. I really wish you were here. I'll email later tonight and let you know how my day went. I think Taylor has some things planned – he's making me blueberry muffins right now. I woke up this morning to three texts: you, my mom and my dad. Made me smile. Anyway, thanks for being my friend and know that I'm thinking of you today.

Text to Kris (3/18)
I miss seeing my scar (a.k.a. formerly "your" scar, but now mine . . . don't forget that or give it away again, please). How was your birthday yesterday? Also, how was the performance today? Did you and Taylor like *The Phantom of the Opera*?

Text from Kris (3/18)
It was wonderful! We both really enjoyed it – thank you for buying us tickets. Birthday yesterday was okay. I was upset because Taylor lost the Ray-Ban sunglasses that I bought myself when we first started seeing each other. They were the best sunglasses I ever owned.

Email from Kris (3/21)
Hi :)

It's a rainy day here in southwest Florida and I'm thinking of you.

Veda got her second set of shots this morning. Unlike Benz, she didn't even flinch. When we got home I put a load of laundry in and tied her leash to the basket – she pulled it the entire way back to our apartment.

I'm thinking when I go down to put the clothes in the dryer, I'm going to sit in the basket and enjoy the ride.

I also had to go to the police department to identify the third guy who broke in. I'm having mixed emotions because I couldn't pick anyone out of the lineup. It all just happened so quickly, and it's been almost a month . . .

Anyway, Taylor and I are going to Tampa this weekend for a skateboarding competition (yay!!) so if you don't hear from me for a few days that's why. Although I might break away from all the female-friendly fun and make some time for my favorite Asian pervert.

I tried to attach some pictures. If I did it correctly, the first one should be a picture my friend Kylie took of me. The second is a picture from my birthday at the beach, and the third is a current picture of Veda just because I love showing her off. By the way, I really don't mind you checking my Facebook. In fact I wish you could just follow me on Instagram lol. But until you get hip on all the social media sites (or at least come up with a good excuse for your wife as to why you're on them) I will continue to send you grainy photographs of myself.

Miss you always.

Email from Kris (3/26)
Have you seen her?

Email to Kris (3/26)
Oh Kris – I'll answer anything and everything that you ask me truthfully. But a few things first:

-   In my own view, I'm a tainted soul. Or if I want to be generous, "amoral" is maybe more fitting. You knew this fact from our first dinner (when I acknowledged that I shouldn't even be there). More relevantly, I've half-joked with you, as our relationship grew, that it would be hard for us to have a committed relationship (even in an alternate universe where I wasn't married), because you frankly knew too much about me. I mean, who the heck would want to have a relationship with some unfaithful soul who would cheat on his wife, had slept with a bunch of escorts and had joined a sugar baby site?

- All that being said, somehow you've become a soulmate to me in such a crazy way that I've stopped trying to figure it out. I mean, think about the setup for a minute. A seemingly random girl from Florida (i.e. the "It" girl from high school), former coke-head, twenty years my junior – falling for some nerdy Asian guy who has so little to do with "her world" that it would be hard to imagine us even relating . . . let alone becoming kindred souls. Makes no sense in any universe that I'm aware of . . . and yet, here we are.

- So that being the case, like I said at the beginning . . . I'll answer anything and everything you ask me truthfully, in the exact same way that I would answer Andrew – if you ever want me to change that, let me know. Though obviously our relationship is much different / better than my relationship with Andrew, in that one aspect of wearing "no mask," you two friends are uniquely the same in my life.

- Yes, I saw Marianne last week. No, we didn't sleep together. To be more frank than I should be, for such a physically attractive girl, I told her that I'm not sure that I feel a physical spark there. In one of those odd moments, I said we should kiss again and see if I'm misreading the situation. We kissed. I asked her if she felt anything, and she said, "Yes," and I responded, "Honestly, I'm not sure." And then I drove her to the airport. No set plans to see Marianne again right now, but no promises that I won't, either. Tainted, remember please.

- On to more normal conversation -- how was the skating competition and road trip this weekend? Fun? Did Taylor actually compete or was it more of a professional event? What percentage of the crowd was male and were you the hottest hottie at the event? (I'm sure you were.)

Ryan

Email from Kris (3/28)

I spent the past two days trying to figure out how to reply to this. I'm still not sure what the right words are, but I'm going to try.

First off, I appreciate your honesty. Of course, I wish you would have told me without having to ask, but it was my mistake to assume that after the New York trip, you would actually consider my feelings and give me the heads up I deserve.

I used to believe we were on the same page. Morally, we were even. You had your wife, I had Taylor. You slept with a bunch of escorts, I have more ex-"boyfriends" than I can remember most of the time. But now I'm starting to see that you're never satisfied. For someone who has everything, you still seem to be searching. You love Sandy, yet you found me. You love me, but you found Marianne. Something doesn't make sense there. Your heart should be full – overflowing even.

Basically Ryan, I have to pull out now before you hurt me worse. We've already been through the why and the how, and I'll take as much of the blame for all of this as I need to. But it still kills me that you see her, and there's nothing I can do about it. I'm not going to tell you not to because I'm not your mother or your wife, and if that's what you want to be doing – if that's who you are – then who am I to stop you? I'm no one.

I love you SO much and I hope you understand that's the reason I can't do this anymore. I'm in too deep for you to still be wandering around. I'm not mad, and you will always be one of my best friends. Like I said in my goodbye letter before you even met her, she's a lucky girl.

And by the way, we never made it to Tampa. I was in the hospital all weekend, and when I asked Katy to email you and let you know what was happening – so you wouldn't get mad and think I forgot about you – it came back as an invalid email address.

I hope you find what you're looking for.

Please don't email me again.

Jesus. I didn't expect that from Kris. I felt a swirl of different emotions. Sadness that I had clearly hurt Kris so deeply. A bit of anger that she couldn't deal with me having another relationship, even though ours was now irregular, given the distance between us. But mostly, I just felt panicked. The thought of losing Kris completely was too painful to think about.

Still, I forced myself to not email back. I figured I would respect her request for space and surely she would contact me when she had calmed down and realized that our friendship was worth too much to throw away.

The next day, since I couldn't email her, I checked her Tumblr blog to see if she had posted anything new.

Post from Kris's Tumblr Blog – Title "Butterfly Effect" (3/29)
I don't know if you check this blog anymore, but I miss you and love you so much. And I never expected this to hurt so much. I feel jealous, sad, subpar, inadequate, and embarrassed. But mostly I feel angry at myself that I let it get this far.

Why can't we just fast-forward to the next lifetime when everything between us will work out? But this is real life.

I half-cringed and half-grinned internally. Kris told me not to email her, but she was apparently still going to use her Tumblr page to make me feel bad. I responded to Kris through Tumblr.

Private message to Kris via her Tumblr page (3/29)
Jesus Kris. Careful about posting stuff like "Butterfly Effect." It could get you in trouble with Taylor. I'll make this short because you asked me not to email (and I'm not sure if this counts).

1) Yes, I still check this blog, hoping you'll post something new.

2) I understand your decision. If it were simply a choice of you vs. Marianne, it wouldn't even be close. But that's not the decision. July 18, 2014. Know what that is? That's the date of your graduation from Edison College next year (assuming, you start again this fall). So call it a year and half before the possibility of seeing each other regularly again, assuming that you even move back to California after community college.

You are one of my best friends – so I'm sorry that I'm not that strong, I'm not that faithful, and I'm not that moral (our own relationship, case in point). Mostly, I'm sorry that I'm not the man you want me to be. As you said somewhat derisively, "that's who I am." Course, the easier solution is to just lie to you on an ongoing basis. But I'd rather have our relationship locked away as one of the purest, most honest relationships that I have ever known – rather than bastardize it. I just won't do that. I wear enough masks in my life.

3) For pete's sake – don't reply to this on your blog. Take the time you need to remember, hopefully, that we're best friends first. Weeks, months, never – I'll respect your silence until then.

Post from Kris's Tumblr Blog – Title "Butterfly Effect" (3/30)
The only positive is that now I can dye my hair whatever ridiculous color I want without worrying about what you think or how out of place I would look during my brief stay in your little world of suits and ties. Lavender it is.

Post from Kris's Tumblr Blog – Title "Butterfly Effect" (3/30)
I have a giant bump on my forehead from the accident that keeps me from being able to raise my left eyebrow so when I try to smile or make an excited face, only half of it moves. Hahaha.

Private message to Kris via her Tumblr page (3/30)
This is ridiculous, Kris. I'm not sure what giving me the silent treatment and then us communicating clumsily over your blog accomplishes, but fine . . . you are successfully punishing me. Congratulations. (And wipe that smirk off your face.) What do you want, Kris? Do you want to be my "spiritual" second wife while you are in Florida for the next year and a half? (I really don't feel like converting to Mormonism.) Yes, I am worried and want to know what happened to your head and why you were in the hospital . . . and while I'm at it (since it's obvious that I'm "social network" stalking you anyway), why did Taylor disappear from your Facebook page? But I guess I'll have to wait until you decide you want to be friends with me again. Don't take too long, please.

And btw – when the hell did I ever wear a suit and tie? You're making me sound like a stiff jerk to your friends who read your blog and know about my existence. Lavender is just fine. Will make it even more uncomfortable the next time we get into an elevator and you start talking about recent middle school memories while there's a middle-aged woman standing right in front of us. Fine.

I recognized that Kris was purposely punishing me. But it still hurt a lot. I had made plans to see Marianne again that week, but I decided it just wasn't worth it. My heart was still with Kris, for better or worse.

Email to Kris (4/4)
Kris,

It hurts me to know that I've hurt you. It hurts me to not know how you are doing. But mostly, I miss my friend (even if it's just over email at this stage).

Couple things, and then I will wander back into the penalty box. First is that I've ended things with Marianne. I have not seen her again, and I emailed her earlier this week that the vibe just doesn't feel right. I don't want to force something that my heart isn't into.

I know, I know. "Whoop-de-doo. Good for you, Ryan." It doesn't change the fact that I hurt you. More importantly, it doesn't change the fact that I'm still the type of person that could do so again in the future (and given our relationship, I'd always be truthful with you if I did, btw). But I will remind you that while that is a possibility – it is a near certainty that at some point, you will do the same to me. (You being in the prime of your youth – and I just have a strong feeling that you're not quite ready to get off the romantic carousel yet and settle down for life . . . though of course, if you did, I'd be really happy for you and Taylor.)

Second, for my part – I've decided I'm going to try to focus on all the things that I am lucky to have (as you so "nicely" reminded me in your email . . . Jesus, Kris, you need to take some anger management classes).

Okay, you may now carry on on with your silent treatment, until you decide you want to be friends / penpals again. I won't bother you again. But at least now that I've gotten that off my chest, hopefully, I can sleep better again (which I have had a very hard time doing).

Ryan

Text from Kris (4/5)

I miss you more than you can even imagine but things are really complicated right now. Taylor knows / read everything. I'll email you when I can. I love you.

Text to Kris (4/5)

Jesus. When you say "everything," hopefully you don't mean EVERYTHING. I love you also – but focus on what you need to focus on. I'm a big boy.

Text from Kris (4/6)

Since when are you a big boy?! Yes, EVERYTHING thanks to your lube talk over email. Lol. I'm at work right now, but I'll be off in an hour and I'll elaborate. I'm pretty sure I'm single, though.

Text to Kris (4/6)

Lube? I was talking about my car! What about your "stick it in my ass" comment??? Jesus – I miss a week and all hell breaks loose. Work? Good for you. Let's talk later then. Most importantly, are you okay physically?

Text from Kris (4/6)

I'm all right. Taylor's car isn't. I'm on break now if you want to call.

I hurried out of my office to my car in the parking lot. I dialed Kris. "What happened?"

"I accidentally left my email account open on the computer about a week ago. So when Taylor woke up the next morning before I did, he read all of our email messages."

"Jesus, Kris. Log out of your email account in the future, please. Too late now, I guess. What did he say when you woke up?"

"He just asked, 'Is there something you want to tell me?' I had no idea that he had read those messages, so I was like 'No?' He didn't say anything after that until we were in his car driving to the skateboard competition in Tampa. He started yelling at me that he had read our emails and knew that it wasn't just a platonic relationship and that I had lied to him. He started screaming at me that I was a whore and a slut and a liar."

"Shit. You should have told him that I coerced you to have sex as part of the arrangement."

"Oh, I totally threw you under the bus. I told him, 'No matter how much you hate me, I hate myself even more for doing this. But we needed the money.' I told him that I wasn't attracted to you, and that I wanted to throw up every time we had sex."

I couldn't help laughing. "Wonderful. I'm glad you threw me under the bus. Sort of. Hey, how do I know that actually isn't the truth?"

"I guess you don't," she mockingly laughed. "Then he started saying how everything was tainted now. He said he was glad that he lost my Ray-Ban sunglasses because they were bought with your money. I told him that the Ray-Bans that I had bought him for Christmas were also bought with your money, so he should fucking throw those away also. He shut up after that."

"Then what happened?"

"Then he just started driving crazy and swerving all over the road. He was so mad, he wanted to scare me. But the wheels on his car are completely bald, so we lost control while we were on a bridge, and we crashed into the center divide."

"Jesus. But you are both okay?"

"My head hit the dashboard. I had to go to the emergency room and they did a CAT scan. I have a huge lump on my forehead and bruises all over, but they said I will be okay. Taylor is fine. His car is totaled, though."

"And how are things between you two now?"

"I think he feels bad about me getting hurt in the accident, so he hasn't brought up the emails again. Honestly, we just haven't really talked about anything at all. We're just silent around each other in the apartment. It's awful."

"I'm sorry, Kris. It feels like it's partly my fault."

"Totally your fault," she said with a quiet laugh.

After the call, I had conflicting emotions. On the one hand, I felt terrible that Taylor's discovery of our physical relationship had led to the car accident, Kris's injuries, and a deep schism in her relationship with Taylor. On the other hand, I didn't feel like Kris should end up with Taylor anyway. From the way Kris described their relationship, I knew that she felt no passion anymore in their relationship. But she was holding on because she was basically afraid of being alone.

To add to the swirl of conflicting emotions, I recognized this might be the harbinger of Kris becoming single in the near future. And I felt a primal jealousy over her sprouting a new love for anyone else. In a way, once I had discovered her relationship with Taylor was unsatisfying, my ego felt protected. But a potential new, more exciting love – that was a whole different threat to contemplate.

We made plans for our next date about a month later, when work would bring me to New York City again.

As the date approached, Kris messaged me updates on her life. Generally, she and Taylor had reached some sort of détente. Silent cohabitation that was void of any love. Clearly, it was wearing on her.

Finally, the day of our date arrived, and like the last visit, I swept past her in the lobby of the hotel without public recognition. Once I got upstairs to the room, I texted Kris the room number.

Date 12

My heart sank when she walked into the room. Though it had been over a month since the car accident, she still had two obvious black eyes. The lump on her forehead where she had hit the dashboard had mostly subsided, though it was still discolored a faint greenish-purple.

"Oh Kris," I said as I held her and kissed the bruise on her forehead. "I wouldn't have expected there to still be so much bruising."

"I'm okay. Anemic, remember?"

Since we hadn't seen each other in over a month and a half, we had decided to just stay in and order room service tonight, so that we could relax and catch up in full.

"How are things between you and Taylor?"

"Pretty horrible."

"I'm sorry. Arguing a lot?"

"No, actually. We live together, but we hardly talk anymore. There's always this constant tension in the silence. I have a hard time falling asleep, and when I finally do, I only sleep a couple of hours because I'm afraid of what might happen."

"What do you mean? What might happen?"

"I don't know," she said softly.

"I've asked you this before, but has Taylor ever hit you?"

Kris hesitated just a moment before responding, "No."

"Have you ever been assaulted by anyone? Either physically or sexually?"

"Once, when I was young, one of my mom's boyfriends lifted me up from behind. I think my mind blocked out what happened next. All I know is that since then, I have an irrational fear where if someone picks me up, I literally go berserk."

"You told me that story before, a long time ago. But you said he just dropped you, and you got hurt."

"No," she said softly. "I don't remember what really happened, but I think something bad."

Another layer of pain from Kris's past that she had hidden from me. I wondered what else I did not know.

Kris looked at her phone and said, "Oh my god!"

"What?"

"Taylor. I told him that I'm staying at Katy's tonight, and he just texted me."

Kris showed me the text.

You've got fucking responsibilities, and if you don't come home, I'm not feeding the fucking kitten.

"We got a newborn kitten," Kris explained as she drafted a text to Katy. "I've got to ask Katy to go feed the kitten. She's just a baby, and she needs milk."

"Jesus, Kris. Ever since you moved back to Florida, it's been one disaster after another. The break-in and physical assault. Taylor finding your emails and the car accident."

"I know. I was so stupid. I . . . had everything in California, and then I moved back to Florida."

"See, you didn't know how good you had it with me," I said with a self-deprecating laugh.

"I didn't," she said with a sad smile. "I wish someone would just tell me what to do now."

"Well, for what it's worth, I think you should consider moving back to California. Ask your dad if you can live with him. Go to a feeder community college that can get you into one of the U.C. campuses. Or maybe go live with your mom in Nevada. And I'm not just saying this so that you'd be closer to me. I just think you need to start somewhere fresh where you can invest in your future again in a healthy way."

Kris considered this for a few moments. "That's an idea. It's just so hard right now to think about next steps with Taylor and living together, but not speaking. It's like we're just stuck. I try to avoid Taylor as much as possible. I basically work until three A.M. every morning, smoke weed, watch the sunrise with Veda, and then try to sleep a couple of hours. Half the nights, I sleep at Katy's place now."

"Ahh, Katy – how is she? I feel like I know her by now, even though we've never met."

"I talk to her about you all the time, and she really wants to come up to New York to meet you."

"We might be able to arrange that one of these times. Maybe I'll end up hooking up with her too," I said with a laugh.

"If you did that, I'd run around this hotel screaming your name so everyone could hear what a scumbag you are," Kris said with mock anger. "So anyway, every night, I sleep just a couple hours, and then run whatever errands I need to that day. Then go back to work in the late afternoon or evening."

"Oh right. Tell me about your new job. You're a waitress at a bar, right?"

"Yup, it's called Players."

"Sounds like a strip club," I said skeptically.

"No, it's just a normal bar with pool tables. Though all of the waitresses are girls, and we're required to wear pretty skimpy outfits and four-inch heels. By the end of the night, my feet are killing me. But overall, I actually like working there, and everyone is super cool. The guys in the back love me, and they're always watching out for me."

"Uh huh, I bet."

Kris sat quiet for a little while. And then she said, "So, I met a guy."

"Really?" I said with a thin smile as my heart sank.

"I mean, nothing has happened, but we've been texting back and forth. He lives in Cape Coral, which is about forty-five minutes away. I was at a party at a friend's house. I went outside for a smoke, and he asked if he could join me. So we just ended up talking on the porch for a while. His name is Harry. He's a part-time model, and he's British."

"So he has a cool accent."

"Yup, automatic points. He said he hadn't smoked in a couple years, but he wanted to have a cigarette with me. We just talked about our backgrounds, and he talked a lot about his family. Family is really important to me. That is one of the things that always bothered me about Taylor. Taylor doesn't speak to his parents anymore since he moved out, and that has always made me wonder if he would be a good father to his own family some day. Anyway, I really like that Harry is so close to his parents, and we've been texting back and forth a lot over the last week."

"But you haven't seen him again?"

"Not yet. Do you want to see a picture of him?" Kris asked as she picked up her phone.

"Sure," I said even as I felt bile rise in my throat.

Harry was tall, blond, and thin with a hawkish nose. Kris showed me a few posed fashion pictures of him.

"Well, I won't pretend that it doesn't hurt, but I want you to be happy at the end of the day, Kris," I said with a sigh.

"Fucking Harry," I added with a genuine smile.

Still, I felt an ache in my heart at the idea of her finding a new love. I thought a minute about how this could change our relationship, or more likely end it.

"So when are you going to see him again?"

"I don't know. Do you want to know when I do?"

"I'm not sure," I said. I thought about it a few moments and then added, "Okay, here's my proposal. You can go on dates with other guys, and you don't have to tell me. I don't want to know. But you have to tell me when he kisses you. If it progresses to that point, I should probably know."

"Okay, that seems fair. And you have to tell me if you go on multiple dates with other girls."

"So I can go on as many first dates with as many girls as I want, but if I go on a second date with one, I have to tell you?"

"Yup."

"Okay, deal. Let me know how it goes with Harry," I said with a sad smile. "Hopefully, this isn't our last date."

We sat silent for a few moments. Then Kris said, "You told me before that you write down notes from all of our dates?"

"I do. Two reasons. First, I don't want to forget anything from our dates. Even when I'm an old Chinese man, I want to remember how special this relationship felt. Second, I figure I might write a book about this someday."

"Really?" she said skeptically.

"Yup, though I'm not sure anyone would be interested in reading it. We'll see."

"Well, I want to hear your description of our dates so far."

"Sure," I said as I moved over to the desk and opened up my laptop. Kris came over and sat on my lap as I logged in to my email account. She laughed as I typed in my email account password.

"What?" I asked.

"You told me before that you've tried to log in to my email account, but you couldn't. Anyway, it's not just your name. It's 'ryanlee14.' with a period at the end," she giggled.

Date 12

After a pause, she added, "I can't believe I just told you that. I don't know how you get me to tell you everything."

I mentally stored her password in my head. I told myself that I wouldn't use it to check her email, but I knew deep down that I would not be able to resist.

I located my running notes, which I kept in an email account. I walked Kris through each of our eleven dates, and we laughed as we reminisced over the memories from our brief but intense relationship.

After I finished reading my notes, I said, "So that's it. Eleven dates."

"Seems like a lot more."

"Has it been that arduous?" I smiled.

"No, just seems like I've known you a lot longer."

"Which was your favorite date?"

Kris considered for a few moments and then said, "When you visited me in LA. I liked having you in my city, driving you around, and going out together. It felt the most like a real date. Like we were a real couple. Yours?"

"Las Vegas, for sure. I liked going to the aquarium with you and walking around. Same reason as you. It felt the most like a real date to me. And, of course, I liked having you take my weed virginity in the car."

I paused for a minute, and then added, "And the worst was the last date. When you got so mad at me and ran out into the streets of New York. I actually was really worried that you would get lost and hurt. Man, Kris, you have a temper."

"I know. Let me show you something," she said as she tapped on her phone.

"What's this?" I asked as I looked at the Wikipedia entry that she had pulled up.

"Borderline personality disorder," she said. "They diagnosed me with this condition when I was in rehab. It means I'm sometimes emotionally unpredictable. I can get out-of-control angry, and when I do, I often black out and can't even remember all the things I said or did."

"Well, with mental conditions, it's always a spectrum. Everyone has some of these characteristics to a certain degree," I said with a natural instinct to defend Kris.

"Yeah, but read the description. I have almost all of those characteristics."

I read the Wikipedia entry.

Borderline personality disorder (BPD) (called emotionally unstable personality disorder, borderline type in the ICD-10) is a cluster B personality disorder whose essential features are a pattern of marked impulsivity and instability of affects, interpersonal relationships, and self image. The pattern is present by early adulthood and occurs across a variety of situations and contexts. Other symptoms may include intense fears of abandonment and intense anger and irritability that others have difficulty understanding the reason for. People with BPD often engage in idealization and devaluation of others, alternating between high positive regard and great disappointment. Self-mutilation and suicidal behavior are common.

I had to admit, the mosaic of symptoms fit Kris pretty well.

"So what did the doctors recommend you do? Are there prescription drugs or therapy that can help?"

"No, you can't really do anything," she said.

I held Kris tightly for a long time, not really sure what to say.

Over the course of the night and the morning, we made love four times. A new record, I pointed out to Kris. Before dinner. After dinner. Before going to sleep (though I was too spent to actually cum this time). And then finally, when we woke up, which had become our morning ritual.

"It's funny, Kris," I said as I held her in my arms in bed, bright sunlight shining in through the window. "I would have expected the physical aspect of our relationship to have tapered a bit by now. But if anything, it feels like it's accelerating."

"I know," she whispered with her eyes closed as she tilted her head up and kissed me softly. "I love you."

I dressed and packed up my things. Kris lay in bed watching me. She didn't need to leave for her flight for another hour.

"You really are one of my favorite people," she said. "My grandma, my dog, and you are probably my best friends."

"Seems like good company," I said as I leaned over the bed to give her one last kiss. "Well, let me know how things go with Harry. Or at least let me know when he kisses you," I said. "Fucking Harry."

Date 13: May 28

Email to Kris (5/3)

Kris – few things:

- My cookie is sore today! "Cookie" is probably the wrong metaphorical dessert. More like my "churro" is sore. Probably because we went to Portland four times, which I believe is a new record (granted, the third time we went to Portland, the plane didn't actually, umm, land, but regardless). Well done, Ms. Strauss.

- I'm warning you right now, you better change your password. I can't actually believe you told me your password. It's like giving a bag of heroin to a junkie and saying, "Here – please watch this for me." Anyway, if you don't change it – I take absolutely no responsibility for my actions from this point forward. None. In fact, if I log into your email account – I'll blame you for tempting me so. Kinda like how you blame me for you leaving your email open for Taylor to read. It's ridiculous and illogical – but I'm going to take that position nonetheless. That being said, I'll try to resist for as long as I can (which will probably be about halfway through this plane ride).

- Will check schedule for next few weeks tomorrow. Think I may be in NY again – not 100% sure. Will let you know and hopefully you can come visit.

BTW, I love you also, Kris. But I want you to be happy above all (even above my own primitive jealousies). So good luck with Taylor – whichever direction you decide to go. Know it won't be easy to talk about given all the history you have. And let me know how things go with Prince Harry (per our agreement, of course).

Fucking Harry. :)

Ryan

Text from Kris (5/3)
Made it to the airport, although I could've slept in that bed all day. Thank you for last night (and this very good morning), and thank you for always listening. You really are my best friend, Ryan. I'll let you know when I get home. I love you.

Text from Kris (5/3)
He killed the cat.

Text to Kris (5/3)
Jesus. I'm sorry, Kris.

I always had the feeling that Taylor could be mean-spirited from the way Kris described their arguments. He would say incredibly cruel things like, "Well, which of us was in a mental institution, Kris?" Still, Taylor killing a newborn kitten out of anger shocked me.

Private message to Kris via her Tumblr page (5/4)
'Ello love. Blimey, I've missed you. I've heard you've been buggering about with short Asian blokes. Toodle-loo for now – Harry (P.S.: I'm gay, and I shag like shit . . . like really gay).

Text from Kris (5/4)
Seriously almost peed my pants reading my Tumblr message from Harry.

Text to Kris (5/4)
Harry tumblr'd you??? Shit.

Just wanted to make you smile today. :)

I have to admit, I struggled a lot over the next few days thinking about Kris starting a new relationship with Harry. By this point, I had been able to come to grips with Kris's relationship with Taylor. If anything, the knowledge that she was unhappy with him made him less of a threat and made it easier to put their relationship in a box.

But the idea of a new, passionate love that could eclipse the light of our relationship was almost too much to bear. Jealousy. It literally made my chest ache when I thought about it.

Still, I tried to be selfless. I mean, if I truly cared about Kris, I should want what's best for her. I would want her to find a healthy relationship with someone who could make her happy in the long run. After all, I knew our relationship had to end at some point, right?

Still, I obsessed. I created an Instragram account and requested access to Kris's account (per her invitation). She had over five hundred followers. When she approved my request, I was able to see hundreds of pictures that she had posted over the last couple of years. Wow – jackpot. This content was even better than reading through her Facebook page, which had only maybe half a dozen pictures. Her Instagram account had hundreds of pictures going back several years, with comments back and forth among her friends. I was able to pictorially trace the early stages of her relationship with Taylor. I saw pictures from her trip to Vegas to visit Max, her prior sugar daddy, last year. I saw pictures of her close friends, Katy and David, whom she often talked about.

As I worked my way from older to newer pictures, I saw a picture of the Tiffany's box that she posted the night of our first date last October. And most recently, I saw some self portraits of Kris dressed up with makeup and wearing hot outfits. These recent "fashion" photos stood out because almost all of the older pictures were candids of her and her friends being silly. Of course, the recent "fashion" photos of her coincided exactly with when she met Harry. Clearly, those pictures were posted for him. Harry, in turn, had started "Liking" all of Kris's recent pictures. The mating dance had begun.

I couldn't sleep the next few nights. Finally, I decided that I couldn't bear standing by as Kris explored a new relationship. I needed some distance to protect myself. So I drafted an email to Kris. I explained that, while I was jealous of her potential new relationship, I also wanted her to find a great love, and so I was going to give her some space. In reality, of course, a part of me hoped that she would read the email, decide she couldn't live without me, and decide to not pursue Harry any further. But I knew that wasn't realistic.

Literally as I was just about to hit "send" to deliver my pathetic email, an email from Kris popped into my account.

Email from Kris (5/6)
Oh my god Harry is so annoying. You won't have to worry about that anymore. And just so you know, there was no time to even kiss him because he wouldn't shut up about himself.

I wish you had a 20-year-old single son or something. I mean seriously, you've set the bar so high that no one compares anymore. Maybe I'm just missing you too much already.

I'm fine. Taylor just didn't feed the kitten and she passed away. I haven't even been able to process that yet. She was a baby and she needed us and I went off to see you, and I feel like it's my punishment of some sort.

"Harry is so annoying." I did a little jig in my heart. Kris's heart was still mine. Everything was okay again.

Email from Kris's account (5/6)
You both are fucking disgusting. I found out recently that you and Kris have had sex on more than one occasion, and she didn't hesitate to mention how it made her want to vomit. For Christ Sake, you're a 40 year old Asian man, hahahah. How could she ever find you sexually attractive? Quit kidding yourself. Does paying young girls to have sex with you make you feel like a big man, Ryan? You are a sad little man.

- Taylor

It took me a few moments to comprehend what I had just read. It was like I had suddenly seen a five-legged duck cross the road, and my brain was trying to reconcile that information with reality as I knew it.

Oh my god, Taylor had broken into Kris's email again.

My mind started racing.

I didn't know if Taylor had confronted Kris yet, so I wanted to warn her.

Text to Kris (5/6)
Assume it's old news on your end, but in case not – heads up, I got a nice email from T.

Text from Kris (5/6)
Wonderful.

Text to Kris (5/6)
You doing okay? Jeez – what happened today?

Text from Kris (5/8)
Good morning sunshine! I'm at a work meeting right now that will take about an hour but call me the earliest you can because it's kind of important.

I made my walk of shame to my car in the parking lot in order to call Kris. I had been a bundle of nerves over the last couple of days ever since Taylor had emailed me.

"Hi, Ryan. What's up?"

"Oh, you know. Not much," I said with a drawl. We both laughed. What else could we do? "Jesus, Kris, what happened after Taylor broke into your email again? Are you okay?"

"I'm okay. He actually didn't tell me he knew until yesterday. The only reason I even knew he broke into my account a couple days ago is because you texted me. Thanks for that warning, by the way."

"Did he read all the bad stuff?"

"You mean your emails about your churro and us going to Portland multiple times?" Kris said with a laugh. "Yes, all that. But more importantly, he told me yesterday that he not only emailed you directly, but he also messaged your wife."

Shit. My world suddenly started to spin. Like a punch in the face, I realized that everything I had worked for my entire life was now destroyed, including my family and my career. And I knew that I deserved it.

Kris continued, "So I freaked out. I said, 'Taylor, show me what you sent. Did you apologize?' and he said, 'Why should I apologize?' I said, 'I mean apologize for me. She seems like a nice lady.' So I made him show me what he had sent to your wife."

I could only half-hear Kris. The other part of my brain was panicking and thinking of ways to control the damage. Had my wife read her emails yet? Could I break into her account and delete the message still?

"So he showed me your wife's account on Facebook. Turns out, he messaged the wrong woman."

Wait. Stop. What did Kris just say?

"This lady's site was all in Chinese, and she had posted pictures of her son. I think she lives in China. Anyway, obviously not your wife."

I started laughing. I was terrified at how close I had come to disaster, of course, but I had to laugh to release the tension. "So some poor woman in China now has a message from some random guy saying that her husband is cheating on her? What did he write?"

"Oh, it was bad. It was all about the sugar baby site, and he said it wasn't the first time you had cheated on her. Bad."

"Did you pretend that the woman was my wife?" I asked hopefully.

"I thought about that afterwards. I should have done that, but I was so relieved in the moment that I told him that she wasn't your wife."

"Oh," I said as my stomach sank at the thought of Taylor trying to track down my wife again. My entire life was now in the hands of a crazed teenage boy in Florida whom I had never met, but who had every reason to hate me. "I think I should email him, Kris."

"What would you say?"

"Just apologize. Try to smooth things over as best I can . . . for you also. If you think that would be okay?"

"I think that would be okay. I'll text you his email address."

"Okay," I said and then paused before continuing. "Kris, I think we should take a little break. In a naïve way, I always viewed the world that you and I existed in as separate from your real world and my real world. It was like a perfect, pure little bubble in which we were free to love each other. But when Taylor emailed me directly, that bubble suddenly burst. And I can laugh about the fact that he inadvertently messaged the wrong woman, but he could easily have messaged my actual wife. Or he might still do so."

"He's calmed down now. I don't think that he will do that."

"Still, it's all too real. Let's just slow things down a little. Maybe we take a week without talking in order to each think things through."

Kris reluctantly agreed. After we hung up, my mind continued to spin. I was in shock at how close I had come to losing everything, and I was still terrified at the risk that I now faced. All I could do was try to calm the beast.

Email to Taylor (5/8)

Taylor,

I don't know how to start this, so I'll just say that I'm sorry and you are right. I have not stopped spinning around in my head since you emailed a couple days ago, and you have every right to hate my guts.

I'm sorry that I got caught up in this fantasy and that people got hurt, and I'm sorry that I may have pushed Kristina further than she wanted. I've apologized to her about that before, and I'm apologizing to you now. It's not enough, I know.

Kristina has told me so much about all the reasons she loves you, how you grew up together, how you shaped who she is . . . and why after all the ups and downs, she keeps coming back to you. Her One. And I certainly never imagined that this fantasy life that I had built up inside my head would intrude on her real life with you.

Stupid, I know. I'm sure it's hard to believe – but I really do feel broken hearted about the pain I've caused.

Anyway, that stops now. No more emails, no more gifts, no more visits. I called Kristina this morning, apologized to her (for a lot of things) and told her goodbye.

If you want tell me again what a horrible person I am and to go fuck myself, I totally get it. I made this bed, and that's your prerogative. Otherwise, I wish you and Kristina the best.

Ryan

Email from Taylor (5/8)
I'm leaving her, fool. I'm unable to ever put myself past all of this, especially since it's happened on more than one occasion. The whole thing is just unbelievable. I hope it was all money well spent. Send her anything you want.

So that was that. All I could do now was hope Taylor wouldn't have another enraged moment and try to contact my wife.

Despite our plan to take a one-week break, it was hard to not communicate with Kris. Not surprisingly, we failed miserably.

Email from Kris (5/9)
I already miss you. I don't know how this ends but it's starting to set in that we won't wind up together. It's funny, because I clearly understood that when we first started this whole thing. I must remind myself that you're not mine to keep . . . But I really wish you were.

Email from Kris (5/13)
How many days left? This sucks.

Email to Kris (5/13)
Okay, fine – I give up, Kris. Who am I kidding that I could go for a week without communicating? (Though I am sort of proud that I made it five days and didn't check my email or your Instagram all today . . . until now, at least.)

Pathetic, but you know what I always say . . . embrace the horror of who we are. Sigh.

Okay, here's my fantasy itinerary for next week.

I'm in NYC from Mon – Thur next week. I was thinking about the potential itinerary in two phases:

Phase 1:

- You take TWO days off from work, and you fly into NY on Monday and fly back to Florida on Wednesday.

Phase 2:

- You get back to Naples on Wednesday early afternoon. You probably have to go straight into work that night.

- Taylor finds out you visited me somehow (again). He goes ballistic (again). Your relationship is ruined. Taylor does a better search on Facebook, and messages my actual wife (as opposed to some poor woman in China who has now divorced her husband wrongly). My marriage and family life (and probably career) are ruined.

- You and I become social outcasts, move together to some no-name town in middle America, and then you leave me within a year once you finally realize that I'm a 38-year-old short Chinese guy with actually just an average-sized penis (at best!).

Thing is . . . Phase 1 sounds great to me. It's the Phase 2 part that I'm struggling with a little.

Anyway, think about it, and let me know your thoughts. How are you doing? I do miss you.

Ryan

Kris went unusually silent for a few days. Knowing that she was going through a difficult time with Taylor and that I was a major cause of that, I tried to respect her space. But as the days grew nearer to my trip, I grew anxious, so I texted her to confirm that she was still planning to visit.

Text from Kris (5/18)
I can't. Not right now. Please don't hate me. Taylor is moving into his own place. I'm scared.

I was stunned – and hurt and mad. I mean, Kris had always made me feel like the emotional center of her universe, and I had gotten spoiled by that. So for Kris to go radio silent for five days and then refuse to come visit me made me mad and jealous about what was actually going on in Florida. Yes, I knew Taylor was her boyfriend, but wasn't it clear that she was actually in love with me? How could she refuse to visit me regardless of what was going on with Taylor? Deep down, I knew that I was being unreasonable, but I didn't care. Like a petulant child, I ignored Kris for a few days.

Email from Kris (5/21)
I'm really hoping you aren't mad at me. I've never said no to you before and part of me knows you would make me forget about everything for a night, but I would just be prolonging what I need to deal with now. I miss you like crazy and even though I've been distant, I want you to know how much I appreciate you being my friend. Taylor is all packed and ready to go. I'm going to California on Thursday until Sunday for my stepsister's graduation. Not sure what your plans are, but maybe we could figure something out. Hope you're doing okay.

Email to Kris (5/21)
Never said "no"? What about the whole anal sex thing???

Look Kris, I could pretend that I'm not hurt or mad – but that's not the truth. And it has nothing to do with you not coming to NY. I completely understand the need for space to work through things yourself (I asked for that space myself in the recent past, you'll remember). And I completely understand how hard it is to say goodbye to someone whom you loved, relied on and grew up with – but just don't want to BE with anymore. But to go from one day saying how you miss me and how I am your best friend . . . to just going to total radio silence with no explanation . . . when you know how much I worry about you . . . that was the hurtful part. It's like my feelings didn't matter. I just wish you showed me the same courtesy and told me that you needed some time before disappearing. That I would have understood.

All that being said, there's only so much that I can be mad at you. And I'll always be your friend in the truest and deepest way (totally separate from whether we continue to have a romantic relationship). And of course, I miss you also.

Good luck this week. Try not to spin too much, or hang out alone, or smoke weed every day. Go work out. Get stronger. Read a book. Get smarter.

You will have lots of fun adventures ahead in your life. Jesus, you're not even old enough to walk into a bar yet. Anyway, you said once that you've invested all this time in your relationship with Taylor and feel like you're walking away with nothing. That's just not true. Every relationship you have makes you smarter about what you actually want in the next relationship, and so each relationship is a step towards finding someone who makes you happy. This is not the end of your life, and you're not going to end up alone. Period.

Have fun at your sister's graduation. It'll be a nice break, and ask her to take you to some graduation parties where you can maybe meet someone age appropriate (and by that I mean, someone neither three years younger nor twenty years older . . . DEFINITELY not twenty years older).

Okay, Kris – thank you for the email. I mean it. It's genuinely helpful, and I understand now. Take all the time you need to get rebalanced in your life.

Ryan

Email from Kris (5/22)
Okay, fair enough. I'm sorry. Things are just really messy right now. We basically live together in silence. I don't know what's going to happen next, and I've never felt more vulnerable. I miss you and love you. But it's hard feeling that way and knowing that my feelings for you have more or less put me in this situation. I just thought it would be really disrespectful to the last four years I've spent with Taylor to come up and see you in the middle of everything. (I know, a little late for my conscience to kick in).

I hope you're doing well and that you didn't get too lonely in NY.

Since Kris wasn't going to visit me in New York, I made arrangements for her to visit me the following week when she was on the West Coast for her sister's graduation. The plan was for her to spend a few days in Southern California, and then her dad would drop her off at the airport for her flight back to Florida. But instead of flying back to Florida, she would fly up to San Francisco. I was sad I wouldn't see Kris in New York, but was mollified she was making the effort to visit me next week.

And then all hell broke loose.

Text from Kris (5/23)
I need your help

Text to Kris (5/23)
Okay – should I call? I've got 30 minutes before my next meeting.

Text from Kris (5/23)
No, the police are here

Text to Kris (5/23)
Jesus – you okay? What do you need?

Text from Kris (5/23)
I need out

I called Kris an hour later, when she texted me that the police had left.

"Kris, are you okay? What happened?"

"Taylor was out to lunch with his mom and I was at home. During lunch, he sent me a text saying that he was taking the dog, so of course, I sent him a text back saying that there's no way he's taking Veda."

"I'm guessing that Taylor wanted to take the dog just to hurt you?"

"Of course. He never cared about the dog before. So anyway, after lunch, he comes into the apartment and starts screaming at me that he's taking the dog. I had put Veda on the balcony, and I was blocking the patio door with my body. So Taylor loses it, and throws me against the wall and pushes my face hard into it. Then he throws me on the ground and starts banging my head against the floor. I was afraid he was going to break my nose, so I tried to cover my nose with my hands. So then he grabs my hands behind me and then . . . he hurt me even more."

"What do you mean by that?" I asked, scared to know. "Did he sexually assault you?"

"Not completely, but he ripped down my underwear and shoved his fingers into me. It hurt like hell."

"Jesus, how are you now?"

"I'm all bruised up. I have two black eyes. My apartment is a mess. He was throwing me all around the apartment, so a lot of the doors and closets are off their hinges. Then in the middle of this, his mom walks in. And I'm thinking, 'Well at least she'll get Taylor off of me.' But then she starts yelling at me also! She's screaming about how I ruined her family and took Taylor away from her. So she jumps on me and starts hitting me. Finally, Taylor starts crying and pulls his mom off of me. I have a jar in my dresser drawer where I keep all my work money, and he just grabs a bunch of my money and then they both run off. So I called the police and filed a police report."

"Has this happened before, Kris? You told me once he never hit you."

Kris paused for a few moments and then said, "Yes, it's happened before. Can I tell you something, and you promise not to be mad?"

"I'll try."

"When you saw me last time in New York, I had two black eyes. That was from Taylor, too. It's been happening for a while."

I was silent, too stunned and angry to say anything.

"You're mad," Kris said.

"No, Kris, I'm not mad. How many times before?"

"How many times has he shoved me around? A lot. How many times did he actually give me black eyes or worse?" Kris said and then paused.

"Half a dozen times?" I offered.

"Something like that," she said softly. I knew Kris had always possessed a deep-rooted fear of being abandoned and alone, and I knew that this fear was consistent with borderline personality disorder. But I still couldn't believe that she had stayed with Taylor for so many years when he had repeatedly been physically abusive.

I had originally pictured Taylor as a sweet but somewhat immature boy who was three years younger than Kris and who viewed Kris as part girlfriend and part parent. That view changed a bit over time based on Kris's description of his behavior – like the time he starved the newborn kitten to death out of spite that Kris wasn't home, the time that he made fun of her stay at a mental institution, and the time that he got mad when Kris had a panic attack and couldn't leave the house to get sushi. So by now, I sensed that there was a mean streak within Taylor. But I really didn't suspect that his darker side went so deep that he would physically abuse Kris over an extended period. I was suddenly glad that I had caused them to break up. Kris shouldn't have to live like this.

I comforted Kris as best I could. I asked her to take pictures of all her bruises and the damage around her apartment, partly as leverage if Taylor ever bothered her again and partly to remind herself never to go back again.

Kris sounded so scared and desperate. I told her to hang in there, and that we could talk about everything when we saw each other next week. I told her again to consider moving back to Southern California to live with her dad or to Nevada to live with her mom, so that she could start fresh and go back to school. I told her that everything would be okay – that we would make everything okay.

Email to Kris (5/25)
Kris, I really do believe that you learn a little bit from every relationship (if you choose to) about the type of person that will make you happy. Every failed relationship is a step towards finding someone you'll be happy with. So it's never wasted. With Derek, you learned you won't be happy with a beautiful guy who's nice but boring. With Charles, you learned you can't be with a chubby Asian guy with a small penis (sorry, couldn't help myself). In my opinion (which, admittedly, is not worth much), with Taylor – I think maybe you fell in love with him because you have this incredibly strong maternal instinct (see Veda and Benz), and you were able to be part parent / part girlfriend to Taylor. But I don't think you really want a maternal relationship with the man you end up with. It creates conflict and stress that can be released in unhealthy ways. From my brief time with you, I think you want someone who challenges you and helps to guide your path in the same way that you can help to guide his path. An equal partner in that sense.

Think about our relationship over the last few months. How fun and exciting . . . and yes, erotic, it's been. Now imagine you get to experience that with a boy who is actually your age and who is free to imagine long-term plans together with you. It's scary, but it's also really exciting. It's something to embrace. You just need to put yourself in an environment where you have plenty of opportunities to meet those types of equals.

You have so much potential. If you focus on making yourself smarter and stronger over the next few years, the rest will fall into place. It will. You're only twenty, Kris. Except for those folks who have married their high school sweethearts, most people HAVEN'T met their future spouses yet. But please, please don't go backwards if you know already in your heart that you won't be happy in the long run with someone. Especially someone who has hurt you and violated you the way Taylor has. Don't settle because you're afraid of being alone.

Get some rest, my dear. Let's talk about all this when we see each other Monday.

Ryan

Kris posted a close-up picture of her two black eyes onto her Instagram account along with a note explicitly identifying Taylor as the culprit. It quickly attracted a flurry of concerned and outraged emails from her friends (and, I can only assume, hopeful male suitors).

Finally the day arrived for Kris to fly up to San Francisco. She actually was going to stay in San Francisco for two nights, though I was only able to meet her for the second night. We texted back and forth often. She was clearly in a lot of emotional pain. On her first night in San Francisco, she texted me from her hotel room that she was lonely. I emailed her back.

Email to Kris (5/27)

I figured that I could write a sympathetic email diving into the heartache of breakups and sharing my sad stories to mix with yours. Or I figured that I could write a distracting email about something else entirely. You've moped enough – let's go with distracting.

We'll have lots to catch up on tomorrow, I'm sure, and I want to discuss your plan from here and how I can help. Don't get me wrong – working at a bar is good, honorable work . . . but you were meant for other things than serving drinks and smoking weed every day, and I worry about your sleep schedule (even if you're not in school right now).

I've been contemplating what I miss most about seeing you. Turns out that if I analyze the time that I spend thinking about you, I estimate about one-third of the time I think about things that I'd like to talk with you about. Those are the times when I add notes to my running list of topics for our next visit. In other words, about one-third of the time, I really miss our conversation and having one of my closest friends there to talk to.

Another one-third of the time, I'm fantasizing about making love to you so tenderly that you can feel how much I care in the way that it manifests in our physical connection . . . kissing you slowly, starting from your ears and neck and working my way down to your breasts, exploring your belly button with my tongue as I rub my stiff cock on your legs, then licking the inside of your thighs, and working my way down until I'm gently sucking on your toes. Then moving back up slowly. Hovering over your swollen pussy with my hot breath until I can't resist anymore, and then pressing my wet tongue onto your salty, sweet pussy. And then finally pushing myself slowly inside of you, and feeling you welcoming me and honoring me as your pussy stretches around my hard cock. And just luxuriously rocking in and out of you . . . as if we could live there forever . . . as if we had all the time in the world.

And the final third of the time, I think about turning you around desperately, pushing you down over the bed, rimming your asshole, thrusting my hard cock inside your dripping wet pussy, pulling your hair roughly and smacking your ass while I fuck you hard . . . until I can't hold out any longer – and then pulling out and cumming on your face and in your mouth as you suck me off. Like I own you, and you own me in return . . .

So that's that. In summary, about one-third conversation and two-thirds some variety of sex. Now, that may sound skewed towards sex, but you have to realize for a guy to fantasize one-third of the time about conversation makes our relationship downright intellectual . . . cerebral almost. Barely physical at all (relatively). So I think we're doing pretty well.

I'm feeling a little under the weather today, but hopefully will be better tomorrow. I can't wait to see you.

Email from Kris (5/27)

Oh my. Quite distracting, indeed. And incredibly cruel since I can practically feel you in the air here. "So close, yet so far." In another world, I would be driving over to make you soup and cuddle up on the couch right now. I really need you to feel better so we can bring these delicious fantasies of yours to life (again). I haven't felt that release since New York. It's just been building and building, but you always make it worth the wait. Egads egads egads egads! Here I am . . . fresh and naked straight out of the shower . . . lonely . . . just waiting to hear the click of the hotel key. Fuck. I'm so wet, Ryan.

Please. :(

I barely slept that night.

The next day, I told my typical lies to my wife about traveling for work and "headed to the airport." I drove to the hotel where Kris was staying and I checked into the room. She was out exploring, so I unpacked my things and then surfed on my iPad in the living room as I waited. About thirty minutes later, I heard the hotel room door open, and I turned to see Kris walk in.

She had two large bruises under her eyes and she looked tired. But she still looked beautiful. She gave me a weak smile and I walked over and gave her a big hug.

We snuggled on the couch and caught up. She told me the details of what happened after the physical abuse by Taylor.

"He tried to break back into the apartment when I wasn't home by climbing onto my balcony on the second floor. In the process, he totally ruined the neighbor's plants on the first floor. Anyway, the balcony door was locked, so he climbed back down and waited in the parking lot until I got back home. Luckily, I saw his car in the parking lot when I got home, so I called the police and they showed up quickly. Taylor didn't really understand why they were there. I think he thought that they were there just to protect me while he got his stuff from the apartment. So we all walked into the apartment, and he gathered his things. In the meantime, the police were trying to pull up the police report I had filed, but for some reason, they had trouble pulling it up. So after Taylor gathered all his things, he's just standing there with me and two police officers, unsure what to do next. He tried to act like Mr. Cool and was joking around with the officers, but they were having none of it," Kris said with a laugh. "Finally, the police officer was able to pull up the report, and he just looked at me and gave me a little nod. Then he asked Taylor to turn around and put his hands behind his back. Taylor was confused at first, but then he realized he was being arrested. He started screaming, 'I don't deserve this, I don't deserve this!' They took him out and put him in the police car, and I could hear him screaming, 'If you ever loved me, don't do this!' It was pretty hard to bear."

"I'm sorry it was so hard, Kris. But he raped you. He did. He deserves to be arrested."

"I know. I kind of feel like I needed to do this, so that there is no way we get back together. He'll never forgive me for this, and his parents will always hate me now," Kris said. But even as she said it, I could hear the doubt in her voice.

I switched topics and asked Kris about her stepsister's graduation weekend. She filled me in on the graduation party that her dad and stepmom had thrown. There were a bunch of her stepsister's college classmates, lots of drinking games, guys aggressively swarming over Kris, putting their hands unsolicited on her legs, etc. She swore that she didn't hook up with anyone, and I laughed at her stories. But I could already feel myself getting anxious, knowing that this was the new order going forward now that Kris was single.

"Y'know, Kris, I used to feel guilty that I might be the cause of you and Taylor eventually breaking up. But now that I know about the physical abuse, I'm actually glad I helped cause the breakup. We've all made our mistakes, but no one deserves to get physically abused. In a selfish way, though, I'm worried for a different reason. I had gotten comfortable with Taylor in your life as sort of your ineffectual boyfriend. Now, though, there's going to be a bunch of new guys chasing you," I said with a sad smile.

"Are you scared?" Kris said with a mischievous grin.

"Of course I am," I answered truthfully.

We made love before going out to dinner. True to my email, I made love to her as tenderly as I could, trying my best to physically communicate how much I cared for her.

As I held her afterward, we talked about her plans to move back to Nevada to start fresh.

"Looks like I'm going to the University of Las Vegas in the fall!" she said excitedly.

"I think that's great, Kris. When are you going to move? The sooner the better, from my point of view. There's nothing for you in Florida but painful memories. Are you going to live with your mom?"

"I'll probably move in a few weeks. Soon as I can figure out how to break my lease in Florida and give work my two-week notice. Yup, the plan is to live with my mom. She's really excited. Maybe too excited, which is a little scary. But I think I'm old enough now that I can live with her and deal with her craziness," she said.

Kris paused thoughtfully a few moments and then said, "You know, you've helped me through all this, and you really are my best friend. It's like you're some kind of a weird parent-boyfriend."

"As opposed to a son-boyfriend?" I laughed.

I spread my hands in front of me and said, "Kris, you've now covered the spectrum of son-boyfriend with Taylor and parent-boyfriend with me. Now what you have to find is something in between. You need, y'know, just a normal boyfriend-boyfriend."

"I know, I know," Kris said with a smile.

We snuggled for a while and then got dressed for dinner. We walked just a few blocks to a local Italian restaurant for dinner. I continued the topic of new relationships over dinner, as I have to admit, it was still foremost in my mind.

"So what type of guy are you going to look for now? I really believe what I said about all of your past relationships being learning experiences that can help you triangulate in on the right guy for you."

"I don't know," Kris said sadly. "I hope it doesn't happen for a while, actually. I'm not ready to move on from you. I mean, I'm never going to get sick of you."

"Yes you will, Kris."

"No. I won't. I know this sounds scary, but I kind of wish we had a son so that we'd always have a link in our relationship."

I opened my eyes wide in mock horror. "You're right. That does sound scary. When I told Andrew about you and I having sex with no protection, he warned me that you might try to trap me by getting pregnant."

"I wouldn't do that," Kris protested.

"I know. It's strange that we love each other so much. I mean, in no universe does this make sense. Given our backgrounds, we should never have even met. And yet here we are."

"Here we are," Kris smiled.

"There's this question that my friends and I sometimes ask each other. If someone offered to pay you money to completely erase me from your life, how much money would you demand? And 'erase completely' doesn't mean that we never see each other again. It means that our lives never actually intersected at all. So we don't even know the other person existed, and whatever impact we had on each other is erased also. I'll go first," I offered. "It's probably different for me, because I have enough money now to protect my family. Having more money would be nice, but it's not that important to me. And you've been the greatest adventure of my life. So it's sort of impossible to put a dollar figure on erasing that. Honestly, I think it would have to be something outrageous, like one billion dollars."

Kris thought for a few moments and then said, "I can't even imagine what it's like to have one million dollars, so it's hard for me to answer also."

"Well, let's say with ten million dollars, you would never have to work again. You could probably generate four to five hundred thousand dollars in interest a year or from investments on that forever. So ten mllion?"

"Fifteen million then," Kris said with a smile.

"I'll take that as a compliment. The very fact that you love me is almost incomprehensible. I figured that there would always be a part of you that would hold me in disdain, because I'm cheating on my wife – especially given the fact that your dad cheated on your mom and then left you both. I figured that a part of you would always hold me in disdain, and that would provide an emotional shield for both of us. "

Kris sat thoughtfully for a few moments. "If it was anyone but you, that would be true. In fact, I'd probably be the first person to tell the wife. But it is you."

"And as Woody Allen said, the heart wants what the heart wants."

"I guess."

"Tell me this. Out of the dozens of messages you would get each day on the sugar baby site, why did you choose me?"

"I don't know. You seemed nice, and you were willing to take things slow."

"Our relationship was slow?" I laughed.

"Actually, yes. A lot of guys want to sleep together on the first meeting. You just seemed nice and funny. I liked that. Anyway, like I said, I hope I don't meet anyone new for a while."

"You say that, Kris, but I bet when you posted that picture of yourself to your Instagram with the two black eyes, it must have been like a beacon to all the guys in the area that you are now single. I bet they are swarming already."

"Oh yeah," Kris laughed. "I got messages from a bunch of guys trying to console me and asking if I wanted to hang out that night. Actually, when I was walking around here yesterday even, two young guys in suits started talking to me in the street. 'Hey beautiful, what are you doing around here?' They actually invited me up to their room, but of course, I said that I was with someone."

"Oh my god. This is going to be really hard on me. Are you going to tell me when you start these new romances?"

"Yes. I mean, do you want to know?"

"I don't know," I said with a pit in my stomach. Finally, I added, "Yes, I want to know."

"Well, we have our prior agreement that we tell each other the earlier of two dates or a kiss."

"Okay, let's go with that," I said. "You know what our problem is, Kris?"

She rolled her eyes at me sarcastically and said, "What Ryan? What is our one single problem?"

I smiled. "Our problem is that we both have a superficial currency so that when we get lonely, we can always fill that loneliness regardless of whether that is the healthy thing to do. In your case, your superficial currency is your beauty. You can use it to get any guy you want to plug the emotional hole."

"And in your case," Kris retorted, "your superficial currency is actual currency."

I burst out laughing. "Yes, I guess that's right. But hey, at least I earned mine! Anyway, my only advice is don't jump at the first guy that you meet who is nice to you in order to plug that emotional hole. You can choose anyone, so make sure he's the right guy."

Kris smiled and nodded.

After dinner, we walked back to the hotel. We made love again. Following the script of my pornographic email, I made love to Kris roughly this time. I turned her around and pushed her onto the bed so that she lay face down with her legs on the ground and her glorious butt sticking off the edge of the bed. I bent her arms behind her and held both her wrists tightly with one hand as I stood behind her and slapped her ass hard. One, two, three times. I heard her moan in excitement. Still holding her arms behind her, I crouched down. I pressed the flat of my tongue onto her wet pussy. Kris gasped loudly. I ran my tongue upward the full length of both her pussy and asshole. Over and over. And then I started to focus on licking her beautiful asshole. Kris moaned louder and squirmed hard. But she couldn't move as I held her wrists behind her tightly. As she squirmed harder in excitement, I pushed her bent arms higher up her back until I could feel the strain of ligaments. Finally, I bent over her from behind, gave her ass another hard slap, and then pushed my throbbing cock inside of her. As I pounded Kris hard from behind, I grabbed her hair and jerked her head away from the bed. I craned around and covered her mouth with mine. She was mine. And I was hers.

"Oh my god, no one has ever fucked me like this before!" Kris gasped.

I flipped Kris over and climbed on top of her missionary style. I lifted both of her legs onto my shoulders so that I could penetrate her deeply.

"Oh my god, I'm cumming hard!" she screamed.

"Yeah, baby," I moaned hoarsely. "I love it when you cum all over my cock."

She bucked hard as she came, and then moments later, I felt myself approach climax. At the last moment, I desperately pulled my cock out and jerked off onto her stomach.

"Yeah. All over me," Kris said as she breathed heavily and smeared my cum in circles on her stomach with one hand.

I collapsed next to Kris and took several long moments to catch my breath.

We fell asleep that night curled up in each other's arms. In the morning we made love again.

Afterwards, we lay in bed holding each other silently for the few minutes that we had before I left for work.

Finally, I said quietly, "You joked before about us running away together." Kris was silent.

"It wouldn't work out in the long run, you know. In an ironic way, because we have been so honest with each other, we now know that we're each capable of cheating. And so, we'd always be paranoid about that possibility if we were together long term. You'd always be wondering when I traveled if I was actually on a business trip. I'd always be wondering why you were surfing the Internet so much," I said with a light laugh.

"Maybe. Or maybe we wouldn't."

"Kris, have you ever heard the fable of the scorpion and the frog?"

"No."

"Well, there's this scorpion that comes to the edge of a river, and he needs to cross it. But he can't swim. So he sees a frog sitting at the water's edge, and he asks the frog to swim him across. The frog responds, 'If I let you ride on my back, you will surely sting me.' To this, the scorpion counters, 'I will not, because if I do, then you will drown and I will drown with you.' The frog thinks about this for a few seconds and sees the logic of the scorpion's argument. So finally, the frog consents. The scorpion climbs on the frog's back, and the frog begins to swim across the river. Halfway across, the frog suddenly feels a burning sensation on his back, and he realizes the scorpion has, in fact, stung him deeply. As the poison spreads and the frog begins to sink below the water, he cries out, 'Why did you sting me? For now we shall both surely drown!' And to this, the scorpion simply hisses in reply, 'It is in my nature . . .'"

Kris was quiet for a few moments, and then said, "So it's in our nature to cheat?"

"Maybe."

"Or maybe it's in our nature to love each other," she said softly.

Date 14: June 12 – 13

Text from Kris (5/29)

Just landed in Houston. Waiting for my connection. Miss you lots. Wish last night could just be put on repeat for a little while.

Text to Kris (5/29)

Sometimes I feel like my life is now comprised of 1) dates with you every 4 – 6 weeks and 2) a bunch of stuff in between. That can't be healthy. Oh my dear Kris – surely, someday our conversation will stall, right? And someday our trips to Portland will plateau, right? But not last night . . . egads, not last night.

Text from Kris (5/29)

I forgot to tell you – they called me Mrs. Lee when I checked out this morning. I'm sure I'm going to hell because every time it happens I have to hold back a huge grin. By the way, if you're ever offered the tortilla soup on a United flight, it's fucking delicious. I'm starting to get used to this whole first class thing. (thank you for upgrading me)

Text to Kris (5/29)

I'm chortling at my desk. It's gotta be some inside joke amongst the hotel reception folks to tease people who they know are meeting illicitly under questionable arrangements. (I mean, who the heck would believe a girl like you would be with a guy like me?) I've never had the tortilla soup – I'll have to remember that. Keep in mind, to fly first class forever, all you need to do is strike a Faustian deal to erase me from your life for the paltry sum of $15 million. At least, I believe you were at $15 million and I was at $1 billion . . . yup, that about sums it up. :)

Text from Kris (5/29)
Oh hush. Either way it has a nice ring to it. ;) About to board my flight. I'll be sure to let you know when I make it home! Love, love, love.

Kris really struggled over the next couple of weeks. We would talk or text every day and, often, multiple times a day. Usually, she would be in tears about being lonely and scared. I could sense her starting to have doubts about breaking up with Taylor. I tried to comfort her as best I could over the phone and with emails. I tried to focus her on the excitement of starting fresh in Nevada in one month, going to University in a couple of months, and meeting someone great in the future who deserved her. But she was in a really dark place, and I felt relatively helpless.

Text from Kris (6/3)
I can't think of anything to say besides I love you, I love you, I love you – because I miss you and can't concentrate on anything but how much I wish you were here to kiss and help me with things and sleep next to me for longer than just one night. Vacation together soon, please. Sweet dreams.

Text to Kris (6/3)
I know it's hard right now in the moment with all the Naples drama going on around you. But Kris – just stay focused and in a few weeks and you'll be starting an entirely new chapter in life. For some reason, you are scared of that new adventure despite the fact that you make friends wherever you go. I may not be tall or "Harry" good looking . . . but I am right. That's what I do. I'm right. It's my gift. And as I said before . . . your greatest adventures are ahead of you.

We made plans to see each other in a couple of weeks when I was visiting New York for work again. It was a two-day business trip. So it was an opportunity for a multiple-day date with Kris, which we had never experienced before.

In the interim, I vacillated emotionally from hurting alongside Kris as I witnessed her pain to guiltily reveling in the fact that in her morose state, I was now her sole love, savior and shining light. I also spent quite a bit of time worrying that one of the many guys now aggressively pursuing her would catch her interest in her vulnerable state.

Still, I wanted her to be happy, and I tried my best to be selfless in our conversations over the phone.

"Kris, I know you are hurting badly right now, but don't worry. I have a plan."

"Plan? Sounds intriguing."

"Well, first we need to define the goal, and then we can talk about the plan to get there. First, the goal is this. I want you to be happy. So you're going to find a happy, healthy, beautiful relationship, and I'm not going to be left a shattered shell of a man. That's the goal. Course, the hard part is figuring out how to get there from here. 'Here' meaning, of course, this state of us being crazy about each other. So here's the plan. The next time we get together, the plan is to strip away all remaining pretense. You can come into the bathroom and poop on the toilet while I'm brushing my teeth. And if I need to fart, damn it, I'll just fart. So we'll spend time together as if we've been together for ten years. Maybe then, some of this fire will fade, and we'll start to properly transition to being what we'll hopefully always be . . . great, lifelong friends. And you can be free to find someone who deserves you."

This sort of emotional drama went back and forth for days.

But then about one week before our next planned date, Kris went radio silent again. I had experienced this before, so I tried to stay patient. But as the days ticked by and our date approached, I started to get upset and panicked. I envisioned scenarios where Taylor had attacked her again, or (worse) she had reconciled and was back together with Taylor. Or maybe she had met someone new. I didn't even know if she was still planning on flying up to New York to meet me. Finally, I broke down and texted her two days before my trip.

Text to Kris (6/10)

I suppose I could act cool and pretend that your silence is easy. But I choose not to put on that mask – at least not today. It's not easy. And though at some point, I'll surely need to take protective measures so as to not lose myself . . . for right now, I'll just ask if you still feel good about visiting me this week in NY. Tickets are booked if you would like to get together. But in the beginning of our relationship, I always used to ask you if you felt good about each upcoming date. For some reason, which I can't put my finger on, I feel like I need to ask that again. Which makes me feel a little bit ... hmm ... "pensive" is probably the closest word. I hope you are doing well.

Text from Kris (6/10)
I'm doing okay. I've been working a lot. Is there any way you can call me tonight? The schedule is being made today but another waitress might be able to switch with me so that I can visit. Remind me of the time frame again? My data is super low, which is why I haven't checked my email or posted anything on Instagram or Facebook lately. Plus it was a nice little break. Taylor is dating my friend Brenda who just started working with me at Players, and he's trying really hard to rub it in my face. I'm sorry if I've upset you, I've just felt kind of lost. I'm going into work now on 4 hours of sleep, and I'll be here until probably midnight my time. So if you get a chance to call after, I would love to hear the sound of your voice.

I was pissed after reading her text. She didn't even remember the exact days of our next date, which was only two days away? She hadn't gotten time off from work yet? Wasn't I supposedly the most important thing in her life? Hadn't she told me that she loved me multiple times a day before she had suddenly gone radio silent over the last week?

Part of me realized how selfish I was being. But I didn't listen to that part.

Text to Kris (6/10)
Sorry Taylor loves to punish you so blatantly – but recognizing it doesn't make it any easier, I know. Jealousy is a given, particularly with someone you dated for so long. And if it's anything like my experience, I'm guessing there is a rotation of emotions from depression, to wanting to get back together, to wanting to hurt him back by dating (or at least sleeping with) someone else. As your friend, my only advice is to move from Florida as soon as possible – start fresh somewhere new. There's nothing in Florida for you but painful memories, a vindictive ex-boyfriend, and temptation to go backwards and get stuck. But I can't live your life for you. So I actually don't know what will happen here. But I'm more than just your close friend. And I'm human also – and I don't like feeling like an afterthought. Let me know about NY either way.

If you don't feel like you want to see me, and you want to stay in Florida right now, I'd rather not twist your arm to come up. Like I said . . . at some point, I need to protect myself too. I can't call tonight – today was crazy for me also, and to pretend to have some medical emergency in order to call you from some random street corner is a little too much for me to deal with right now. Please get some rest tonight – everything is harder when you're too exhausted to think.

It was probably the curtest message that I had ever sent Kris. The trip was only two days away, I had bought her tickets, and she was still being noncommittal. Frankly, I thought she was being rude. Of course, I was also terrified that she wouldn't come, given her emotional turmoil, and that made me feel both vulnerable and angry.

The next day, there was still no response confirming that she was coming up. The trip was tomorrow.

Text to Kris (6/11)
Kris – let me know where your head is at. I deserve that if nothing else. I can't do anything about the airplane tickets at this point, but I can try to sell the show tickets that I bought. I know you are going through a tough time, but I feel like I'm being whipsawed here.

Text from Kris (6/11)
Yes, I will find a way to make it.

Okay, our last texts did not have a great tone heading into our date the next day, but at least she was coming.

On the plane ride to New York, I started thinking about the volatility of Kris's emotions. Kris would swing from periods when she would tell me multiple times a day that she loved me to periods of complete silence for days at a time when she completely ignored me. She would transition in seconds from declaring herself incredibly happy to be free of Taylor to the next moment being incredibly depressed and uncertain about their breakup. I remembered her stories of becoming so enraged at times that she would literally black out.

Then I remembered her telling me how she had been diagnosed with Borderline Personality Disorder (BPD) during her stay at the mental institution, and how this condition affected her ability to control her emotions. And I realized that I didn't know anything about this condition.

I suddenly felt guilty that I hadn't even made the minimal effort to learn more about a condition that could be so fundamentally impacting someone whom I supposedly loved. To begin to rectify this, I downloaded a couple books about BPD onto my Kindle and read them on the plane ride.

I've always been skeptical of psychological disorders. To a certain degree, everyone has the key traits of many psychological disorders. Fear of being alone. Losing control when angry.

So when someone says something like, "I have borderline personality disorder," my natural reaction is usually something like, "Oh stop blaming a 'disorder.' Just get control of yourself." Not the most admirable reaction, I acknowledge.

But as I read the book on BPD, not only did I realize that Kris exhibited almost all of the key behavioral symptoms, but I also learned that people with BPD can't control their emotions. That's actually the primary manifestation of BPD. Anger, depression, happiness are all experienced by the BPD patient in the extreme. Personal relationships are viewed as completely good or completely bad, and that perspective can flip back and forth in moments. That inclination to view relationships or situations in black-or-white terms even had the clinical term "splitting." This behavior fit Kris exactly. As sad as it was to admit to myself, part of the reason that I loved being with Kris was because she made me feel like I was such a wonderful person. She was always complimenting my looks, my intelligence, my sense of humor, the size of my cock. In a way, I suppose she had "split" her view on me, and I had thus far been categorized as completely wonderful.

BPD patients also had an intense fear of abandonment and being alone, so much so that their romantic relationships often overlapped. The clinical term for this behavior was "shingling" (e.g. shingles on a house that overlap). This fit Kris perfectly. She had admitted that she had not been alone between relationships for many years. The most recent example, I suppose, is that she had gone on that date with Harry while she was still living with Taylor. In a way, she was testing if Harry could be her next boyfriend before she fully pulled the ripcord on Taylor.

In the end, though, the violent altercation with Taylor had driven Kris to the breakup before she had another relationship firmly in hand. And so the past couple weeks of being alone had driven Kris's deep depression that I had witnessed. Oftentimes, patients with BPD came from broken homes where a parent had left early, and the remaining parent wasn't completely supportive. In Kris's case, her father had run away with another woman when she was just a toddler, and her mom was an abusive alcoholic who had wrestled with her own demons her entire life.

"Unconditional acceptance" is what psychologists call the psychological security that parents usually provide to their children. "Unconditional acceptance" is the feeling that most children have that no matter what happens, their parents will always be there and will always love them. But many patients of BPD did not have that "unconditional acceptance" growing up. "Love" from their parents, if they were even around, was often completely conditional. Conditional on whether they were drunk, conditional on whether they were in the mood to abuse the child that night, conditional on whether the child got in trouble at school. And without this "unconditional acceptance," the child can develop the extreme fear of abandonment and the emotional volatility that often accompanies BPD.

"Unconditional acceptance" is also the key to recovery for BPD patients. In order for patients to regain control of their emotions, they need someone to prove that they will always be there, no matter what the patient does or how they act. But the BPD patient will make it difficult for someone to prove "unconditional acceptance." Their fear of abandonment makes it hard for BPD patients to trust other people. So when someone shows them true kindness, the patient often pushes that person away because the patient can't trust that love. For example, a BPD patient will often pick a fight with the very friend who loves her the most. In return, the friend will often get hurt and angry because he doesn't understand the cause of the patient's behavior. And this anger, in and of itself, is damaging because it just "proves" to the BPD patient that the friend's love is not unconditional.

It's a terrible emotional cycle. And I was determined to help Kris break it, by proving that my love and friendship was a bond that could never be broken. No matter what she did, no matter what happened, I would always be there.

Little did I know how soon my convictions would be severely tested in this regard.

On the plane ride over, I sent Kris an email.

Email to Kris (6/12)

Saw an update that your flight is delayed 30 minutes. Everything okay otherwise? I've been doing a lot of reading and thinking. We have lots to catch up on, I'm sure – but I just want you to know that no matter what, as your best friend, I love you unconditionally. See you soon.

This is great, I thought. I understood Kris so much better after learning more about BPD. I would shower her with "unconditional acceptance." In retrospect, if I were to psychoanalyze myself, maybe I was spinning ever deeper into my own "hero complex." This was just another chance for me to rescue Kris. Maybe. But I think, for the most part, I just wanted to help someone I loved.

When I arrived at the hotel, I checked in and walked through the lobby towards the elevators. I saw Kris sitting on a stone bench in the lobby. I walked by her with a smile.

"Excuse me, Miss. Do you know which way the elevators are?"

Kris blushed and pointed to her right.

"Thanks," I said with a grin. "By the way, are you here alone? Do you need any help?"

Kris smiled and gave an embarrassed shake of her head.

Chuckling, I took the elevator up to my room, texted Kris, and a few minutes later, I heard her knock on the door.

I gave her a broad smile and hug as she walked in. She looked tired. We sat down on two chairs in the living room facing each other.

"So what have you been reading about?" she asked me.

"I've been reading a few books on borderline personality disorder, actually. To be honest, when I didn't hear from you over the last week, I got pretty upset. To go from telling me that you loved me multiple times a day to suddenly going radio silent was confusing and more than a little hurtful. I felt like I was on an emotional yo-yo and that you were pulling the string. But then I took a step back and told myself that if I truly cared for you as a friend, I should be more understanding of the fact that you are going through an extremely difficult time right now. And then I also remembered that, a few dates back, you told me about being diagnosed with borderline personality disorder. And I realized that if I really loved you, then I should learn more about this condition so that I could understand better and hopefully help more."

Kris stared at me with a weak smile.

I continued, "So, first and foremost, as I said in my email, you should know that I will always be there for you unconditionally. It's important that you know that. Second, I know that it is tough breaking up with someone you've dated for so many years, and I know it's extra difficult right now because he's being so vindictive. But I have to tell you, Kris, I think it's a good thing that this happened and that you broke up with Taylor. Don't take this the wrong way, but Taylor just does not have a good heart. A man who can let a kitten starve to death out of spite, rip your pants down and stick his fingers inside of you, and rub your face in a new relationship immediately after you've broken up – in no universe could that man have a good heart. No matter the motivation, no matter your own violations, and no matter your history of hurting each other. And it's the little things also. Like when you told me about the time he wanted to take you out to sushi, and you had a panic attack and you asked him to get take-out. Instead of trying to understand, he just got really mad. Or the times that you would argue, and he would maliciously make fun of you having been committed to a mental institution. In no universe can he possibly have a good heart."

I leaned forward as I continued. "If he really loved you, he would take the time to actually learn about BPD. I've barely known you for half a year, and I've tried to learn about it. He's known you for half a decade, and he couldn't make the effort to try to learn, understand and help."

I felt a few tears run down my face as I spoke, and my voice quivered as I thought of Kris being emotionally and physically abused throughout her life.

Kris sat silent for a few moments. She let out a little sigh and then said, "So, I've met someone."

I stopped breathing. I just stared at her waiting, but already knowing that whatever came next was going to rip me apart.

"I didn't expect it. I mean, over the last week, all these guys have been pinging me, but I just wasn't interested. I was too emotionally lost to deal with any of it. But a few days ago, at work, one of my regular customers slipped me a note written on a napkin. I'm totally a sucker for that stuff. The note said, 'I know you are going through a tough time, and you don't have to say yes. But I would love to take you out sometime and show you how a woman should be treated.'"

I could literally feel my heart constricting as Kris spoke, but I tried my best to maintain a supportive look. "Unconditional acceptance," I reminded myself.

"His name is Rob. He's a big Kentucky boy. He's five years older than me. He's probably a foot taller than me, even when I wear heels, and he has strawberry blond hair. So, he's really not my type in that respect. But some of my coworkers knew him from high school, so I asked them what they thought, and they said that he was a nice guy and that I should totally go out with him. So after my shift, we went to McDonald's and just talked. I actually told him all about you."

"Not all about me," I said with a weak smile. "I mean, you didn't actually tell him about how we met and the nature of our relationship?"

"Actually, everything. I told him about how we met on that website. I told him about how you had your wife, and I was dating Taylor. So we were sort of each other's swap. He thought that I was just some innocent young girl working at the local bar. So when I told him that I was having an affair with a thirty-eight-year-old Asian man who is married and paying me a lot of money, he was pretty shocked. He said one of his good friends was a thirty-six-year-old Asian guy, but now he didn't know if he could introduce me to him," Kris said with a laugh. "We talked in the parking lot of McDonald's for an hour, and then I told him that I needed to go home to take care of Veda. Then he asked me if he could kiss me, and I said yes. It was nice."

I felt a hard lump in my throat, but managed to ask, "And since then? Have you gone out on more dates?"

"No, just that one date. But I want to see him again," Kris said softly. "I actually didn't know if I was going to tell you about Rob, since I'm not sure where it will go. But we had that agreement to tell each other if we kissed someone else, and then you were being so nice to me right now and saying all those wonderful things. Katy told me not to tell you."

"Aah, Katy. I'd expect nothing less," I said with a laugh. "Well, I must say that I've thought about this scenario. I mean, it was a certainty that you would meet someone else at some point. Though to be honest, I didn't expect it quite so soon. I actually didn't think you would tell me when it happened. So thank you for proving me wrong."

"Anytime. Best friends don't lie to each other."

I leaned forward in my chair toward Kris with my hands clasped together in front of my mouth. I had a hard time collecting my thoughts into anything coherent.

After a minute, I just said, "Kris, I'm happy for you. I want you to be happy. But if it's okay, I'm going to take a walk outside. It's a lot for me to process."

"Okay," she said quietly with a nervous look.

I took a walk around the block and picked up some wine coolers and snacks at the deli on the corner. I felt better as I walked. To be clear, it hurt like hell. I could physically feel my chest constricted in pain. But I told myself that this had to happen eventually and that our relationship was never going have a "good ending." So maybe it was better for this to happen now. Sooner rather than later, and this was as good of an ending as any.

By the time I got back to the room, I felt better. I unpacked the groceries onto the living room table. I opened two wine coolers and handed her one.

"I'm okay, Kris," I started. "But do you still want to stay here with me these couple of nights?"

"Yes," she said. "Do you still want me to stay here?"

"Yes. I think so," I said, honestly still a little confused about what I wanted. "You know, you could have told me before you came up here."

"I know, but then I was scared that you wouldn't want me to come visit. And I wanted to see you again."

"I understand. But you got so mad at me that one time when I didn't tell you about Marianne before you visited. Kind of the same thing, you know?"

"I'm sorry. I just didn't want it to end like that," she said sadly.

"It's okay," I said with a wry smile. "I'm glad you came up."

"I'm going to take a quick shower," Kris said as she stood up.

"Sounds good. Okay if I take a shower with you?"

"Sure," Kris said with a smile. "That's what best friends do, right? Shower together?"

"I guess so," I laughed.

I kissed her deeply as we both undressed, and then we moved into the shower.

With my mouth still covering hers, I soaped up her breasts and caressed her nipples with my slippery fingers. She moaned loudly and reached down and stroked my cock slowly with her soapy hands.

Breathing heavily, I turned Kris around to face away from the showerhead. I placed both of her hands against the back wall and I bent her over. I knelt down, positioned my face behind her ass, and pressed my tongue flat against her pussy. She moaned loudly. I worked her clit slowly from behind with my tongue. I felt her pussy get increasingly wet, and then I moved upwards and licked her asshole. She gasped loudly. Encouraged, I continued to massage her asshole with my tongue. I moved my tongue slowly at first in small circles, and then with increasing pressure. She squirmed hard against my tongue.

When she couldn't take any more, she stood up straight and turned around to face me. She pulled my head up and covered my mouth with hers. She then crouched down and put my throbbing cock into her mouth. I groaned at the rush of pleasure. As her mouth moved slowly up and down my cock, she looked up at me with her beautiful green eyes. My cock ached so badly that I struggled not to cum right then. But if this was the last visit, I told myself, there were a couple of things I still wanted to experience with Kris.

"Kris, lick my balls please."

Without hesitation, she pushed my cock up with one hand and moved her mouth lower. She began to lick my balls gently. I experienced the most exquisite feeling as she worked my balls with her tongue. It felt both ticklish and achingly erotic at the same time.

We dried each other off and moved to the bed. Kris lay on her back and I worked her clitoris with my tongue again as I simultaneously rubbed her special spot inside with my finger.

"Oh my god, Ryan. You really are the best," she groaned as she climaxed once.

My turn. I climbed on top of her and began to fuck her missionary style. As I felt her excitement build again, I sat up and leaned back as I fucked her, so that my cock rubbed the top of her vagina. She screamed and came again on my cock. As I felt myself near climax, I pulled my cock out of her dripping pussy and climbed upwards on the bed. One more thing I wanted to try with Kris.

I knelt to the side of Kris's head and stroked my cock. She turned her mouth toward my cock and pursed her lips in anticipation. I stroked my cock desperately. As I exploded, Kris covered my cock with her mouth and sucked me hard. She swallowed all of my cum.

This was, without a doubt, the most intense erotic experience of my life. I collapsed on top of Kris, and we held each other tightly.

"I like this sheen of sweat that we have after we make love. When we hold each other, the sweat on our skin makes it feel like we're totally connected," I said.

"Mmm-hmm. So soft," Kris said as rubbed my chest gently with one hand. After a pause, she added with a laugh, "I don't think Kentucky boy is going to be this soft."

"Jesus Christ, Kris," I said as I sat up, suddenly angry. "That's not funny. I'm trying to be mature about this, but I don't need an image of some big Kentucky guy fucking you."

Kris sat up also, realizing her mistake. "I'm sorry. I'm sorry. Just try to imagine that he's some big, ugly, fat guy."

"Is he?"

"No," she said.

I calmed down a bit. Sort of. Well, might as well get this over with. "Okay, so tell me more about him."

"He was in prison for a couple of years. I think for dealing cocaine, which is funny because he doesn't look like he's ever done drugs in his life. Now he's a welder, I think. Or he does something with his hands, which I was surprised by because he's really smart. I know he could be doing something else with his mind. But it's probably hard for him now because he's got a felony record."

I tensed a bit at her description of Rob. Kris must have sensed my skepticism because she quickly added, "But he's really sweet."

"Look, Kris," I said. "I don't care if he's made mistakes in the past. I'm all about redemption.

"And I know that love can spring in unexpected places," I said with a wry laugh. "I just want to know that his intentions are good."

"They are," she insisted. "He's a true Kentucky gentleman. I mentioned that my car was filthy inside, and the next day, while I was working, he surprised me by completely cleaning the inside of my car. Then Katy emailed me today that she let him into my apartment because he wanted to steam clean my carpets and fix all the damage that Taylor had caused. He's really nice."

Kris sat thoughtfully for a few moments and then said, almost to herself, "But I worry, is he too nice? I can't date anyone who's too nice because I'll run all over him."

"Am I too nice?" I asked.

"No."

"Great, thanks," I said.

Kris just smiled. "You know what I mean. Two days ago, I was hanging out with him at a pool hall, and I told him that I was coming up to New York to visit you."

"I thought you only had that one date with him at McDonald's?"

"Oh, this wasn't a date. I was just hanging out with Rob and a couple of his friends before I had to go to work that night. He's really good at pool, and I'm really bad. So he was teaching me a bit."

"How did he react when you told him that you were coming to visit me?"

"He got really quiet. So I started to cry. I mean, he's so much bigger than me, he could really hurt me. When I started to cry, he begged me to stop. I told him that I was afraid he would hit me, and he said that he would never hit me. He wasn't even thinking about yelling at me. He said that he understood that we weren't dating yet, but if this worked out between us, it was important to him that we never went to bed angry. And I told him that if this worked out, I wouldn't continue to see you."

I thought about her last statement.

"It's weird," I said. "Somehow it felt okay before that you were cheating on Taylor while I was cheating on my wife. But now, for some reason, when you are starting a new relationship, it feels like it would be impossible to continue our relationship."

Kris sat quietly for a few moments. She then looked at me with tears rolling down her face. "I think before, I was cheating on Taylor because there was something missing in that relationship. But now I need to find someone who can love me in the way that you can't."

"I know, Kris," I said as I hugged her and gave her a kiss on her forehead. "I want you to find that also."

We had dinner in the room that night, and we made love again before going to sleep. I came inside her this time.

"You're lucky I'm having my period," Kris said with a smile. "You've never been good at pulling out."

"I know. It's just like a black hole with an irresistible gravitational force. It's so incredibly hard to pull out at that moment when I climax."

"Ha, ha. Black hole," Kris chuckled.

In the morning, I woke up earlier than Kris and got ready for work. Before I left, I gave Kris, who was still half asleep, a quick kiss goodbye, and then I put an envelope with one thousand dollars in her purse in the living room.

Text to Kris (6/13)
Morning, love. Have a fun day exploring New York. Depending on how my meetings go, I may be able to come back to you mid-afternoon. Will let you know. I left a little walk-around cash for you in your purse.

I finished my meeting around 2 P.M., and as I made my way back to the hotel, I texted Kris to let her know. She said that her phone was dying and that she was lost, but that she would see me soon.

I got back to the hotel and she wasn't there. After about an hour, I began to worry that Kris had not been able to find her way back to the hotel. I tried calling her multiple times, but went straight to voicemail. That was not surprising since she had said that her phone was dying. But still, I became increasingly anxious. After another half-hour, not knowing what to do, I started wandering the streets around the hotel, knowing that it would be almost impossible to find her. I soon made my way back to the hotel and just waited.

Finally, around 4 P.M., I heard the card key click in the door, and Kris walked in.

"Jesus!" I said, "Where were you?"

"What do you mean? I went shopping," she said as she laid down a couple of bags from Juicy Couture and Free People. "Well, you should have told me. I'm really mad at you. The last message I got was that you were lost, and that was a couple hours ago."

I saw a hurt look briefly cross Kris's face, and then in seconds I witnessed her mood transform into a defensive rage. "You aren't my parent!" she screamed. "I can find my way back. I'm not a baby. And if I was really lost, I would have just asked someone!"

Instinctively, I could feel my own anger escalate, but then I reminded myself of Kris's BPD condition. I reminded myself that patients with BPD often try to push people away because they are afraid of being hurt. "Unconditional acceptance," I repeated mentally to myself.

Instead of responding, I just took a deep breath. Kris misinterpreted my sigh and became even angrier.

"If you are going to sit there and sigh at me, I should just catch the next flight back to Florida. Jesus, Ryan, you're so fucking needy! You need to know exactly where I am all the time. Like if I don't respond to your emails in one day, you get all paranoid."

By now I had collected myself and just focused on calming Kris down.

"No, Kris, I get mad because I worry about you. I worried that you were lost today. I worry when I suddenly don't hear back from you over email for long stretches because I'm concerned that you might be hurt again. Okay, Kris," I said as I stood up and wrapped my arms around her. "I'm sorry. You're right. I'm not your parent. I'll try not to worry so much or be so needy. But I still love you unconditionally."

Kris started to cry. "It's just that when you get mad at me, or when Rob got mad at me, I worry you're going to hit me. So when someone gets mad at me, my first reaction is to get mad back."

"No, Kris, I'd never hit you," I said as I held her tightly and just repeated, "I love you unconditionally, even if we're not together anymore."

She sobbed on my shoulder for a while. After a few minutes, we were able to laugh a bit at our own histrionics. She caught me up on her day. She had explored Central Park in the morning and then went shopping on 5th Avenue, where she bought a couple of sundresses.

"So what Broadway show did you get tickets for?" she asked as she changed into one of her new dresses.

"A musical comedy called *Avenue Q*. It's got puppets, but apparently very adult humor. I actually have no idea if it's good, but it's gotten good reviews. Also, in the past, I've bought you tickets to *Wicked* and *The Phantom of the Opera*, which are shows that I've seen before. So, in effect, I was sharing experiences with you that I've already had in the past. This time, I thought it would be nice to go to a new show that both of us could experience together for the first time."

Kris gave me a bright smile.

We walked to a sushi restaurant a few blocks away for dinner. As we sat down, I did a quick scan of the other patrons. There were a couple folks who gave Kris and me curious glances, but no one that I recognized.

"So what's your plan now, Kris?"

"You mean in terms of Nevada? I'm still moving in a couple of weeks. I told Rob that his timing couldn't be worse."

"But the heart wants what it wants," I finished for her.

"I guess that's right. Rob can come with me if he wants, but I'm moving to Nevada and going to university in the fall."

I thought about that for a few moments. Kris had known Rob now for three or four days, and she was already talking about moving together to Nevada. Not atypical of her personality or the common expressions of BPD, I knew. Kris could never bear to be alone for very long, and given her beauty, she never had to be alone.

"Well, Kris, this doesn't behoove me to say, but my advice is this. When you get back to Florida, you should spend as much time as you can together with Rob. Moving together is a big commitment, and it's not a lot of time to figure out if you are compatible. But by the end of a couple of weeks, at least, you should have a feel for whether the relationship is accelerating or reaching a plateau. Also, I'm going to need a little time also to deal with this on my end. Frankly, I think you need some space also. It's not possible to truly throw yourself into a new relationship if we're still talking all the time."

Kris just gave me a sad look and started to cry. "You really are my best friend, you know."

"I know. And you are mine, Kris."

It was still sunny early in the evening at this time of year, so after dinner, we strolled to the theater, which was about a ten-minute walk away. We still had some time before the show, so we stopped at a Starbucks around the corner from the theater. Kris ordered one of those calorie-bomb iced coffee drinks with whipped cream and I ordered a chai tea latte. There was a little park next to the theater. We sat down on one of the park benches to people watch as we drank our beverages.

We tried to pick out strangers from the passersby whom we guessed the other person might be physically attracted to. After pointing out a half dozen girls for me, whom I all rejected, Kris sighed and said, "Are you ever going to show me a picture of Marianne?"

I was a little surprised. I hadn't thought about Marianne in a long time.

"I'm not sure what good can come of that, but okay," I said as I pulled out my Blackberry. I did a quick Google search for Marianne under the name she used as a model. A series of her professional model photographs came up.

Kris looked at my phone. "Oh," she said with a little surprise in her voice. I guessed that she was taken aback by Marianne's beauty. I quickly closed the browser with Marianne's pictures and put the phone back in my pocket.

Kris sat silent for a few moments and then asked, "Wait, real or fake?"

"Don't know. I never found out," I laughed. "There just wasn't that spark there, y'know?"

I gave Kris a light kiss on the lips.

Kris seemed to brighten at that, and then she added, "Well, I'd still do her."

We enjoyed the show. It was hilarious, actually. But we spent a lot of the time erotically teasing each other in the dark. I would stroke the inside of her naked thigh with my fingers as she sat next to me.

At one point, I heard her breath quicken, and she spread her legs apart in her chair as my fingers tantalizingly moved up her thigh. But I stopped just short, and instead, I leaned over and whispered into her ear, "I want you." Kris nodded, breathing heavily while staring straight ahead at the stage.

At intermission, I went to the bathroom and Kris went outside for a smoke. I waited in the inside atrium for her to return, but started to get a little worried when the chime sounded, indicating the imminent start of the second half of the show. I walked into the theater to check our seats in case I had missed Kris coming back in, but she wasn't there. So I went back out to the atrium. After a minute, I saw her walking towards me across the atrium floor from probably thirty yards away.

There are a few images from our relationship that I will always remember, and this was one of them. Kris, in her pretty new sundress, walking back to me. Young. Beautiful. Completely mine, at least for just this moment.

I walked towards Kris also. As we met, without a word, I put one hand gently around her head and the other around her small waist. I pulled her against me, and we kissed for what seemed like an eternity that was still too brief.

After the show, we held hands as we walked back to the hotel. I knew there was a risk of running into someone that I knew on the street, but I didn't really care. I knew that this was our last night together.

When we got back to the hotel, we made love again. Kris came multiple times first, and then she got on her hands and knees on the bed and presented her perfect pear-shaped ass to me. I remember Kris pushing her bottom against my cock as I fucked her hard doggy style. Nearing climax, I pulled out again and groaned for her to turn over. As I came, she again covered my cock with her mouth. I tried to pull away as the feeling was too intense, and I pleaded, "Too much! Too much!" But Kris was unrelenting as she sucked every drop out of me and swallowed it all.

We held each other afterwards in bed and Kris laughed.

"Too much! Too much!" she mimicked me.

"It felt like I was being electrocuted!"

"I know," Kris said with a smile.

After a few moments, I said, "When I got home this afternoon and you weren't here, I watched a show on MTV where this teenage girl was having sex with her boyfriend. In the middle of it, she started imagining that she was actually having sex with another boy. Have you ever done that?"

"Imagined having sex with someone else while I was having sex? Yes," Kris said with a smile.

I opened my eyes mockingly wide. "Have you ever imagined having sex with someone else while WE were having sex?"

"No," Kris laughed. "But I have imagined having sex with you when I was having sex with Taylor."

I have to admit, that made me happy.

"What about you?" Kris asked.

"Yeah, I've imagined having sex with you while having sex with someone else."

"You imagined having sex with me while you were having sex with one of your other sugar babies?" Kris teased.

"No, no other sugar babies. And besides, if I had to imagine you while I was having sex with another sugar baby, that would sort of defeat the purpose of having another sugar baby."

Kris laughed. After a few minutes, she asked, "So how many dates have we been on? Do you still keep notes on each one?"

"I do. Like I said, I'm going to write a book someday. Thirteen. Thirteen dates."

"Thirteen dates," Kris whispered. "You have no idea the impact that you've had in just thirteen dates. Without you, I'd still be with Taylor. I'm a different person because of you. You've changed my life."

Kris started to cry again. I held her tightly, and I cried also.

"I don't like this at all," Kris said. "You said that you need to take some time. So we are never going to talk again?"

"Did I say never? I didn't say never. We just both need some time apart right now. Believe me, it will be harder on me than you. The idea of you with someone else really hurts. You know, the selfish part of me just wants you to stay single and pine away for me forever. But the part that loves you wants you to be happy and find someone

Date 14

whom you can be with permanently because I know that I can't. But it still hurts a lot."

"Well, you'll still have two, and I'll only have one."

"What do you mean?"

"I mean, eventually you'll find a new relationship to replace me," Kris said. I could hear anger rising in her voice. "You know, Ryan. There are parts of your life that I pity. You have a perfect family, but you're obviously still searching for something."

I denied it, but I knew Kris was right. I just didn't know what I was searching for, and it made me sad.

"Like I've said before, I will never try to justify our relationship, Kris. In any organized religious or moral code, I know this would be considered wrong. But I'm a moral relativist. So I believe that as long as we're not hurting someone else, everyone should decide what is right and wrong for themselves as individuals. So when I look back on our relationship, and I think about how much we love each other, it's hard for me to believe this was wrong. It . . . just . . . is. And I'm so thankful for it."

"Why can't you just admit that you married the wrong girl, Ryan? You couldn't wait around twenty years for the right girl," Kris said with a wry laugh.

I gave her a sad smile back. "Do you remember, on one of our early dates, you told me about one of your dreams in which I was dancing with you at your wedding and you were crying?"

"I remember."

"Well, I promise Kris, we'll make that happen. When you get married, whether to Rob or someone else, I'll find a way to come, okay?"

Kris smiled, "You can't ever take that promise back, you know?"

"I know. And when we dance at your wedding in front of all your friends and family, I'm going to kiss you like this," I said, and I gave her a deep kiss.

"And then my husband is going to kick your ass," Kris laughed.

"Worth it," I said. "And you have to hold your promise that this scar on your back is always mine. Even when you get married, this scar is mine."

"Okay," Kris said with a sad smile.

"You know, Kris, whomever you end up with long term, you should tell him about your BPD condition. If he loves you, he'll try to help you."

"Okay," she said softly.

"Maybe the reason that you get into these roller-coaster relationships is because of BPD."

I felt Kris stiffen in my arms and then pull away.

"What the hell does that mean!" she growled.

"Retreat, retreat," I told myself.

"I just meant that you sense emotions more deeply than other people. And so you are particularly sensitive to the ups and downs in relationships."

"I'm broken, then? Is that what I am?" she screamed.

"No, not at all. I love you unconditionally and completely, including the fact that you feel emotions so deeply."

She calmed down after a few minutes, and we snuggled in bed again.

We fought and cried a lot that night. I think in a way, Kris was trying to make the breakup easier by ending on an angry note. But I deflected her anger each time. Unconditional acceptance. I wanted her to always remember that.

As Kris finally settled in to sleep in the wee hours of the night, I stood up and said, "Okay, I'm going to go poop."

"Poop? This I have to stay up for," Kris laughed.

"Nope, I'm going to run the hair drier as I poop, so you can't hear it. We've held out pooping in front of each other this long, why ruin the magic now?"

"I actually pooped earlier in the lobby bathroom when I went downstairs for a smoke." Kris admitted with a smile.

"Well, I guess we're even then," I said as I handed Kris an Ambien pill. She swallowed it without any water and was asleep in minutes.

I awoke in the morning to bright sunlight streaming into the bedroom. Kris was curled up in the crook of my arm. She was awake and crying already.

Date 14

"It's today," I said simply, tears running down my face also.

We dressed. Kris packed up her things. I walked her to the door. We hugged and kissed one last time. She walked out the hotel door, turned once, and whispered, "I love you."

"I love you too."

And then I closed the door behind her.

Epilogue

Email to Kris (6/14)

Thank you for coming up to NY. As painful as parts were, it was maybe also the most fulfilling of all of our dates in some ways (the final count is fourteen, btw). The most real, the most raw, the most emotionally naked. (Though I still couldn't bring myself to poop in front of you, and I even gave you an Ambien to knock you out before I let loose in the bathroom . . . and you, for your part, pooped in the lobby . . . so don't kid yourself . . . we're even on that front.) I know that someday you will find someone great, Kris. And just maybe that "someday" is actually today. And just maybe that "someone" is actually Rob. Who knows? But you deserve to figure it out. And we both need some space right now. You, in order to not be shackled emotionally while you explore the early heartbeats of a new relationship. Me, in order to remember how to breathe on my own again (which I failed at miserably last time).

One thing that I needed to clarify because I felt miserable that I totally fumbled what I was actually trying to say last night. I did NOT mean that you feel false emotions because of BPD. I would never say that, and I know that's not true. I meant the exact opposite, and I just articulated it so terribly . . . I'm usually better in that respect. I honestly meant that you sense emotions more keenly and more truly than most people – like an emotional tuning fork. In ancient Greece, they used to have these oracles who were born with the ability to speak to the gods and divine "Truth" for the unwashed masses. (Usually, they were virgin girls . . . so okay, maybe the metaphor isn't perfect.) But it's a gift, Kris. At least it was to me.

Next steps – you put an "Out to Lunch" sign on the door of our relationship and go open the door to new one. Rob sounds like a wonderful spirit (and quite handy also!). I deleted my Instagram account – I know myself, and I wouldn't be able to resist otherwise. As promised, I forwarded what I thought were the funnier or more meaningful emails between us to our joint Gmail account and filed them all in a folder labeled "Kris." That's the legacy of our relationship, so I won't ever delete that account. (Plus, I'll need the material eventually for the book.)

We'll always be a part of each other's lives, and I do remember my promise, of course. (Actually, to clarify . . . was it just a "dance" at your wedding, or was it a "makeout session + dance" . . . I forget where we settled out?)

I will always be standing there if you need me to help. In some ways, I like to think that through our relationship, we were able to help each other "find" our true selves. And in that respect, I'm just really proud of both of us. :)

It's been almost two months now since Kris and I said goodbye in New York.

The first month and a half were pretty brutal. I couldn't sleep, and I lost a lot of weight. The hardest part was that I had to maintain an outward facade of normalcy with my family, my friends and my colleagues all the while that I was torn apart inside. The only friend in whom I could confide was Andrew, and he was a true friend, empathizing with me along my road to recovery, without judgment. I know it's just adolescent heartbreak. And I know that I have only myself to blame. But the hurt was real.

Kris never moved back to Nevada. She had an argument with her mom, and so she and Rob ended up moving to his small hometown in Kentucky in order to live with his mom instead. According to her, she was going to work at the local diner for a few months to save money, and then she and Rob would move to Nevada for her to start university in the spring semester. I tried to be supportive, but inside I was sad that she had delayed her educational path to a better life yet again. I loved Kris, but she was terrible at organizing and planning for her future. My fear is that she ends up never going to university at all. Maybe she'll end up living in Kentucky permanently.

Epilogue

At first, we would try to not talk or text in order to give each other space. Usually we would make it a week before one of us would break down. She had her moments of doubt, when she would text about how much she missed me. I would write her emails describing how much I was hurting and how I missed her also. Silly stuff, I know, and not worth describing in great detail.

But as time passed, the stretches between our communications became longer. And time was the great healer, so I gradually felt better, more whole, more myself.

Still, we've had our histrionics as we worked through letting each other go.

Email to Kris (7/20)

Hi Kris. As always, I'll be honest with you and put up no emotional facades. Truth is, I've written you a number of emails over the last month, but I didn't send any of them. It wasn't fair to you starting a new relationship, I felt. But for reasons you'll see, I need to send this one.

Have you ever seen the movie *Always*? Stephen Spielberg movie from the late eighties (don't say it). It's a romantic drama about a woman (Holly Hunter) who loses her pilot husband (Richard Dreyfuss) in a forest fire accident. But the spirit of the husband is trapped on earth. So he watches his wife grieve over his death, and eventually, he watches his wife start to fall in love with someone new. But he has some limited ability to communicate with his wife from the spirit world. So she still feels his presence hovering around her, and therefore she's emotionally unable to move on. And the husband, for his part, can't let the love of his life go either – so he does everything he can from the spirit world to sabotage his wife's new paramour. At the end, the wife effectively gives up on life. And this makes her husband realize that if he truly loves his wife, then he has to let her go so that she can be free to move on and be happy.

It's worth a watch, if you haven't seen it. But I guess I just told you the whole plot (sorry!).

Anyway, I'm sure you see the analogy. But maybe not in the way you think. See, I actually feel like I'm the wife here. I still feel your spirit everywhere, and it's made it hard to move on. No, neither of us died, so no need to over-dramatize. But in a way, that makes it uniquely painful – because there is no closure. No one died (thankfully). There was no big fight (though you tried in NY). And we didn't fall out of love with each other over time (if anything, it felt like it was accelerating during the last few months). So no closure at all (we'll get to that in a second).

It's hard to describe how painful the last month has been for me. I certainly never could have fathomed it. It's been a process that has ranged from the sublime to the ridiculous. Sublime in certain mornings, when I would wake up and I could emotionally elevate your happiness above mine and feel genuinely happy that you found someone whom you are so excited about. Or sublime in moments when I would look back on memories from our relationship and just be inspired by the unexpected magic that life can sometimes bring. But ridiculous in other moments, like when I walked by my assistant and called her "Kris" accidentally (three weeks ago). Ridiculous in moments like when I relapsed and stalked all of your old teenage pictures on your mom's Facebook pages (last week – cute, btw). And ridiculous when my assistant booked my travel, and I almost asked her to change the hotel reservation just because I have too many memories of you in the Palace hotel (this morning).

So it's a process, and I'm still working through it, honestly.

But I know that I genuinely love you, because I want you, first and foremost, to be happy. That's not to say that I don't have moments when I selfishly wish that you had never met Rob. But the larger part of me truly wants you to find someone who can make you happy. You deserve it, as much as anyone deserves such a thing. From the way you describe him, Rob seems like a genuinely good soul, and I try to focus on that. So I hope it works out with you two.

Kris – I'm not Taylor. I don't want to rub anything in your face. If anything, it hurts me to say anything that could hurt you even in the slightest. In the same way, I appreciate you not rubbing Rob in my face (figuratively, of course . . . I mean, it would be horrible to have some six-foot white dude actually physically rubbed against my face . . . Jesus, how the hell do my friends put up with me?).

Epilogue

So I'll keep this part brief.

Her name is Vicky. We've seen each other twice this week (once in Orange County and once up here). Since I know you would wonder anyway – she's pretty, but not as pretty as you (frankly, that's an almost impossible hurdle). More importantly, though, for the first time in what seems like a long time, I've been able to smile a bit and laugh a bit and be completely open with my thoughts and emotions. I told her all about you and how I'm still removing that shrapnel. She's really sweet and understanding about it, and said she really wants to help heal me. (Jesus, where was all this when I was younger?) But I still feel your spirit hovering everywhere (at very inopportune times, I might add), and so I don't know if I'll see her again. I thought about not telling you until I had figured it all out – but as you said, best friends don't lie to each other. And we had our "two date" agreement to tell each other. So I wanted to honor that.

Kris – I need you to let me go. I need you to tell me that your relationship with Rob is accelerating, that you're crazy in love, that you love me as a friend (but are no longer in love with me), and that you want the best for me and therefore truly want me to move on. I feel like that will help give me the closure that I need. Please.

You and I are friends now, not lovers – I've learned to accept that. And I might not see you again in this lifetime (except for your wedding, of course) – to be honest, I'm still struggling to accept that.

But you should know that no matter our distance in space and time, I'm always there to help if you need it. Emotionally or financially. (Or even sexually . . . no? Oh well, can't blame me for trying one last time.)

Joking aside, Kris – I'll say this only once and ask you to remember it. If you ever need a helping hand, please just ask. Don't be embarrassed and don't feel like it degrades our friendship in any way. We both know that by the end of our relationship, money was the least important aspect to both of us. It's just that life deals people different cards. I've studied and worked so hard to improve my hand in my life, and what gives me happiness now is to help people I care about. You're one hundred percent correct that money does not buy happiness. I know lots of unhappy rich people. But it can ease things. And as long as we're friends, you should never feel trapped or desperate. Never. You're smart and beautiful, and have the ability to make any guy you want fall in love with you, and you aren't even old enough to walk into a club yet. You're going to do great, but if you ever need a helping hand to get through uncertain times, just let me know. My financial support was never contingent on us being lovers. It was just contingent on us being friends, which I'll never give up.

Anyway, that's it. Verbose even for me.

Ryan

Text from Kris (7/20)
Some of your message came in the wrong order and I feel like a few pieces are missing, but I get the gist of what you're asking for. But before I do so, I want to make sure it's the honest truth – so give me some time. (No, not weeks – I won't put you through that again.) Just long enough to have some time away from Rob and think clearly without any distractions. Maybe I'll take Veda on a walk if I feel better tonight.

I had to go to the hospital again and shockingly, I still don't have insurance! My car insurance money went towards my prescriptions, so I might break down and ask for a little help this month, but we'll see how many days I'm scheduled to work next week. Anyway, I promise I won't leave you hanging for more than 24 hours. I hate it when you're in pain, especially when I know I caused it. Vicky sounds nice. Talk to you soon.

Text to Kris (7/21)
Please ignore my message from yesterday. I feel stupid for sending it. It's not fair to put this on you. It's my problem, not yours – I'll deal with it. Sure, the honest truth from you would be good to understand at some point – but on your schedule, not mine (whether that's days, weeks, or months before you're ready to tell me). Plus you're sick, and I hate the idea of me putting more stress on you. I'm sending you a little help to get you through this month. Feel better. I'm fine.

Ryan

Text from Kris (7/21)

First off, thank you. And wonderful timing because Rob's mom just got laid off this morning, so she won't be able to help much for a while.

I actually packed up my entire car a few days ago, dead set on going anywhere but here. I'm driving myself crazy with nothing to do but

think. I've been overanalyzing everything and it's made me panicky. So now I get to distract myself with unpacking it all again lol.

As far as Rob's concerned, he's not perfect. He's OCD, so he's always moving my shit around, and he likes stupid action movies, and he cut all of his pretty hair off. He drives me crazy sometimes, but I really do think he's perfect for me. If anyone can put up with me day after day for the rest of my life, it's him. As usual, things between you and me aren't as easy to define. I'll admit some days, I try and block you out completely. Rob deserves so much (more than Taylor ever did), and I feel guilty for even talking to you sometimes because although he's understanding, I know it makes him uncomfortable on some level.

I think of you as a best friend that I love, but it's hard to say if any part of me is still IN love with you, especially since it's been so long since we saw each other. Can you be in love with two people at once?

Rationally speaking, there's no point. You're far away, and you're (still) married. We had our run – a great one at that. I don't want to ruin the memories with awkward feelings. To answer your question as best I can at this point, if it were a choice between you and Rob, Rob would win.

You and I were never meant to be together in that way forever. You know that. You were the one to always remind me of that when I would not-so-jokingly suggest we just run away to some island together, remember? But that doesn't mean I don't smile when something reminds me of you. And it doesn't mean I don't still tear up at your kindness and the way you cared for me like no one ever had before.

No new person or any amount of time is going to change that, Ryan.

Promise.

Text to Kris (7/21)

You're welcome, and also, thank you Kris. That's what I needed to hear. I'm happy that you found a perfect match for you.

I agree about the great run we had – I will always be thankful for that. I always knew in my heart that it was unfair for you to have just a fraction of me and for me to want all of your heart in return. And I recognize, as you said, that you and I weren't meant to be together forever. As the old saying goes – a fish may love a bird, but where would they live? Sigh . . . certainly not in Kentucky.

Just so you know, when you would "not-so-jokingly" suggest we run away together, I would "not-so-jokingly" actually consider it. But I couldn't hurt my family like that. I had my chance, and this is my life. And it's not perfect, but I do love them. Besides, I always figured if we ran away together, I would probably run out of jokes by the second week (third week tops), and then where would we be?

Okay, Kris – let's not over-dramatize this any more (Jesus, I'm not sure that's even possible . . . I can almost hear the "For Good" *Wicked* song playing in the background). We're friends, and we'll always be friends at some level, I hope. And maybe someday, we'll be able to laugh about all this, and Rob will be so secure in your relationship that he won't care if we talk once in a while.

But not now, for either of us. We both need to move on. But I'll always be there if you need me . . . and vice versa, I hope. Because that's what best friends do. And no one will ever replace you either, Kris.

Promise you also.

Text from Kris (7/21)

I'm drunk and I was really hoping you weren't mad at me because you really are my best friend.

Text to Kris (7/21)

Not mad. I want you to be happy, and I'm glad you found that with Rob. I'll send you a free copy of the book when it's done. :)

Epilogue

Text from Kris (7/21)
And I'll send you one of mine in return. :)

Text to Kris (7/21)
Yeah, but I don't think Rob will ever be THAT secure that he'll want to read my book. Sometimes I read it instead of watching porn at night.

Night Kris. You're gonna do great.

Text from Kris (7/21)
Goodnight my dear.

I haven't talked to Kris since that last exchange. "Goodnight my dear."

Maybe that's a fitting end. I never did explore a relationship with Vicky. I just wasn't emotionally ready to start something new.

It's funny. When I first started this relationship with Kris, I remember thinking how nice it would be to find an "in-between" that could be the best of both ends of the relationship spectrum. On the one end, I had hoped our relationship could be an exciting physical relationship without the emotional emptiness that I had experienced with escorts. On the other end of the spectrum, I had hoped that we could develop a true friendship without the emotional baggage of a committed long-term relationship.

But emotions are called emotions for a reason. And I've realized that the downside of developing a true emotional connection in any relationship, even one that we know cannot last, is that it hurts like hell when it comes to an end. It's just the law of gravity, I guess. The higher you go up, the harder you come down.

And I know that I should feel guilty about my affair with Kris. I know that there should be some moral to this story . . . that I learned what I did was wrong and, as a result, have recommitted myself to my marriage.

But my story is not meant to be one of redemption or absolution.

It's a story of love. And it's the story of a friendship that made no sense in this world, but was as real as any friendship that I have ever known.

I have thought a lot about Kris's comment on our last date that I was searching for something. She was right. I was searching for someone with whom I could be completely myself. This was the one relationship in my life where I could be completely maskless. Where I could share all of my darkest sins, and Kris could share hers in return. And we loved each other, not in spite of our flaws, but because of them.

I still miss my friend.